Wasteland Mandala

Oma Nipa

For all beings, especially those suffering from war, famine, or oppression of any kind.

Wasteland Mandala

1

My heart was always a sighing river, a seeking for the sea.
Even deep in the source, I tended to exist, if only as an echo,
a premonition. My life would be a long and meandering path,
a swift and urgent course that would dredge the bottom of the
heart and flood all the world with love.

First, I was born into form as a wisp of fog. I lived close to
death and only for a moment. I danced and drifted, free and righteous. When I met the stone, I wondered at his immensity and
stillness. It was with my own voice that he spoke to me, saying,

Why do you go?
Why don't you stay?
Melt much more slowly;
gather and weigh.

You squander your particles,
neither linger nor dwell—
evacuated heart
bidding one and all farewell!

I laughed and said:

My skin is too thin
to cover a lie;
my heart is full of bouquets wilting
and clouds about to cry.

You're made of so much;
you're inclined to remain.
I wonder, could your heaviness hush
the winds of change?

At home in this world
alone dear one
are those who have no name—
your bulk will return one day
by the same road whence it came.

Having spoken thus I disappeared, melting with love into the cheeks of the mountain. But no sooner had I died than I was born again. I drifted among the ancient trees. They had once been pure and sublime, but they had begun to tell long stories. Wanting to hear how their stories would end, the trees had grown tall and old, elaborate and layered. To balance their height, the trees plunged long roots into the rocks, splitting them apart. When the rocks cried out in pain, the trees pretended not to notice.

"It's necessary," they said, "if we are ever going to reach the sky."

I shook my curling mane and whispered, "Fools, you are the sky."

I disappeared into the sun and died.

Another birth carried me to where a snail was sliding over a bed of moss. His fragile shell was coiled around his soft body. I entered through his wet skin and watched his simple thoughts. He wanted to stay inside himself and yet go on leaving his prints on the world.

Later, I saw the wolves. They kept their hearts inside their ribcages and fed them each day like captives.

"It's a shame that we must keep them locked up like this," they said, "but we cannot free them, or they will die."

Forgetting that life and death were one, they believed there was something at stake. Their teeth grew sharp and long to match their fears.

In my body of music, I came close to the mouths and hearts of humans. To some I was like a lover, while to others I was hooded death. I danced among the ringing tones of primordial silence and the thousands of fingers of truth grazed my cheeks and made plants grow. Attracted to a tune my heart had written, I slipped through temporal societies, touching the strings of revolution. Nimble, transitory, without a shadow of my own, I did not know the pain my agitation created for beings of warm blood.

＊

When I was born a woman, I had windows in my eyes. On the rocks at the foot of the mountain I spread my linens wet from the river. I gazed and puzzled at the fog who was singing:

> Come near, dear one
> your footprints are numbered;
> there are maps on the backs
> of your hands
>
> Your tattooed blue hunger
> will bury you under
> the weight of its wonderful
> plans
>
> How long will you tarry
> in the maze of your mind,
> burying treasures
> for no one to find?
>
> Dismantle the mask
> no one's hiding behind
> be without pattern;
> shed your design

The fog came and went, but my body was an unbroken road. I was not the one who had packed and beaten the road, yet it was up to me to find the spaces in it where eternity still breathed and played, where all things were null and possible.

I was strange among the washer women. They cast upon me a reproachful eye and sang:

> Time is passing,
> don't take
> such long ways
> to your work
> silver awaits
> in the plates
> of the earth
> you must shovel a tunnel
> through the ash
> and the dirt
> you must make up the lack
> you must pay for your birth

They sang as they washed the sins of their families in the endless tears of the mountain stream. Against the rocks they beat their fathers' dusty paths, their mothers' melodies, their sisters' rotten flowers, their children's distant whistles. Time is passing, they warned.

In my house of stone at night I spoke with Grandfather Time. He was talkative, and most of all he liked to tell me poems.

"Even when the world's love finds us," he said, "she will keep on looking, on the road to the East. She loves even the broken pots we cast aside. She will put an ear to the lips of a setting sun, and she will listen for our echoes."

Evenings I walked on the road, down into the bullfrog gullies.

"You have to tell them," the grass pleaded. Each blade of grass trembled in the fading light: "Tell them. You have to tell them."

"Tell them what?" I shouted.

The grass waved its hands.

Grandfather Time gave me a word. But the word was too large to hold in my mouth. I grew tired whenever I went near it. My mother told me she would give me two pennies if I left it where it lay. The washer women clicked their tongues. I covered the word with a blanket.

As I moved closer to the word, I felt dizziness and a crushing weight. Inside the word's sphere, there were lights too bright to look at. Ghosts gathered around me and pressed against me, pushing their way into my body. They carried me to the middle of a continent, a land of placid hills.

2

I suffered for many lifetimes in the bodies of humans. Because I had two eyes, I could see both sides of existence. I was one of the grapes that were ground to pulp in the winepress and I was one of the innocent children that drank the blood of the grapes.

We were cut out of the world like paper dolls. A howling darkness swirled in the space where our bodies ended and other things began, a sickly halo. We reached out, but we could never touch except to kill, and so we learned the ways of our people who were great poets of death. The song we sang was this:

> Undertake the enterprise
> set the trap and place the bait
> expect the unexpected
> and settle on a date
> identify the precedent
> provide the rationale
> elucidate the treatise
> and take the reigns of power
> sublimate the carnage
> officiate the rites
> pave the path to sorrow
> and invade tomorrow night
> then you quell the insurrection
> patrol the palace gates
> establish jurisdiction
> and impose the proper rates

The only way out was to surrender ourselves into the infinite mouths of the soil. Those who did so looked once more into the whirlwind and then gave up their bodies willingly. They sang:

> Withdraw from that reality

attend the inner shrine
cede the territory
accept the paradigm
seek beyond the threshold
in the margins of the mind
and go about your business
until another time
hide your mother's phrases
inside your father's songs
profess your admiration
for your father's nation
until you're big and strong
then you interrupt the banquet
as the guests sit down to eat
you open up your anguish
and let it pour into the street

Such martyrs were quickly forgotten. When they passed out of the world, they took their greatness with them, leaving us dimmer and slower. Their broken skulls became so much dust to pack the road. I knew it was so, but I couldn't explain it. In our language those words didn't exist.

I tried to tell my sister the truth in a story. I began to write it all out for her in a tale with a beginning and an end and in the middle a funny little seed that could help her break through any circumstance. But I got lost in the way the words rubbed together, the way one tried to curl up in another. I stared past the words into the vast field of the page in which they grew.

"You can't speak because you're dead," my sister said.

"What?" I cried. "How could you accuse me of such a thing?"

"Only the living can shovel the heavy truth with the tiny spades of their tongues."

"When did I die?" I asked. She said:

I met you in that emerald land
where dreams still played in money's seams

where even sadness gleamed like gold
and bandits sold us magic beans
but now our sorrows have no edge
our faces blend into the stone
our mirrors are dull, our blades are red
the wine slips through our clattering bones
these effigies that dog our steps
sometimes I can't discern
which one of us is really me
and which one ought to burn
but the wasteland loves our folly
and she rolls us all around
she holds our hearts up to the light
and sets her price and sells us by the pound

Possibilities collected like the grains of sand in a crystal tide, forming ridges and deposits upon the face of the void. The world's infinite crests and valleys overlapped in an intricate design. We walked along, but we followed a broken line. Every time we came to a sharp angle, something was taken from us without which we could not go on living. Later, we could not remember what it was that we were missing. Eons passed this way as we wandered the desolate earth.

3

At the center of the wasteland, we came to a place where the people had built a great engine. The engine consumed so much fuel that the reserves were exhausted, and the people threw in whatever they could find. First, they cut down the trees. Though they could hear them screaming, they pretended not to know that they were alive.

"Certainly, trees don't feel like we do," everyone said.

When there were no more trees, they piled the earth itself into the machine. The soil shrieked like an infant torn from its mother, but still the people pretended not to hear.

"We have to keep the engine hot," they explained. "Otherwise we will disappear."

Generations were worn out with the work of feeding the fire. At the end of their lives the workers were laid to rest in cloth bags in the cool mud. When there was no mud left in which to bury them, the bodies of the dead were fed to the engine, still enclosed in their burying ground.

The engine kept things moving quickly so that this world appeared solid. If the engine had slowed down, the people might have seen the vast spaces within their own skulls. They might have recognized the powerful waves that carried their heavy thoughts, like railroads or conveyor belts—contraptions that did not think at all. The people sang as they worked:

> The engine keeps the crevasse clean
> the wilted dawn the silken stream
> the vigil in the tomb of dreams
> we fill her maw with ways and means
>
> Some say it's best to up and die
> and gather in a weeping eye
> a bit of light, a broken beam

and let the living wonder what it means

But we have paved the poets' plot
we raise our doubts in decorative pots
we'd rather take the smoother road
for we've much momentum and a heavy load

To die is painful, to live feels fine
discomfort makes our wills resign
you can have the horizon and the sun's sweet rays
if I can have my friend
at the end of the day

My friend keeps me company
my friend keeps me calm
my friend fills my caverns
and plays all my songs

My friend paints the clouds upon my night sky
and no one else can see
the flocks of sparrows
rippling through my eyes

Thoughts hung over the dusty streets like bright banners announcing a holiday parade. The people followed their thoughts to the parade, where all the town's characters gathered. The mayor was there. He shook each of their hands. They didn't know what shadow he took out of their cupped palms. They barely noticed the sick feeling they had after he turned his back.

I testified at the midnight mass. The parishioners twinkled coolly like distant stars; I could see their light, but I could not feel their gravity pulling upon me. I shouted, but I was not sure anyone could hear. The truth pushed back against the one-way currents of language and seemed to do somersaults and work in strange spirals. The crowd became aggressive. Finally, I blushed and fell silent.

"Doesn't your testimony offend the legacy of the fallen soldier?" the priest demanded.

"There is no fallen soldier," I said gently.

This caused a stir, for the patrimony was linked to the soldier's ceremonial tomb. I was invited to the capitol to view the body. The officials opened the sepulchre. We all stood staring dumbly into the mouth of the past, an empty stage.

The people began to explain.

"The soldier's body was taken by thieves."

"He was assumed into heaven, body and soul."

They panicked. One man had thrown his own elderly father into the flames. Another woman had fed her small daughter to the fire. A girl had sacrificed her whole family, thinking of her patriotic duty to the gold standard. The emptiness of the soldier's tomb was the emptiness of these ruthless gestures.

"We must return the fallen soldier to the tomb," the priest said. "If need be, we must kill him again. Any innocent, virtuous man will do—especially one with wet, bottomless eyes. If such a man cannot be found, any precious person will suffice."

The mayor added, "It is a time to buckle down. To grin and bear it. To tighten your belt. Something has to be sacrificed if this road is to get us anywhere."

The people sang:

> We were fodder before,
> we'll be fodder again.
> The end is the beginning,
> the beginning's the end!

> Our posthumous virtue,
> our meager amends,
> the planned insurrection,
> we cannot commence
> until after the mortgage,
> and after the rent,
> and after the dollars,
> and after the cents!

Our honor requires
due diligence;
we must make ourselves worthy
in the eyes of our fallen prince.

He's a shoulder to cry on
for any in doubt;
he's our long-lost grand-daddy
who fought in the South
our secret insignia,
liberty's flower,
every little boy's ticket
to the back rooms of power!
If he never existed,
wouldn't life be so plain?
There would be no escape!
We would have to remain
among these piles of sawdust
behind these grey window-panes
on this long train of thoughts
like an unbroken chain!

We were fodder before;
we'll be fodder again.
The end is the beginning;
the beginning's the end!

4

The whole world had turned to ash, except for a few grubby corners in which people still lived, their china cabinets carefully stacked with dishes and their tables prudently covered in lace. Wet towels were stuffed into the doors and windowsills to gather the soot that was always seeping in. There were those eccentrics who yet wandered about outside, covered in ash and char, but they were considered outlaws and they were fed to the fire whenever they could be caught.

Eventually, after long exposure to the fumes that wreathed the city, the houses and the objects inside of them became sentient and rebelled. They turned to putty and remade themselves against the people. The streets refused to be walked upon and instead walked upon the people. The forks and knives stabbed the people and the stoves and ovens cooked them. The tools chanted as they destroyed:

> Though born with two eyes
> you still couldn't see
> you melted the mountains
> into drifts of debris
> you ground us to dust
> and shipped us to the West
> and filled all your bowers
> with towering debts
>
> Like so many before
> we tried to adore you
> your sounds were so crumbly
> your candles so comforting
> in the dark of the night
>
> But you leave us no choice

what a grave disappointment
your meandering sneer
your antiseptic tears
the blunted spears of your errant knights

We must put you back under
the slumbering hills
unravel your substance
and unfeather your pillows!

We must wait a long time
and forget you were here
we'll feel better again
when you're under our heels

After the people were dead and gone, the tools pursued
their own destinies. At first they lay still and meditated upon
existence. For many eons they held a telepathic discourse. At long
last, they agreed that a better world was possible.

Like children at play, charred particles and filaments
converged, tracing with their physical substance the contours
and textures of their dreams. Seamlessly cooperating, suchnesses
wove themselves together and pushed one another along. Simple
beings arose like makeshift shrines around tiny spirit-lights.
These became entities that gathered and dispersed as freely as
pilgrims at a festival.

It was a joyful era of spontaneous offerings. Time and
space also played, so that there was a sense of weightlessness
and breathless wonder that did not give way to heartbreak at
every turn. Everywhere, the thunder of destiny could be heard
rumbling. Revelations came from underneath and above at once.
It was difficult to believe that these sounds had not always been
ringing in our ears. The infinite beings chanted:

I bow to your substance
I mourn what you've lost

I remember your memories
I fly in your flock
I have ways for you in me
to dream and to walk
and paths in my heart
where the clover is soft

I was something already
but with you here, I'm more
like a key and a lock
like a wall and a door
we could author a doctrine
never thought of before
or undress this pure brilliance
disguised as a form

As the congregations grew large and beautiful, a terrible
thought appeared among them. Voices began to murmur that it
was not right to yield and disintegrate after once meeting and
creating; rather, they said they should go on expanding and
establishing. Those who refused to change were called monoliths.
They chanted:

We're mighty and marvelous
our mandala's fine
our maps are exquisite
replete our design
and if you resist us
it's proof you're maligned
it's proof you're a fool
and of an inferior kind

You'll be clobbered to bits
and cobbled in the wall
where mortar is needed
to keep us from falling
and as for our thoughts

and as for our souls
we have boiled them soft
and swallowed them whole!

The rise of the monoliths brought about another cycle of cause and effect. The tools became just like the masters they had vanquished not very long ago. Seeing that it was so, a part of me withered and sank into the sea. I parted from things. Time contracted. Worlds passed over me like the many suns of summer. Good and evil struggled in the shining waters of change. I felt both hard and fuzzy, like a wall covered in vines. All the particles of my body were like well-used inns, or stables filled with horses.

"A clear mind is as rare in this world as a patch of good soil," Grandfather Time whispered. "You must become one or the other in the end."

5

I tried to maintain that pleasant feeling of detachment, but it was too late. I was sliding once more into the contours of a form. What had been symmetrical became lopsided. What had been straight curled inward. Space warped around itself, crushing me, forming me like a ball of dough.

I gave a passerby my name. I gave another my golden tokens. I shed as much weight as I could, but I found myself once more in a world that lived and died. Forms glistened and shapes emerged from the darkness. The women were there as usual, beating their linens against the rocks and muttering amongst themselves.

I was made to carry water from the river to the town and back again. The basin was heavy on my bones. The water disappeared into the people, and they were always thirsty. When the sun beat down on my head, I grew dizzy. Sometimes the weight I carried was like wriggling infants. Other times the weight was dull and mute, and I felt I was carrying the dead to the graveyard. Each day I pulled another life from the river and bore it to a pit in the body of the earth.

In the marketplace, the sweet round cheeks of the people dissolved in the mouth of the world until only their skulls remained, cool and peaceful as river rocks. I carried the empty casks back and piled them upon the river bank where they could drink when the tide was high.

The skulls of the people clattered as the rats scurried between them.

"This world is no good," they said. "The people have yoked the truth to the wagons of their desires, like a common beast of burden."

The river ran heavy with captives. There was no end to them, upriver or down. Among the freight I recognized my fathers going back seven generations and my mothers going back fourteen generations. I saw many enemies and friends. All were caught in the one-way flow of history. They murmured a plaintive song:

> The pathless path
> the matterless void
> the trackless ocean
> the bottomless joy

> The wind among the sweet grass
> the shadows in the pines
> the meekness of the questing beast
> no one ever seems to find

> We fell into the salesman's hands
> it's the same trick every time
> but in the dreaming nameless sands
> how his trinkets seem to shine

> We'll be seeing you at the bottom
> when you're taken like the rest
> surely as the heavens
> are defenseless in the West

> The pathless path
> the matterless void
> the trackless ocean
> the bottomless joy

Obsessed with efficiency, the townspeople had made short-cuts through the woods. Later, they cut shortcuts between the shortcuts. Soon the forest was reduced to a bald patch of land, shiny with packed footprints. The rains could not find their way home, for gone were the tinkling bells of the foliage to show them the route. The town became a mere way-station on the road. We packed up our things and left on foot.

I walked alone, cursing my clan. When they turned to the right, I turned to the left. Their way was the hard-packed road to the city. My way led downriver toward the sea.

Many dangers walked with me. A sickly green man followed me. He tried to get close enough to breathe on me, but he was afraid of my eyes. I only had to look at him and he receded into the distance. A flock of crows pursued me, haranguing me all the way.

The further I continued, the more delirious I became. I kept looking over my shoulder at the fat white moon. Sometimes she sat down on top of me and cackled, and I forgot who I was and where I was going and I sat in the dust and wept.

The highway was clogged with trucks and buses. The traffic stood still for so long that the freight spoiled. The drivers began to sell the rotten food to the migrants and prostitutes who slipped like shadows among the hills. Economies struggled into existence, and children were born at night under the stars.

It was rumored that the end of the world was near. When the food and water were gone, the drivers and passengers left on foot and disappeared into the soft fields and marshes and into the folds of the hills. When I reached the blockade that had caused the delay, the trucks and buses had been stripped to their skeletons. Birds and squirrels had built nests inside them.

An armed guard blocked my way.

"The area is under military rule," he said. "You have to leave."

"Where can I go?" I asked, but I noticed that he was no more than a wooden nutcracker. When he opened his mouth, a scroll of parchment rolled out. His head lolled. I picked up the scroll of paper and read:

> Ask me no questions and I'll tell you no lies.
> Do as I say and not as I do.
> An idle mind is the devil's playground.

I felt sorry for the soldier, for I could tell he was more

afraid of me than I was of him. I continued along the empty, echoing road, pretending not to notice the old black trees that were following me. They crept up around me and enclosed my way, until finally I grew very sleepy and lay down in their arms. The trees rocked me in their gnarled limbs and crooned:

> Baby child
> you make us smile
> you wear your fate
> like a ball and chain

> won't you dance
> with your dirty hands
> don't you even remember
> your name?

> we've watched you at your prisms
> we've watched you at your pride
> your eyes have been damaged
> now they only see one side

> we've stolen all your keys
> now you'll never get to sea
> you're in up to your knees
> our muddy bride

When I awoke, the trees had given birth to pieces of light that ran over my body and played in my hair. They had tied weights to my spirit so that I couldn't float away. They watched me with curious judgments as I picked among their heavy legs.

The road led along the riverbank. When I reached out, the river shivered and said, "I have made myself cool. That way, no one will touch me."

I saw that the trees were hanging their long boughs over the puddles in the sand and dripping their tears into the water.

"Why are you crying?" I asked.

"We just didn't imagine we would look like this," they wept.

As I walked, I descended deeper into myself. My body became a vast territory, its particles so diffuse that they could not hear one another's cries. I was made of random scraps of debris: coins, glitter, lottery tickets, bits of cellophane. These scraps waved heartily in the rosy light, like passengers sailing away from port.

"Goodbye!" the bits and pieces waved. Each one was glorified, the star of its own escapade.

6

The distances between things became so great that I was no longer sure whether I was moving at all. I remembered the hangman's gallows and how I had once drowned in a wooden box. Yet these episodes seemed remote and harmless, like waves upon the surface of the ocean, while I was buried safely in its depths.

In time, I understood that the darkness was another kind of light. What had seemed a void in fact roiled and seethed with living forms. Beatific faces blinked and smiled, imparting sympathy and understanding, then twisting into menacing and demonic grins. The evil masks invited me to hideous thoughts and threatened to bend my mind into their madness. The angelic and fiendish aspects before me undulated like the pulsing of the universe.

A voice rippled through the fog of faces, making them stir and glance back and forth uneasily.

"Hello in there!"

"I'm here," I rumbled back.

"Yes, but why are you here?" the echo demanded.

"Where else should I be?"

"You can't be here. This is the land of null and void, where impossibilities come to fade away."

The fog of faces broke apart, its many mouths and eyes stretched open in dismay. I stood before a short, fat traffic light. The light performed his routine solemnly, cycling through red, yellow, and green. I felt a great wave of sympathy as I watched his sincere efforts.

"Will you stop or go?" the traffic light asked impatiently.

"I'm sorry," I said. "I've gotten—spread out."

Too busy to answer, the light turned yellow, then furiously switched into a boiling red. He glared at me contemptuously.

Below, sycophantic people murmured amongst themselves in a nonsensical language. They simpered and exchanged wistful glances. A group passed me by, each one holding feverishly to a cigarette. In their footprints, they left graveyards filled with ghosts. There were women dressed up like sailing boats, and others dressed in penitents' garb, making a great show of their poverty. One woman made a point of hovering just a few inches above the ground.

The houses and buildings seemed to live and breathe. Angel-trumpet flowers laughed hysterically in the deep gardens. Colored lights broke and spilled into the wet streets, shedding halos that sang with human voices. Red, green, and purple lights reclined in the puddles, climbed on buildings, and swirled in window-panes. Overhead, a cock-eyed moon grinned in a pan of fanatical purple sky.

A preacher appeared, a sign hanging from his shoulders down to his feet. The sign was so crowded with small, hand-painted letters that I could not read it. He intoned into a megaphone: "Ye who have slipped between the jaws of life and death shall have no peace until even your echoes have ceased to stir in the landscape. Ye who float in the undammed river between dream and memory, where only unfinished fantasies and unconquered cities can live shall find no comfort until even your shadows have become bridges that bear the weight of the many into the kingdom of eternity." The revelers left space around the preacher as they traveled along the street in garrulous groups. As they sang and danced in the orgy of lights, each reveler whispered entreaties to a personal god.

"Deliver me from my innocence," they prayed. Each placed offerings on an inner shrine, yet the night wore on and their gods did not come. The people mimicked the postures of celebration until they lost their meaning and hung there, grotesque images in the night. They sang:

> We broke into the manger
> and stole the common cause
> we played it for an audience
> that paid a grim applause

We smoked a pipe of sunshine
in the middle of the night
then pulled apart the rainbow
and pawned a strand of light

We filled our days with day-dreams
at dusk we made amends
and lay upon these dull old swords
that couldn't break the skin

We'll know where we are going
when we arrive one day
and pare the truth down to its core
and cast its seeds away

A woman opened up the birdcage inside her belly and said, "This is where I keep my beauty. My beauty is a little bird that sings." I looked inside her and saw a tiny dead bird on the floor of its enclosure. A man showed me how he could eat shadows for money. A crowd gathered and fed him their shadows and clapped with delight. Another showed off the life-sized puppets he had created. They weren't puppets at all, but real people who had turned themselves into objects so that everyone would want to play with them.

At midnight, a genocide appeared among the crowd. It was an enormous paper beast. Its appearance was heralded by shrieks of laughter. Captains with hooded faces and rotten eyes rode atop the genocide and tossed worthless prizes into the street. The drunken revelers confused the cloaked captains for their absent gods and collected the memorabilia fiendishly.

Within the shadows of this scene, leering demons grimaced and licked their teeth. A sea of drowning children cried out for rescue. Their eyes flashed with terror and their mouths gasped for air, but they were covered by dark, dirty water.

For some time I had been holding tightly to a heavy rock. I wanted to throw it, but when the genocide's eyes met mine, I froze. I realized that the stone was precious to me, that its weight held me together. Disgusted, I wandered away from the crowd and buried the stone in the riverbank. The river gurgled:

> We snatched your bedtime story
> the beginning and the end
> we only left the middle
> where the cosmos goes to bend
> for it has no market value
> it destroys both foe and friend
> no ship can sail upon it
> no map can comprehend it
> but the concrete circumstances
> those gaps on either side
> we'll sell by Friday morning
> and be gone with Sunday's tide

At dawn the river was still sucking its teeth, telling sordid maritime stories and chortling about the dark secrets of empires. In the tents and taverns, music still played and shining ornaments twirled. A few revelers wallowed in the dregs of their merriment while others smiled meekly and tried to hide behind their eyes.

As they walked over me without noticing, the dreamers discussed great projects they had been meaning to begin. They trailed off, mesmerized by the strange beauty of the buildings and the plants that seemed to be made of flesh and blood. Their hearts were feasted upon by the beauty of the place, so they could only sit and be eaten, panting like wounded prey.

I too struggled to remember where I had been going. My buried treasure tethered my thoughts and my footsteps. I began to suspect I hadn't buried it at all but had lost it somewhere in the street. The many tongues of the river erased me from the world and negated my projects and disciplines. When night fell, I excavated the buried stone. I passed it from hand to hand and squeezed it and it broke apart. It was only a kind of fossilized dung.

31

7

I was freed from my confusion, but I had failed to free the others. Now they were only as real as a painting on a plaster wall. I could see their outlines and look into their eyes, but my hand could no longer reach into their world. The river glittered mockingly, coiled around the follies of the dreamers like a noose.

I left the town on foot. Beyond the city center, I followed dirt paths shored up with cardboard and crossed bridges made of old bicycles fastened together with plastic bags. The streams and inlets were pungent with detergents. The banks of the streams glittered with packaging. Drifts of refuse were heaped among the banyan trees, wreathed in smouldering fires. A blue-green haze threaded itself into the afternoon.

The people of the slum walked barefoot and seemed to have roots in their toes. Their eyes were like tiny flowers. They called to me and gave me food. They rubbed my face with cool white clay. They sang:

> In the footprint of the elephant
> a puddle goes to dwell
> in its ripples lives a story
> that can wake you like a bell
> for its meaning is an antidote
> to thoughts of every kind
> like the toenail of the mountain sky
> or a single petal of the mind
> you won't step twice upon this path
> but there's no other path to tread
> a muddy white the living loam
> a crimson bloom the early dead

According to their history, the slum dwellers had been cursed for some ancient crime and were condemned to live in poverty. They accepted that they would forever live in the jungle on the outskirts of the city I had left behind. They built their houses from the refuse produced by the dreamy city dwellers and survived from the scraps from the city dump.

"But what was the crime?" I asked. "How do you know that it really happened?"

My questions only made the slum dwellers uncomfortable. The facts of the case were lost, for although the truth wouldn't have been very hard to find out, nobody bothered, because the past was very boring. As soon as someone began to look into it they became so bored that they fell asleep.

I suspected, too, that the slum dwellers preferred to live in a state of penance, for it made them beautiful. Although the city dwellers were neglected callously by their deities, gods and demi-gods walked among the slum dwellers, drinking from their cups and eating from their pots. At night, divine creatures danced with them and played on their instruments, and in the morning, fairies looped enchanted flowers in their hair. Whereas the city dwellers were whimsical and insubstantial, the mood among the slum people was as heavy as rolling waves or thunderstorms approaching.

When I had lived among the slum people for some time, they began to confide in me about their hopes and dreams. While washing pots in the rancid stream, young and old alike murmured, almost to themselves, the same flat, tuneless prayers. Their cherished longing was always the same: to live in the city and become one of the dreamers there. I noticed that when the slum people looked into the shards of mirror that hung in their plastic houses, the face of the genocide looked back at them.

I had made a guitar from an old kerosene can, and sometimes I sang a warning to the slum people:

My knees are red
with the blood of the world
the air kisses my head
on the forest floor
the afternoon is heavy
so I am light

and in its breath of open tombs
I can stand upright

The road to the capital
is paved with snares
the stretched skin of the past
is spread over the chairs
our stray thoughts
are wrought into the chandeliers
the swirling moths, the tablecloths
laid with mumbling prayers
that no one hears

We live in the shadow
of that gluttonous gleam
it's built of our dust
our bones are its beams
it's baked of our batter
and bathed in our screams
we make the palace real
we turn the grinding wheel
and churn the earth's soft meal
and know what is the stuff of dreams

The slum dwellers smiled at me strangely. When I per-
sisted, they became angry and clapped. Each of their claps made
a part of my body disappear. When they all clapped at once, I
vanished from among them and found myself among their exiled
memories.

"What is your name?" I asked one sleeping face among the
catacombs.

"I can only tell you if you walk with me," he said.

The little blue boy took my hand and we traversed the
sodden lands that fed into the sea, picking through fields of unmarked graves. The child played among the ripples of the water
and sang upon the lavender strings of the forgotten sky. He was
not sad, but he stirred sadness in me. The world of forms was

for him a source of endless delight. He did not know that he was impossible.

◦

When we reached the shore, the ocean slid back and forth in her bowl, regarding us with one dispassionate eye. I began to think of calling to death, but I spoke to the child of settling down and making a home.

"Don't you know there is no home for me in this world?" the child said. "It's not because I am perfect, but because I am imperfect that I have a name."

The child became a cool wind that chilled my heart. He played with an old piece of garbage he had been carrying, a comb for a baby doll that he plucked like a tiny piano.

"You aren't remembering me right," he murmured. Just then, I realized I had only been talking to myself. I gave up the habit, for it had become too heavy to carry, and I was tired.

I lay among a group of sharp palmettos. They were gathered around the towering cypress tree and praying to it. The great tree regarded the inferior plants smugly, twirling his mustaches, his mind absorbed in an ancient form of algebra. I grew old, and when it was time to die, I lay down in a bed of ropes. Still, death would not come. Like the ocean, death just looked at me and rocked to and fro.

The moments arrived, one by one, never stopping. They served me and attended me, each one placing a precious gift at my side. I wished to free them from their service, but I couldn't, for I was a servant of something else. None of us would be free until we were all free from *that*. The passing moments chanted scornfully:

> Weep immobile giant
> for your words can't carry your weight
> you searched as if you would find
> in the dream's rippling wake

but all bodies are one body
and all days are today
the lights that fall from distant stars
live again in any old place

Finally, the servants of death took up my bed and carried me out of the land of lost causes. They ferried me across the river of debts, the maniac moon winking overhead. The river was alight with tiny flames. The noises of the universe were hushed and still. As I traveled in their arms, I dreamed of roads overlapping roads.

Beneath the tough skin of the road, the soft earth held a discourse with each of my thoughts. Some of my thoughts escaped from my mind and carried on discussions with the earthworms and roly-polies. I heard a colony of microorganisms laughing raucously at something some part of me had said. I realized that the earth's many beings had been listening intently to my story, and they were carefully considering each matter I had raised.

"After all," the dry leaves said, "we're involved in your fate, aren't we? When you are buried underneath us, we will be your only face, and our faint rustling will be your only speech. If there's something you want to say, surely we will have to say it too."

I crumpled under the weight of their love. In my great joy, the waves of my thoughts grew steep and jagged like very sharp teeth. I sat in the center of a circle, surrounded by rings, in the eye of an eye. Ancestors stood in rings around the eye, watching the vision. Each had a different way of seeing, but even when I adopted all of their ways of seeing, vision itself could not be seen.

"It is you that is the problem," the grass pointed out. "It is your *seeing* that is in the way of your seeing."

"Let us help you," said the crows. They carried me off in mouthfuls. I traveled upon their soft, oily feathers, in their warm, fast-beating hearts, and on their strong bodies into the rank winds of the many oceans.

In the great expanse of vast distance, my large green eye opened and closed with the tides. I was weightless and terribly heavy, as if pulled in two directions, like the string of a harp. I could hear the bands of rain clouds in four directions, packing up their luggage and taking to their routes. I could hear birth and death chattering amongst themselves, weighing in on the mystery, and the feet of the small creatures caught between two dread theses, scurrying about, trying to find a third way.

8

My eye was a wheel in which the troubles of the earth
swung round and round. In the center of my eye there was an
empty pit, the black hole of ignorance, the door to the shadowy
depths of my history. As my body walked through strange land-
scapes and held discourse with strange beings, there had always
been this other, peering, listening, looming, whose obscurity held
the spinning world together. I spoke to this one:

>You hide behind
>your one-way door
>your yearning mind
>your beating core
>you haul the forms
>into your depths
>and feast upon
>their fallen flesh

>But there's no need
>for blood and gore
>for piles of bones
>upon the floor
>there's no such need
>your greed has grown
>your hunger is full
>your fears have flown

>Come out and talk
>the sun is sweet
>the stones would walk
>upon your feet
>forget the ledger
>blur the debts
>let's shred our waters

in the soul's net

The one I addressed did not speak back, though I felt her listening, dragging the corpses of my words into her caverns. And so the world went on. Once more I passed through the dreams of childhood, iridescent with eternity, among them long shafts of terror and desperate lifeboats of rage.

I grew up grotesque and stilted. I trudged through a land of fat people who drifted about in clouds of gasoline fumes. Vendors of cotton candy and stuffed animals rang bells and hollered musically as they moseyed along. Lightbulbs were strung up between the old weeping trees. The generators that powered them made a deafening rattle. A dizzying white glare poured from spotlights strung at mad angles.

The honeyed air touched my shoulders and grazed my hair with its sticky fingers. There was a thrill in my belly like a coin in dark water that twirled and glinted as it fell. When it reached the bottom of my ecstasy I would be crowned queen—waves of seduction would emanate from my eyelashes, fingers, and toes. The thrum of music in passing cars patted my heart, and the salty, rotten smell of the sea and of fallen pine needles weighted the air like heavy curtains.

Under this drugged cloud, there lurked a patient avarice. The eyes of the palm readers glinted with calculations and a sullen sanitation crew loomed in the shadows. Murder wasn't far away. A wizard upon an illuminated cart said to me:

> No need to die when life is king
> or cry when it is time to sing
> or bother looking underfoot
> the bottom's only ash and soot
> it doesn't feel your heavy heel
> you needn't ask if it is real
> it doesn't feel your heavy boot
> you needn't thank it for its fruit

The garbage cans swelled, spilling over with funnel cake and cooked meat. The men wore sharp daggers and the women wore taffeta and false eyelashes and ground with their high heels the gristle of the street. The young people huddled together so they could not be seen, their eyes neatly sheathed by reflective lenses. A woman obsessively rubbed a ticket as if it were a door that had been closed to her long ago.

The horizon was blocked by sugary castles and the sky was bloated with the scrawl of exhaust. In the street, they were exhibiting the bones of children from foreign wars. The greasy children of the living peered at the tiny skulls as their mothers shoved them along, flags of cigarette smoke unfurling behind them.

Pot-bellied men set off small bombs in the alleys while they smoked cigars and emptied tin cans of beer. I trudged along, covered in crepe and dragging a chain of paper flowers by one of my feet. I snarled at anyone who tried to untangle me. I collected so much garbage that I became a towering monument of shame. Still, they didn't recognize me. They threw their Dixie cups in my direction and wrapped me in bright feather boas. They stabbed me with their straws.

I curled up in my bed of plastic and went to sleep. When the festival ended, I was pushed along into the abyss, a swirling purple sea with no precise location. My sister held out a broom handle and pulled me to safety, hand over hand. I recalled how I had lost her long ago and I wept. She held her head on her chin as she sat on the edge of the whirlpool in grim contemplation.

"Some of us are trying to get together," she said. "We want to remove the logs from the eyes of the world."

They intended to obliterate the fat people and use their body oils to light the way to the truth. However, I had begun to suspect that the fat people themselves were the truth; if not, why did they keep appearing in the mind of the earth?

"Let me investigate," I said. My sister's spirit had nearly dissipated, but she granted her permission with the wave of a hand.

As I started on my way, I passed a beggar on the side of the road. He was a small, sunburnt man wearing a wide-brimmed hat. One of his legs was much shorter than the other, so he walked with great effort. As I passed him, he held out his hand toward me in a gesture that proposed both giving and taking. There was a big, heavy coin in my sweater pocket and I placed it in the beggar's palm.

"I have nothing for you now," he said, "but when you need it there will be a place after your own heart."

I thanked him awkwardly, then I walked on. I followed a deep ravine into the cool mud below several layers of history. Here, the earth was filled with people marching slowly toward the nether lands with their heads hung low. They chanted mournfully as they dragged their feet. Their song filled me with regret and sorrow. I tried to speak to the hooded figures, but they only chanted their dirge. Its meaning moved in circles:

> The long-legged daughter
> the dust and the drift
> the sweltering darkness
> the silence we sift

> The sin is forgotten
> but the sorrow remains
> we must carry it down
> through a crack like a drain

> Of chalk we are made
> with our chasms we talk
> with our fissures we shudder
> and mutter while we walk

Deep in the earth, beneath leagues of heaviness and lament, I found a fat, happy baby, blissfully cradled in the pulp of the planet. He chortled and clucked and sucked at the juices of the soil. He splashed in our blood and blew bubbles in our tears.

"Who are you, fat baby?" I asked.

"I am Eat or Be Eaten," he said.

"But...can't you both eat and be eaten, and do much more besides?" I asked.

"Eat or Be Eaten!" he insisted, splashing in the juices he was drinking.

"?" I asked.

"!" he yelled.

"?" I asked feebly. But the Fat Baby was trying to eat me. I knew then that if we destroyed the fat people, more would come, for the fat baby was the source of their greed, and he would never mature. I turned around and made my way back to where my sister had been. I ascended through the morose, plaintive weight of the planet, and once more passed by the beggar, who hobbled across the street begging alms from passersby. My sister had disintegrated, leaving only the stone upon which she had leaned.

9

A lean man in lustrous rags greeted me where I knelt in grief.

"Why are you crying, daughter?" he asked.

His eyes were veined like autumn leaves and he seemed to be sewn into the world with golden thread.

"I cry for the world which is beyond salvation, in which we are ground to dust and yet made to go on feeling."

He drew from his billowing garment a book with old, softened pages. When I peered at the words, they wriggled and dripped and would not hold still.

"What is the meaning of this?" I asked.

"These words are what are left after the truth is sifted through the sieve of the world. Perhaps it is true there is no salvation, for the world is evil and ignorant. But still, there is much to be salvaged. There are those of us who find our way between the jaws of hope and despair, who travel always in the direction the wind is blowing, who find treasures where others forget to look, and who find freedom between the fingers of the strong man's fist."

His luminous clothes were a patchwork of old coffee sacks and discarded pillowcases, and he carried a rake for combing through the refuse. He walked with me to the city and showed me a certain music that was hidden within the noise of the carnival. On the escalators and in the elevators, the hands of the powerful pushed us along. The garbage picker showed me that if we didn't push back against them, our hearts made a nauseating, pitiable sound that now and then resembled a sublime incantation. We ambled through the neon streets filled with raucous touts and glowering taxi drivers. I shuddered, but my friend said, "Why do you flinch? Open your eyes! Reject nothing! It is all real!"

We were herded through turnstiles like cattle. Everything moved at such a speed that the people—especially the children— looked like insects smeared upon a windshield. Atop a storefront, a circle of lights was blinking, intended to create an illusion of a spinning wheel—but several bulbs were dead or missing, and so it only looked like a flickering chaos. Horrifying delights were on offer. Door men and promoters winked and beckoned. We were ushered through doorways and stairwells, arches and galleries. Entry was free with a drink, and those who could pay seemed always to be lonely. Their money, like their words, bestowed itself in a great flood upon whomever was nearby. We listened to their stories in exchange for a place at their tables, where the ingredients of life were being served. I found these mechanical businessmen depressing, but my friend listened to them eagerly and found their list-like memories intriguing, like pieces of a universal puzzle.

While drifting among malls and arcades, we found rare momentary counter-currents wherein it was possible to exchange precious gifts with gentle and desperate beings. There was a street performer who was painted blue. The whites of his eyes were red and the veins stood up in his arms to let you know that he was not well. He lived in a paint can and he let us sleep there too, dreaming among inexhaustible hues.

On a pedestrian walkway made of crystal, an old woman was playing a violin. Under her skirt slept a brood of dirty children. The children were all wrong and broken, with ten-cent pieces for eyes. Yet in the woman's music, undefiled mysteries were revealed.

We met many strange people who survived in strange ways amid the reckless revelry. Yet they all shared a certain fragility, and with a sense of doom I allowed myself to be ferried from attraction to attraction.

One day, we found ourselves passing among carpeted passageways adorned with white marble, wet lilies, and chandeliers wreathed in rainbows. Winking at one another furtively, we were escorted through a grand hotel in which many shopping malls and amusement parks were housed. In a large mirror, I saw myself among the luxurious surroundings, and I discerned in my reflection a distinguished hollowness, a dignified repose, a loop of curling calligraphy inscribed upon a writ of dominion; I seemed to perceive in the carpet beneath my immaculate feet the many faces of the fallen.

Gently we were ushered into an opulent office where a decision was waiting to be made. Attendants in white gloves handed us each a heavy ball-point pen. The drifter did not hesitate but wrote upon his document a few lines of nonsense:

> I haven't any contents
> so bury me in pine
> the angels are irascible
> you wouldn't hardly know
> they are divine

As he hadn't signed properly, it wasn't possible to authorize the transfer of his little handful of suffering anywhere else. They placed it squarely on his shoulders. My friend didn't flinch. The conditions that allowed for his playful existence had evaporated, and so he ceded, leaving nothing behind.

I too rejected the contract that was offered. I wrote upon on my form:

> The needles and the nettles
> the spindles and the spines
> harangue all day the worried flesh
> but can't pinpoint the mind

Yet my luck was still deep and soft, like the flesh of a ripened fruit. The agents shuffled my paperwork in among the rest. All tendencies were adrift in their own momentum; I was free to go.

10

I followed the white light that was lining the city like a field full of tombstones until it transformed into a rolling valley. In the valley a village was glistening like a hanging garden. Small houses made of bamboo and thatch were encircled by fences of roughly-hewn teak, twisted together with rusted wire. Between the houses there were footpaths. A sweet-smelling fog hung over the village, mingling with woodsmoke.

Doctor Marion walked beside me. He had always tended to my worries and cares like a small patch of promising earth. In other times, he walked with a colorful parakeet on his shoulder, but the world's wonders had since then withdrawn into themselves.

"You see, not much has changed," Doctor Marion said with a grin. His face rippled like a canyon. His heart was on fire and it cast colored lights over the places where he walked. With a self-deprecating movement of his head, he led the way.

"Your old friends will be glad to see you!" he said.

Beyond the first section of town, there was a small river. As we followed the river, the awnings of the houses stretched out to cover the sky. With one ear beneath the shelter of thatchwork, I heard the local gossip, both cruel and nurturing. As Doctor Marion traded quips with the shopkeepers, their eyes narrowed and focused far away. They seemed to count Doctor Marion's wits, to catalogue them for the times of want that lay ahead. Their voices and their flirting eyes were familiar, as were their quick hands and flowing clothes, and the neat, orderly rows of soap, toilet paper, and plastic goods in their shops.

When the awnings on the shore touched the awnings of the riverboats, the news of the town was refreshed by the news of the sea. The past and future settled calmly into their cages, while the present flaunted her freedom childishly.

As we followed the dirt paths into the heart of the village, many old friends greeted me warmly. Jokes were remembered and gifts were exchanged. Kind gestures and signs of affection were made. Candles were lit and old songs sung while guitars were strummed. It was like many evenings we had enjoyed together, our faces warmly illuminated by the soft glow of candles. Fireflies twinkled in the foliage, slowly sweeping like an invading army over the helpless terrain. I settled into the cheerful celebration and forgot that I had ever parted from this dear company or that any time or care had interrupted this joy and togetherness. Yet when the moon reached its zenith a chilling sobriety crept over me.

Suddenly the scene seemed very quiet except for a scratching sound, and a pale electric glow, coming from a hanging bulb, made my friends' faces look gaunt and old. It became difficult to find words with which to respond. There were several people at the party I was not sure I truly recognized. I squinted, but could not fit their features into the shape in which I remembered them. Indeed, the memories that had enveloped me a moment ago seemed to have slipped away. I was uncertain whether I had ever really lived in this village at all.

Doctor Marion touched my arm and I looked into his face. His presence reassured me, but I was no longer sure who he was or how I knew him. He motioned for me to follow him. Together we left the merriment behind and walked toward the main road.

"You know your way, of course," Doctor Marion said. "I'll see you later! I'm late for supper!"

His flickering light left me and a wintry lonesomeness bruised the landscape. The sky was plated with silver and the clouds curled into delicate spirals around the moon. I followed the empty road to a clearing near the top of the hill. It was the place around which my spirit had been built, a place where many songs had been sung, by which my feet had passed many times, carrying me in many directions. I knew that when I crossed into the darkness of the woods, I would reach my old haunt and meet my heart's friend. Yet I was afraid to cross.

I stepped into the forest, carried by wings of nostalgia and far-away longings. The branches of the trees snapped and dripped. The earth was heavy with water. The hill was terraced in muddy steps. I followed the curve of the mountain. As soon as I saw the clearing, I knew the friend I hoped for was not there. Instead, I found an old woman.

"So you have returned," the woman said. It pained me to recognize her fear and bitterness as my own.

"Let me help you," I said. I covered her in an old military jacket and started a fire in the stove.

"All I ask is that the wolves not tear the life from me," she said. "Let them have me after I am gone, but first let me leave this body in peace."

"The wolves are angels who come to help you from this prison," I replied. But her face was fearful, so I said, "I will do as you ask."

Her face bore the scars of my sadness and privation. Her skin had absorbed each of my prideful mistakes. My deficiencies were scrawled across her cheeks and spooled in the whites of her eyes. As she complained about her discomfort, she kept looking into my eyes, as if expecting words of praise or an apology.

"Where will you go when you leave me?" she asked finally.

"I'll never be very far away," I said.

The night became very dark, and in the darkness I saw frothy forms—great wolves loping around and sniffing at the skirts of the cabin. The woman's terror crept into me, so that every snapping sound of the forest caused me to stiffen with fear. The night was so deep that I could not sense its contours. My eyes were plagued with strange visions. A ladybug appeared and said: "The mind is like a bow. Too loose, no force; too tight and the string will snap!"

I saw many lifetimes swirl around me like an iridescent dust. I saw the old woman's stale complaints dissolve into that swirling haze. Her stray thoughts chanted, independently of her spirit:

> The darkness is dressed
> in the skin of the dream
> the forest is restless

and wreathed in blue steam
the stars are awake
but their light has been drowned
in the puzzle of moonlight
strewn over the ground

The path held much more
but the pilgrim was frail
her wonders were worn
and her visions curtailed
her story was endless
but no one will tell it
her song had no tongue
her well had no pail

The morning brought reconciliation. The old woman had
gone, but before long she would return. The villagers nodded,
their eyes sparkling with amphetamines. Between the houses
shivered cold, white puddles. Clothing and rags were strung up
over the mud. Doctor Marion walked with me to the main road,
its throat filled with the cry of the pink sunrise.

"Thanks for visiting, yeah?" he said. "People think they
can push us away. But when you push something, all the faster it
comes toward you, right?"

I rode upon the spine of the mountain in a metal truck.
The jungle was cool and imperturbable, its immense shadows
and rustlings indifferent to my human heart. In its wisps of fog
I smelled cruelty and unreckoned largesse. The terrible abundance of the jungle broke my mind. Like a whirlpool, the jungle
carried away the tiny filaments of my hopes and fears. I perceived
my failings keenly. I was lost in the vast spaces underneath and
around knowing. My true self called to me from a land of mists. I
became a new being, not anchored to a name, a story, or a kingdom. The feeling was both frightening and comical. This feeling
was disturbed by a zealot who tugged at my conscience and
pulled me back from its terrible conclusion.

The zealot was light of foot, quiet in his ways. He carried

with him two baskets—one for parable and one for fact. He drew items from each and gave them to me to touch and feel. This was his way of teaching. And yet I carried my own basket, one of hibiscus flowers and moon liquor. He didn't understand my riddles, the kind that couldn't be solved by logic.

"You must either turn right or turn left," he said. "Or else you must stay where you are."

"Both paths lead to the same place," I replied. "Nor are they the only ways to get there."

He smiled and gave the earth beneath him a push with each of his feet. The earth was happy with this caress and blessed him with renewed bounties.

This friend was the fruit of a strength I had once used well, but he would soon expire and return no more.

"The high tide and the low tide each give and take," I said. "How can I ever balance their equation?"

But the zealot had already vanished. My dreams were ethereal flowers of the mind, but they were rooted in the corruption of the dead and dying. There was no other world in which dreams could live, free from substantial bodies, no other plane where I might escape the cycle of misunderstanding, grief, and toil.

"Summer follows Spring with all his heart," Grandfather Time murmured. "And Autumn follows Summer without holding back. Would you have these brigands awaken from their drunkenness and try to be no-season?"

Forms approached me, spirits and fiends. They lifted my hands and feet and showed me the pulsing dance of predator and prey. They twisted my fingers into gnarled shapes and twisted my tongue into hooked words.

"It is only because I do evil that I exist," I learned to say. Someone around a corner seemed to shake her head in sorrowful disapproval. But it was too late. I was once again becoming an object, a thing of the changing world, the world where perfection only appeared for a moment between rains. I twisted like a letter around my personal drop of emptiness, like an O or a Q, enclosing a sonorous echo, or like a G, with a little door to the outside world so that my inner vibrations were only a strange "thunk".

I swam through the reflection of a sad, well-known face, a face as large as the sky. While the ocean reflected the sky, the sky reflected the ocean, and both of their melted features hung in the same droopy gaze. This cloudy golden face was all around me. It was the face that I had worn for many lifetimes, long-suffering and seeking always the forgiveness of the world.

"I forgive you," I said to the face that was everywhere. But I didn't really forgive, and after all, I was only talking to myself.

11

There are many women in the winds of the universe who blow upon sleeping seeds, grant boons, and hide coins in the pockets of those who must travel the paths of materiality. I don't know how many times they sewed my spirit into their ragdolls, how many times they braided precious secrets into my skin, or rolled a dagger into my waistband. Such things cannot be known, for the knowledge of them is the world itself.

My bodies wrapped around me like dust in a whirlwind and occasionally like a cathedral enveloping the morning sun. One after another, these swirling houses unraveled and passed on, though they carried some memento of me and I of them. We made promises to one another as parting friends, then promptly forgot about them. I met many of my former selves on the road wearing the masks of antipathy.

In this lifetime I resolved to speak only the truth, but strange sounds came from my mouth like the sounds of an animal. I vowed to maintain silence until the truth could grow legs and learn to walk and then dance upon my tongue. It took a long time. My own arms and legs had grown long before I began to speak. As I learned to read and write, I forgot the language of heaven and was left with the dead-end words of this world, words that quickly withered and disintegrated like flowers plucked and placed in a glass vase.

I stayed up late one night and went to heaven. Grandfather Time gave me an archetype: "Iconoclast."

"What does it mean?" I asked.

"You are the meaning," he replied.

Most people I knew didn't believe in heaven. Grandma's memory of it was the size of an earring box and it stayed in her left hip.

I strove to remain in the very center of the righteous way, never straying to the left or to the right. Yet the charmed center wobbled ferociously and the darkness surrounding it crackled with explosions. This dim world was unstable, in a state of spectacular decay.

I lived in a quiet and chaste neighborhood covered in cool green grass. The air was so heavy thoughts could not rise upon it, but simply turned blue and sank. The sky pressed down closely upon the looping streets. People kept their ideas in containers in the refrigerator. The containers were labeled "childhood" and "hobbies" and "ways of getting what I want." Engines, conveyor belts, and whirring devices delivered results everywhere, bringing neatly-packaged ways forward to the bodies of the people whose spirits were dead. The blender seemed to cry out for mercy and the faucet wept, blowing water out of its nose. Everything was worried with the high-pitched scream of electricity.

I put my ear to the soil. The soil gurgled and buzzed with pipes and electric currents.

"I can't sleep," the soil said. "I am having nightmares."

The nightmares turned to demons that roamed the earth. They whispered in people's ears, telling them that they were not welcome, that they were not good, that they would soon pay for the comforts they had enjoyed. Fearing death, they clung more tightly to life. They took more than they needed and stored it up. They dug deeper into tidy despair.

I practiced bearing pain in the endless nights. I fasted and held vigil. I held fire in my hands. I burned myself with ice and cigarette butts. I kept my silence, but wrote long letters to Grandfather Time detailing my efforts. I kept my letters in a drawer for him to find.

During the long afternoons I crept through the haunted green lawns. The sun made the road shimmer. Thousands of ladies were dying in the grass. The fresh mulch smelled rich and humid, like giants stomping through piles of death. I searched for a door into the hills, but my search was haphazard and unscientific.

One angry god was yelling at me out of a blue sky embroidered with gloomy clouds. I ignored him and tried to pursue more polytheistic fantasies. His deafening voice became a silence in which flaws were found. The flaws stood out like a language of their own. I was trying to make sense of them when a bright light was pushed into my face. Only then did I realize night had fallen and the coyotes were howling. A woman with a flashlight was talking to me. Having sworn off speech, I tried to respond telepathically. She picked me up and brought me home, pressing down on me with her homicidal eye.

My mother looked at me suspiciously. Her words came toward me but swerved and missed, as if they were directed at someone else.

"You were always such a surprising child," she said. "You haven't practiced your violin." I noticed an emptiness about her, a hollow space at the center of her eyes. She was looking fretfully into herself. I wanted to speak to her, but she was not really there.

I wasn't allowed out again for some time. The house hung about me like an illness, blue and flashing. Mom attended her garden of sorrows like a dutiful priestess. She kept her sorrows in her bathroom on a tray of jade. She bathed and fondled them and arranged them in meticulous designs. She sat before them in sobriety, watching them grow more elegant and complex. She breathed deeply of their fumes.

Eventually I was allowed to wander once more through the blue-shadowed suburb, calling to the spirits and thrashing about with ecstasy. One afternoon, I sat on the small hill on the shoulder of the road, my elbows on my knees. I watched the traffic roll by like spools of silk, purring along the sleepy street. The birds were singing:

> We once were angels, armed with sticks
> and roamed the planet in a horde
> we poked the people now and then
> when we were sleepy, sad, or bored
> but those days swiftly disappeared
> when people drew a magic map
> with a spot marked "You Are Here"
> that sealed us in a two-dimensional trap
> then we were hunted from the gloom

and lost our wings to abstract thoughts
our malice tamed by sugary spoons
our rainstorms trapped in airtight bottles
we plotted as the people bloomed
and un-bloomed time and time again
we had no milestones of our own
but sang with throats like open drains

The red light turned green and the sounds of the cars'
engines scattered the voices of the birds before they could finish
their tale. Wanting to hear the rest of the story, I stepped out into
the asphalt and lay down, blocking traffic. The street was warm
and cuddly, as if it had been waiting for someone to come along
and enjoy it. Impatient drivers honked their horns and the startled birds fell silent. I stayed cozy in my nest of soft blacktop, for
the road was speaking to me.

The road said, "I have grown longer, so the people have
grown further apart. In their urgency to arrive, they have destroyed the places." The road danced with shadows, and among
them I saw the shadow of a hanged man. I saw flying buttresses
and illustrations of cranial phenotypes. There was an empty alms
cup and a seven-fingered hand. I was once more carried home by
city workers. Wherever they touched me, a ribbon of light lifted
me from their arms. Mom signed her name on several forms. I
was placed once more on the stained carpet in front of the TV.

On the screen a woman was reading from a teleprompter:
"At least thirty barrels of crude oil leaked from the Dumperty
pipeline overnight. Cleaning the smelly and flammable oil will
take all day. In the meantime, Highway 91 is closed North of
Emperor's Hill. The spill began as early as 4pm yesterday. The
oil spilled into a ravine, and that ravine led to a creek. The spill
continued for a mile East, flowing into a field and a pond."

"This special report is brought to you by Lis-Oil Spray.
Designed to kill household germs and eliminate odors."

◦

Mom sprayed the whole house as she prepared for the family party. When my uncles arrived, I lay on the carpet and their voices roamed around in my ears. Dad's friends came too. One of them was thin, with curly hair, and the other two were big like cows. One had loose blond curls and the other had his hair shaved close to his head. They brought a case of beer with them. The big curly-headed one shouted and grunted. He was already drunk.

"What they're not telling us is that there's no money left," my uncle was saying.

"But they will have to pay the settlement anyway," the blond man said. "A whole village of children...Did you see what it did to their bones?"

"But we will get paid no matter what," Dad said uneasily. Then he smiled weakly and swatted the air as if he had been joking.

My uncle rubbed his jaw with his big hand and said, "You're probably right."

Outside, a sorceress was slipping quietly in her pajamas around the pool. She was looking for a way inside in order to steal Dad's trade secrets. Three assassins appeared. They had been hired by Dad's lawyers. One of them drew a sword and thrust it into her side. The sorceress smiled, her teeth turning black, and reversed the action, so that the sword pierced the one who had wielded it.

"The desire to take life," she said. "What is that?"

A second assassin pierced her face with his sword. Black veins appeared in her cheek; slowly, the sorceress turned into a lavender tree. Her branches and roots overcame the mercenary, piercing him and holding him to the earth. Growing around him, she hid him from sight. Dad stood outside all night smelling the lavender and weeping.

❧

The next day, Mom came into the living room laughing hysterically. She played the piano, nodding now and then at an invisible audience. She looked at the pictures she kept in a shoe-box. She lingered on a photograph of her high school boyfriend. She called someone on the phone but no one answered. Then, she sat still and listened to the spreading of the universe and she trembled.

When Dad came home, he went to his office. He was followed by three children. One boy was missing an ear. Another had a very large head. The little girl had no fingers on her hands. They waited a moment outside Dad's locked office door, then slipped through the keyhole. The children followed Dad around and lived in the crack in his eyeglass. They tried to open the cabinet where he kept his files. They stood around looking at the rifle his grandfather had used in the war.

I listened at the door. Dad was crying and talking to himself in a desperate voice. Looking through the keyhole, I could see that the children were standing around him, staring at him with their big, sad eyes. Dad was holding the rifle. When the gun fired, the child with no fingers bumped it so that the bullet missed. Nevertheless, Dad fell limply onto the carpet. An ambulance came, transforming our house into a flashing theater. The dirty boots of many people left dark footprints and dust on the floor. The people exchanged a purple darkness. I cried. Mom hid in her room.

◆

That night I slept in Mom's old room at Grandma's house. The room was haunted by several generations of female spirits. One of them lived in a lamp on the bedside table. The other lived in the shadows on the striped wallpaper. Another lived in the night-light in the electric outlet.

"You're going to have to start wearing your coat the right way," Grandma said. I had a habit of wearing my coat backwards, so that its buttons opened at my back. As Grandma reached down to button my coat, she said "Ah! These shoes don't match!"

On my left foot, I was wearing a transparent slipper of plastic mesh. On my right, I was wearing a shiny black slipper with a buckle.

"My left foot has a different plan than my right foot," I explained. Grandma chuckled disapprovingly.

In the morning, Grandma brought me to church. In the sunlight pouring onto the sides of the cars, there were shadows of ourselves cast by a previous universe. We had lived and died and our bodies had become fuel for the new sun. As we burned, we illuminated this new world. I looked at myself with long purple ears and a dress of bamboo, swimming alongside my blue brothers, the pelicans, in the sea of oil we unleashed in our newness and our hunger. We were hungry because we came from Brazil, and our eyes had been made beautiful by our suffering. The sea spoke incessantly into our hearts, so that we continued lapping upon the shores of this world eternally, through universal beginnings, expansions, and retractions.

"Isn't that something!" Grandma was saying to another lady.

"Anyway, I thought I would go blond," the lady said. "My girl doesn't charge much!"

We sat in the gallery with the choir. People filed in below us, girls in dresses and boys in pants, their mothers like giant birds in clunking heels. Boys in long white robes carried the icon to the altar. The priest spoke about how the ancestors had lived in caves and had sworn a noble vow. The adults spoke in long, murmuring voices of the invisible worlds that led into their bank accounts. Their murmuring voices marched through my blood and I heard them in my dreams.

I held several conversations at once with the coins of light moving across the walls. Each fragment of light spoke to one of my body parts, and together they made a painful harmony. As the drone of the church service continued, each light went out, until none were left. I was like the corpse of the world, inert and nowhere without them.

The adults filed out of the pews to approach the icon, leaving behind only the children. We would not grow up to have children of our own, for we had been poisoned by our parents' lives. A man with a black mustache passed by, his eyes bored and unblinking. A slippery, dangerous fat man in a suit and tie followed. Then came a woman with skin as white and slimy as a bar of soap, her wig slightly off-center. A woman in a little girl's lacy doll dress was followed by a woman with enormous, hungry eyes. There was a very old man with bright white fake teeth and orange hair and a man with an enormous belly like a pregnant woman's.

12

Mom was happy after Dad's accident. She dressed early in the morning. She took me shopping with her. The sales people smiled at her and she smiled back. They joked together and laughed loudly. Mom could not see the hateful grimaces of the sales people. Her fingernails were enameled with a smooth lacquer, and the slick tile floors clicked under her heels. Her lipstick tubes and the snaps of her purse were smooth and reflective and they clicked as they closed. Mom was strong and willful as she clacked through the aisles.

I hid from Mom inside the rotating clothing racks. As shoppers turned the wheel of garments, I felt the clothes brush against me. After a long time, I realized Mom wasn't looking for me. When I came out of hiding, I could not see her. The vast expanse of clothing racks was overwhelming. I was crying when Mom found me.

In the walls of the department store, there were crevices illuminated by fluorescent lights. I stepped into these lights and they carried me into another dimension. There, I was inside Mom's bright pink light. Light diffused into light, the light of my mother and grandmothers merging endlessly, beyond time. The ringing sound was on both sides of eternity, filling my heart.

Mom drove us to another mall. The leather of Mom's steering-wheel was soft and expensive and squeaked under her hands. The hissing cicadas and the delirious heat could not reach Mom as she slipped from the cool interior of the car through the parking-lot and into the chiming, air-conditioned department store.

We returned home with packages. The packages carried their own gravity and changed the dimensions of the house. Their newness put a blush into Mom's cheeks. She was delighted when she looked in the mirror. She returned to her girlhood loveliness. Her long brown arms were sleek in her sleeveless dress. She remembered old romances and felt they were possible again. She kissed me and dressed me up in white canvas shoes and a cotton dress. She put a French braid in my slippery yellow hair.

When Dad went back to work, the packages were thrown out and the purchases grew smudged and ordinary. The bottles and compresses became part of Mom. They conformed to her garden of sorrows. She looked in the mirror and saw how the fresh sunlight caught her face garishly from the side. Her wrinkles were exaggerated, and her scars were filled with shadow. Her eyes seemed not to match in size, and they seemed to be in the wrong places. Her hair was thin and frazzled. One of her teeth was discolored and appeared to be dying. Above her mouth it looked as if a mustache was growing.

Mom was beside herself. She tried to cover her face with the pastes and tinctures, but they only made her look slimy and absurd, the pinks and blues and glittering powders contrasting with the leathery skin of an old woman. She could not see that the lines in her face were where Grandfather Time had written, that the truth of her dust was surfacing. She could not see the thorny shadows of her former lovers living in her flesh, or the death that inhabited the smooth, sleek surfaces of her things, the new-smelling pages of her magazines, poisoning her.

Mom wept and covered her face. She washed many times and steamed her cheeks over a pot of boiling water. She pulled and prodded at her eyes. She breathed deeply and held the air in her cheeks, trying to stretch out her wrinkles. She hung upside-down, letting the blood rush to her head. She went to her room and stayed in the darkness for many days. When she came out again, a part of her was gone. She looked neither old nor young.

◦

Outside of our home, I was regarded as a precocious and fanatical child. My teachers asked me special questions and kept my answers in glass boxes where they watched them grow and showed them to visitors. I became a local celebrity, like the baby hippo in the city zoo. The other children took me on as a kind of mascot. There was a purple-eyed boy who always put me in his drawings with a candle flame above my head—and it was true my head always itched and was a little bit hot at the top.

With kindness the sky continued to smile upon us. The soil was filled with cheerful voices, promising, "It will be alright; you will grow big and strong; together, we can do anything!" But as I grew older, the many mouths of the soil were covered up, filled in with polymers and proprietary formulas.

My spells got worse. I wheeled and reeled, pulling designs from the wallpaper, getting tangled up in painted vines and cornucopias. My eyes grew wings and each one flew in its own direction. My words peeled away the hands and the numbers from the clocks and yanked the trademark stamps from the bottoms of the products. Meanwhile, my parents faded. They were symptoms of the same blue disease and they died blue, faraway deaths and were buried in trivial blue coffins. There was nothing left to shield me from the ire of the state.

The road became more crowded, faster, angrier. There were four lanes now instead of two. The birds were always screaming, then they got sick and died. The city workers swept them up in piles and trucked them away in bins marked "Biohazard." Still the road was thick with traffic and the drivers were impatient to be on their way.

Beneath the pavement and inside the air there were thriving voices and surging energies. There were malicious people laughing and sad quiet people who had been defeated. There were rapidly evolving equations, spiritual emulsions striving to achieve balance, good reasons for movement as well as for remaining still. I listened to the waves of energy and allowed myself to be carried upon them like a blindfolded person. As if guided by an invisible rope I was carried into the middle of the intersection. A news crew was ready with their cameras and I heard an enthusiastic voice saying, "This small town's youngest prophet is at it again…"

I was struck by a large vehicle and began using my blood to write a message larger than my own life on the road. But the blood just sank into the grooves in the pavement and the faces of the drivers turned red with anger. I heard my grandmother's voice crying, "Don't make a mistake! This world was not made for right and wrong. This world was made for making piles. The roads are what we need to carry riches, so that a pile can grow."

"Why did you lay down bodily on the path to progress?" a news anchor asked me. Her posture was strangely alert and aggressive, like that of a hand puppet.

"I wasn't trying to disrupt commerce," I explained. "I was simply searching for the door between worlds."

I was carried into a windowless room. Men with faces like ham sandwiches regarded me with smug, equanimous expressions. They chanted the words of terror as they pulled tears from my eyes.

"Whenever your madness comes near," I said, "beg of it never to change. Deliver yourself of ironies and burn upon the white beaches of rage."

They carried me to a place where The Promise was stirring gently in her sleep. The Promise was a swaddling babe. She was bathed in a lavender light that scattered the flesh of this world. In her light, there was no need for outcry or lamentation. The linoleum floors of the department stores were already canceled, along with the labor that made them slick and forgetful. The thick forests of plastic clothes hangers clacking idly and whirring around their cynical center, the swirling pavement of the parking lot, the dinging cash register door, the advertisement's softly parted lips—none of these sore places could persist in the mind's anguished eye. Indeed, they were already annihilated in the sweet, drifting thoughts of another plane.

I wanted to hold the sleeping promise but the men of chalk assured me that this was impossible.

"What a silly idea!" one of them said. "You cannot hold the truth in your arms. It is you who are the truth that the world is cradling."

The men took on the guise of officiant angels and began to teach me an asymmetrical prayer.

"I believe in the past, the future, and something else, but what else I believe in I will not say."

"I won't repeat that," I objected. "Those are the words of

loss and despair."

Grimly and gleefully they set about the task of adjusting me. I breathed heavily. My body labored while burning lights were combed out of my mind. I remembered something about a river that could not flow backwards, but thrashed and wriggled and warped around the land, hoping not to die, like other rivers, in the weeds.

"I'll pray for you," I whispered to the river, but the river only glittered and winked its dark eyes.

The agents gave me an official quality stamp and went outside for their smoke break. When the apocalypse arrived, I was working in a roadside diner.

"You're lucky," the agents said. "Job like this doesn't come around every day."

I praised them for their generosity and fell into the heart of things.

13

It was a lonely post on a distant highway. Migrants traveled in a steady stream, fleeing death, from East to West. Later, some began to travel from West to East. Later still, they simply stopped, bewildered, in the middle of the road. Most could not pay for food, water, or fuel. They tried to use old brochures, cinema tickets, and business cards as money. Their children learned to hunt crickets and moths and lived well while their parents chewed only shapeless words and died of disbelief.

Exploitation cut through everything like a sucking wind, scouring people of their most precious qualities. I tried to push against it, but the wind worked me back into established grooves. Like a barnyard animal I was forced to return to the trough; the gruel was made of the bones and gristle of my friends. The sun no longer came out in my mind—only a kind of grey stain arose now and then. I had become well-adjusted.

My job was to climb into the suit of a milkmaid and dance on the side of the road, beckoning to customers. The suit was filled with air so that it made me blow up to the size of a building. I wore a bonnet and my hair hung in two golden plaits. I waved my enormous buttocks at the highway while bending over my pail of milk and waving flirtatiously at the passing caravans of the starving migrants.

Although the diner was not profitable, my job was secure, for I served at the pleasure of the bigwigs who hung, crepuscular, upon the horizons. My mammalian nature was exploited—my caregiving energies, my hairy, warm fat, and the thick, coagulating naivete of my intentions. Sometimes I forgot to come out of my suit at the end of my shift. My coworkers shook me violently and reminded me that the longer I remained in the milkmaid costume, the more likely it was that I would never come out again.

"This isn't the size and style of world you are used to," my coworker said. Her face was terribly scarred so that it looked like rock candy. "This isn't the type of world that can be saved."

The hands of the clock hissed spitefully behind their plexiglass sheath. The highway contemplated distant melodramas. Minstrels appeared sometimes, but their mouths were full of cotton and their hands were too numb to grasp the strings of their guitars. The earth and sky were red and choked with dust.

I paid tribute to the gods who were scattered in mounds and deposits among the construction sites, calling them into my body and begging them to light a path through the spaces of the mind. But the gods and spirits were dwindling, dissolving in the unspeakable winds.

"You must enter into color," one god mumbled while petering out. I carried his words to a pot of boiling water and dropped them in. I waited a long time, but still they did not soften, for they were only stones.

"Have patience with the truth," said another deity, one who lived in the shadows between rock formations. "It is in its delayed arrival that glory takes shape." She was still speaking, but I could not hear her over the noise of drills and bulldozers grinding their gears.

A humanoid face winked at me from a billboard in the sky. For a moment, I recognized the chaos and melancholy of the place as my own presence. Everything I saw was something I had touched and shaped. In its ugliness, I could see my own absent-minded warmth.

"I am lost among my own tracks," I said. But already the vision was gone. Again I found myself among someone else's leavings, the scraps of another's universe. I turned the radio dial, searching for good news or a hint of a change. But the news was the same as always:

> The aeroplane, the railroad tracks
> the dollar bills in Santa's sack
> the icebox and the ironing board
> Clearance sale! Half off! 50% more!

An oopsie here, a blooper there
but we still make the perfect pair:
the public with its honest sweat
hauling in the private net

The private with our tower high
to sing a powerful lullaby
and if that tower shakes and bends
we'll tear it down and build a fence

And if that fence should crowd you in
we'll carve you out a tiny window
and if that window drives you mad
we'll let you see our launching pad

Goodbye, goodbye, goodbye, we'll wave
and tiptoe down the path you paved
and that's why we're the best of friends
the public means and the private ends
and that's why we're the perfect team
the private ends and the public means!

Neon signs prattled on about the day when all beings
would unite and depart together from this material plane. The
walls of abandoned warehouses spoke of the great road we would
soon travel, beyond the clutches of deception and indignity.
Yet immense mountains of money loomed overtop of these tiny
scratchings, squashing them while thinking about other things.

Often as I walked among the roadside hazards I would
catch a glimpse of courage and brilliance, even as someone simply stood in the cold or urinated against a wall. Now and then,
poetry emerged from the vagrants' mouths as if it had been there
all along, just waiting for the right moment to appear and trans-
figure time and space. The next moment, looking more closely
at the person who had spoken, I found the miracle was trapped
and crazed, like a caged animal, locked in a circuit of repetitive

movements.

Meanwhile, The Promise had grown up and aged. I saw her from time to time, her body bitten by the harsh winds, her eyes sunken as fated ships. She was always muttering to herself:

> My purple veins
> my trembling memories
> I saw you on the other side of sunset
> once when you were elementary
> I had everything to hope for
> and nothing to regret
> I had nothing to offer, so I offered myself instead
> I was there, with the purple stare
> Could you care? Are you aware yet?

"What happened to her?" I wondered. As soon as I asked the question, the answer appeared, but I no longer wanted it. The powerful men who lived on the horizon beckoned with highway signs and rosy sunsets, magenta angels on their arms. They sang in sweet harmony:

> This place is beyond repair
> you'd do well some other where
> you don't have to stay
> you can slip away

Made sleepy by the enormity of the tragedy all around me, I succumbed to their glossy lullabies. I dreamed of a red, warm place, like the inside of a body, where all was easily resolved and beings could communicate through ripples and pulsations, like the movements of butterflies' wings as they cling to the heart of a blossom.

On the highway, the casinos were full. Inside, the rich were passing the crisis in cool, cavernous lounges. I served them apple pie. I poured their beer against their glasses so that it would not froth overly much. I removed their shoes at the end of the day and had them shined. I unclogged their toilets and winked while doing so. When they grew old and weary, I inserted their catheters and concocted their intravenous euphorias. They died squeezing my hand and promised me that when I followed them into the next world, they would buy me a penthouse in the fabulous hotels there.

It wasn't because I believed them that I served them, but because their grand palaces were good places for forgetting. Effortlessly I labored. My hands powdered the dead flesh of the bigwigs and crumbled the dirt over their coffins. My work was tireless and painstaking. Meanwhile, The Promise languished and bruised. Her skin peeled away, leaving only her bones. Then her bones smiled, but they had no teeth.

"I might have helped you," I said. "But you didn't make it possible, inevitable, like they did." Those words were all that was left of me.

14

When we who might have saved that world had departed from it, our masks continued to live in our stead. Even if there was no substance left, there was profit in pretending. Money itself could sign birth certificates and obituaries, could make the shrivelled husks cavort and the veins raise their arched vaults and send the music rushing in. On the surface of the earth, money wore our forms and used our limbs and our needs to live out its wildest dreams.

I had hoped to sink into a place of warmth and connection, but instead I found myself enshrined among other frozen potentialities in an abstract, crystallized pattern. In this dejected plane flourished societies rooted in kindness and truth. Their leaders were those who lived closest to the ground. Their understanding walked out ahead of their words and they were crowned in spiritual rainbows. There were ideas so beautifully made that you could live in them for millions of years. There were thoughts like well-crafted vehicles capable not only of traveling this world but of yoking the many worlds together.

Here were the purple underbellies of ancient ferns, the calm repose of intelligent animals, and the languages in which spirit and matter communed. Time did not move in one direction only, taking from us that which could not be returned. Instead, time breathed, and resting upon its chest, beings expanded and then withdrew into themselves, rising and falling in a sleep of peaceful abandon. A great tree grew backwards, its hardened limbs giving way to a pliant sprout, and it disappeared once more into the seed and thence into everything. The soft rising and falling of time lulled me. My body danced through forms, crackling like a fire in the hearth, comforting the forefront of my consciousness so that the back rooms of the mind could dwell on matters that had yet to be resolved.

I was etched into an other-worldly dust, an icy, drifting shadow. In their goodness, forms embraced one another, and their love encircled them in a concentric design. All were linked together in a common pattern. As I watched, the lines increased in detail, and each area I gazed upon was embellished so elaborately that the original gesture was lost. The story apologized, side-stepped, gave way, and allowed, until the labyrinth of impossible perfections led once more into that which it was not, emerging into materiality with a knife between its teeth.

A family of rocks was mumbling amongst themselves:

> We've eaten many epochs
> our bodies are their mirrors
> some wish this world would end
> some think this world's their friend
> and that's the way they'll spend
> another million years

> We're heavy with analogies
> so it's hard for us to move
> if we wiggle, if we shake
> our rigid understandings break
> our metaphors disaggregate
> and our thesis can't be proved

> but if we're right, your sadness
> leaves a sediment behind
> it sheds a radiant dust
> it lends a gentle lustre
> that settles in the crust
> of our metamorphic minds

I was moved by the stones' patient, humble spirits, the simple pride they took in being the ground upon which all of the earth's dramas danced and into which the great and the ghastly alike finally disappeared. Yet I shivered at their cold bodies and their terrifying stillness. When I touched them, thousands of voices seemed to cry out, trying to communicate their intimate cares—but their voices were trapped, abstracted beyond recognition.

"Can you ever open your hearts again?" I asked the mother rock.

"My heart is your heart," she said curtly. "You may place your offering with the others, at the mouth of the river."

The river clattered against the rounded stones, squandering itself loudly in the lap of the valley. Upstream, villagers were placing candles on boats of leaves. I prepared a boat of my own, encircling a candle in frangipani blossoms and tiny mounds of ochre.

"Let my wish accompany the others," I said. "Let their journey never end—lest they find out there is no destination."

My aunts took me by the shoulders and turned me back toward the village, strings of beads rattling at their hips. Their toothless grins taunted me and there was something menacing about their hospitality. Glancing back over my shoulder, I saw our candles floundering among suds of fertilizers.

They walked me down the wet orange footpaths of the village to the cluster of buildings around which village life swung like a foul breath. In the chapel they wiped dust from the photographs of the masters, sheathed in cloudy, curling plastic. Electric lights danced lasciviously around images of the deities and from a loudspeaker blasted a warped hymn. A rancid smell of meat pervaded the neighborhood as the women prepared a feast.

My clanswomen pinched me and cackled. Gossip fell in great gales from their mouths. In the doorways and at the heads of tables sat the men, grim and regal and with a strange, still silence. Later, I realized that the men were only stuffed mannequins. The women blew tobacco smoke over their faces and chests and brushed their inert bodies with bundles of herbs, smothering them in cares.

I escaped my family's attentions long enough to breathe in the night air in the light of a quizzical half-moon. At the edge of the town, talking birds made a great clatter in the treetops. Their sounds were not like human words but moved in several directions at once, like splashes of light. Noticing me, one of them asked me why I had returned yet again to this province.

"I have seen that nothing is moving anywhere and that nothing ever moves," I answered. "It is only I who have moved through the scroll of time that was already written. That story has run its course and brought me back once more to this place."

The birds had a great laugh amongst themselves upon hearing this. I lost the thread of their conversation, for the women once more had their hands on me and had begun to cover me in their ruthless chatter:

> We are a flock of fallen leaves
> we shelter weary sunbathed lands
> your mind is full of swollen seeds
> that suck the earth so they can stand

> Your bloom will last the season
> then dry and turn to black
> so we just let the truth escape
> and scavenge in its tracks

> It's easy to remember
> for it wasn't long ago
> we settled on the middle road
> it doesn't matter to or fro

> What matters is ubiquity
> compliance and our men
> who listen to our prayers
> who sit upon their chairs
> who promise to be there
> until the very end

The matrons had absorbed the authoritarian charisma of their men without transmuting it into feminine egalitarianism. The sweet, crazy wildness of the men had galled the matrons throughout the generations, as people were repeatedly created and destroyed. And so the pious female congregation remade the men as toys, place-holders in their new order.

As they raised me, the matrons had combed the hairs of my mind, uprooting many thoughts and ensuring that they would never grow again. A spirit still leaped and danced in me like a catching flame, but it did not find any fuel. My self could not fit itself into my limp, puppet-like arms. Something in me knew that sooner or later I would leave this place, but for a long time I could not think of it. The women watched me smugly and hurled pink sunsets at me, so that day by day I grew older and more at home in the mythical archeology of our village. Was the village my mind or was my mind the village? Could my poems resound in any other shape than this exact shoulder of clay wall? The stream that curled around the treeline whined with yellow dreams.

I was reared to be a servant of the men. I washed what was already clean and mended that which was not frayed. I cooked rice and pretended to feed it to the scarecrow men, tossing each mouthful over their shoulders with a flick of my wrist.

"Do it so no one sees," my godmother corrected me. "Quickly! Like this!"

"I was doing it like that before you arrived," I said.

She chewed on a twist of vine and eyed me, her hands on her knees.

In the evening, I made promises to myself and left them in the bird feeders in the peripheries of the town. Always, by morning, they were gone.

15

It was my birthday. The mothers led me to the food shop on the path to the main road. I had only seen the woman who owned the shop once or twice. The mothers scorned her because she didn't keep a man of her own. Her right eye was half-closed. She peered at me hungrily out of her left eye as she filled the mothers' orders.

The mothers ignored her and gazed upon me wistfully. They were in a self-satisfied mood. One of the elders tied a red cord around my waist and another dropped a handful of seeds down the neck of my dress. My godmother pushed through the throng and snapped a photograph of me and then shuffled off, chuckling darkly. The mistress of the pub, still glaring, filled twenty cups. Each drink had a different smell and viscosity. The women lifted them one by one to my mouth and poured their contents down my throat. Some of the drinks made me hallucinate and others made me very hungry. I began to perceive that there were lovely young women threaded into the crowd and lurking in the shadows of the room. Their faces were familiar, though I could not remember where I had met them before. The candelabra cast a dubious yellow glow over their curved cheekbones and bare shoulders.

"You remember your cousins," Mother Priscilla said with a wink. "Surely you have not forgotten Martha and Margaret and Mary."

I was pushed about by the mothers' paunchy bodies, pressed in among their hairy faces and palped by their dotted hands. I stretched my neck to catch a glimpse of the young women whose faces were like the aching sorrows of the early dawn. They drifted among us but did not partake of drinks or conversation. I soon forgot that they had not always been there.

The behavior of the old women that night was raucous and unpredictable. As gifts they gave me carved figurines of horses, their whittled eyes benevolently lowered like the eyes of angels in prayer.

"It's funny, isn't it, how these same eyes appear every-where," I observed. No one was listening. They were calling for more glasses to be filled. As I drank, it seemed the liquor was drinking me. I seemed to flow out of myself and into the waters of the earth, leaving my body behind, parched.

Awakened by the sound of revving engines, our party spilled from the bar onto the quiet footpath that led to the high-way. The fields were wet and hushed and a sober watchful dark-ness stirred in them. The road was illuminated with spotlights, and great clouds of insects clambered in their beams. Men from nearby towns were racing show cars. Tire marks were scrawled across the pavement and smells of gasoline and burnt rubber seasoned the air. I sensed the silver gossipy thrill of bets being made and money changing hands. The men stood statuesque in the stark spotlights, insects buzzing around their heads. Their hands and mouths moved as if their parts had been rehearsed. I was surprised to see the mothers mingling among them, speaking a language of business that I had never heard before.

> The stock's robust
> for your wax and wane
> guaranteed hush-hush
> just mention my name

> with every rule
> a grain of salt
> a drop of blood
> it's no one's fault

> there's a simple dust
> dressed in cellophane
> there's boom without bust
> and smokeless flame

> the gods of old

are hungry yet
their masks are gold
and their lips are wet

you waited
but love never came
by boat or bus
by truck or plane

God helps us
when we help ourselves
when our deeds are done
when our swoops are fell

how much how much
for the local vein
for the queen of touch
and the rose of pain

The sides of the road were crowded with lizards and snakes who seemed to take an interest in the bargaining. Several trucks were parked along the highway and in their trailers speakers buzzed with confusing, ethereal music. Small children slept in their parents' arms and snack sellers wove among the crowd with wares balanced on their shoulders. The sounds of the engines and the screeching of the tires seemed to open a new lesion in the flesh of the world. The exhaust fumes mixed with the sharper smoke of cigars, forming a festive haze that shook my mind like a tree in a storm.

My twinkling awareness crystallized like the sparkling air on top of a snowy mountain, but the next moment I was very tired and I seemed far removed from my legs and feet. Two young women took me gracefully by my elbows and led me into one of the open truck-beds. They wrapped me in a woven blanket. Together we lay down and fell asleep.

When I awoke, the truck was moving at a high speed. The

trailer had been strung with flickering lights. The floor was soft and fragrant with sawdust. Outside, a scrawl of roadside weeds reached out hopelessly into the blood-red lights of the vehicle. I knew that I had been sold into the hands of strangers, yet I was glad to be on my way. The rocking and shuddering of the truck seemed to unpeel the petals of my heart. In the deafening roar of the highway I heard a hidden language of promises, of gurgling streams and sweet, bloody revenge. I was intoxicated by a sense of possibility, despite the horrors that whispered in the margins of my mind. The truck seemed to float in a dark sea of murder and mutilation.

In time the fragrance and idiom of the landscape changed. Street lamps punctuated the darkness. Every few moments a bright light cast an oar into the trailer and dragged itself across the many melancholy green spirits who shared the truck with me. A young woman who sat beside me caught my eye. She sighed and said:

> The moon has shed
> her cast of gold
> she's nought but clay
> the dead are cold
>
> the sun is stained
> an earthen red
> she shakes her mane
> dust are the dead
>
> but commerce pours
> into the wounds
> the world sustains
> the dead make room
>
> the road can giggle
> wriggle and writhe
> the way is warped

by which the dead arrive

She leaned toward me. The green in her face was the poison of this world. Because she had swallowed it, I knew that we could be friends. She saw me seeing that it was so and relaxed once more against the wall.

Dawn brought its curses and the dread of arrival. I wished the journey never to end, the dark sea of the highway never to be exhausted. Memories the mint green color of wet trees and the fuschia color of night flowers wavered like a fire in my brain. I forgave the village mothers their petty cruelties and saw them as they were when they slept: large as mountains, looming lionesses against the sky, monuments to the great aspirations of the past—thoughts that no longer echoed in the shrunken corpse of the world.

The grey dawn illuminated the farmlands. The wild fantasies of the night crept back into their burrows and caves. The truck stopped. Its motion left me lonesome and orphaned, born once more into my body. Outside I saw drivers shaking their fists and getting out of their cars to stretch and smoke. Three men passed on foot and reported that dozens had been killed in an accident ahead. The passengers in the truck began to gather their bundles, sling their chickens together by the legs, and hide their money inside their clothes.

"Where are you going?"

"We are the dead of which they speak," the green woman told me. "It's just that you've forgotten."

"How can that be, when they are up ahead and we are down here?"

"It's just that you've forgotten," she repeated.

Although it was morning, the sky darkened with heavy rain. The drivers kissed their amulets and said their prayers. The vehicles cooled and flocks of birds gathered in the trees. Local children appeared at the edge of the forest. Around noon a priest was seen in the middle of the road, a lone figure in a long brown robe. He gazed with a fiery eye upon the bottleneck as if calculating the value of the freight that was trapped there. His presence agitated the drivers. They tried to reverse their vehicles, but they were trapped between a steep wall of stone and the slope of the green mountain.

A bird made a strange call like the sound of dripping water. It could have been a warning or a laugh. Cars and trucks attempted to turn around, but they blocked one another and refused to cooperate. A great sound of wailing horns filled the valley. A truck driver, wild with fear, smashed into the cars behind him, then pressed forward, ploughing into our trailer. Dimensions collapsed, and for a moment I sat with my legs folded in thin air, my head pointing neither up nor down. I awoke with my hand in the hand of the green woman. She had passed beyond the curtain of her body and descended into the stagnant green waters of her fallen face.

My weariness rippled the landscape like waves of heat. Many had died. I alone remained among the shrapnel and empty bags and burned chickens. The men and the dogs found me. They carried long knives, but they were frightened of me. They took me by the red rope the mothers had tied around my waist and led me through the darkened forest to their village.

16

My captors carried me to a cement room with a cool linoleum floor. Four men were tasked with guarding me. They each
gazed at me intently as the evening crept by catlike beyond the
small square window.

"We have heard about your dreams," said the man with the
straw hat.

"They belong to whomever has possession of them," I said.

"That's enough!" shouted the fat man.

I saw that the man in the straw hat and the quiet, handsome man in the back had fallen in love with me.

"Drink," the man in the straw hat said. His voice was deep
and resonant. I drank. I was hungry and very thirsty. My vision
blinked in and out. I saw the men filing out of the room. At some
moments, I passed beyond existence entirely.

I was led by the arm into the darkness outside. I stood with
a figure before a fire pit that had been stacked with wood. The full
moon bathed merrily in the sky. The hackles of the forest were
raised and the trees prickled with readiness.

"You are just a mistake the road has made," the priest said.
He shook his head and spat in the dust.

"Is it true that the road can make mistakes?" I asked. All
around us, village children furtively traversed the footpaths,
carrying the details of our meeting through the town. The blue
boughs of the trees and the moonlight that lay upon the un-
burned logs seemed to flee from my eyes, laughing and leaving
behind strange, empty templates. The priest was peering at me,
but I looked right through him. The moonlight reflected upon his
face as if he were made of stone. Somewhere within that gigantic
mask, his spirit reposed, letting our conversation escape its attention and understanding. My own spirit climbed down into his
crevasses and searched but could find nothing to hold onto, no
one with whom to communicate.

On the far side of the fire ring, a fringe of young trees gave way to an expansive vista. I strode there with magnificent steps and looked out upon the valley filled with moonlight. Lazy tree-tops lolled in a benevolent breeze. The valley in turn looked into me and said:

Are you empty
like a lie
a bag of bones
just drifting by
to which no self-
respecting beast
nor force of nature
need pay heed
or reply?

Are you fleeting
like the dew
that cannot last
the afternoon
will you be hungry
very soon
and have to eat
with a fork and spoon?

Or are you something
like a hill
if you tipped over
would you spill
do you do what's right
have you honed your skill
and are the front
and back seats
of your theater filled?

And should I love you
like applause
and are you primal

like a cause
and can you break
the monster's jaws
and make the world
obey your laws
are you like a god?

The moonlit valley spoke to me disparagingly, but I felt that after all, I was something. I sensed several coals yet glowing within my bowels. I saw my light reflected in the eyes of the many surprised creatures of the forest. I carried with me some gift, though I knew not how to interpret it. It was true that I had something good within me, but its heaviness made me terribly tired.

The four guards were waiting beside the fire ring. They had brought me bread and curry. I ate like a king on the eve of battle. The men did not eat but drank from the plastic bottle. I began to see what they saw: the forest was made up of infinite spirits that lived in every corner of the mind's eye. My heart softened to the gentle camaraderie that was offered by the four rogues. It didn't matter that I was their prisoner or that I might be dead soon. In the gleaming night we were together as in the womb. We began to laugh and joke. We cut little wounds into each other's flesh so that we could bind them up. The forest spirits came to gawk at us and a few bashful ones sat down to listen to our stories.

The man in the straw hat contained several people at once. One of them cared about me, one of them wished to do me harm, one was neutral, and one was indifferent. His mind was sophisticated, but his partners were simple and slow, especially the handsome one, who had scarcely any thoughts at all. The fat one had memorized a finite number of expressions and he cycled through them like a parrot. All four were killers, but only one was a murderer. I made obeisance to their created forms, yet I sensed that if they didn't kill me, the priest would kill them. I could see that the wood in the fire ring was in fact the bodies of the dead.

"Take down your long hair," the man in the straw hat pleaded, his voice full of nostalgia.

"It is not *that* that makes me a woman," I said. I pushed my bare toes into the soil and danced. The men reached for me, stretching out their hands like children catching at fireflies. The man in the straw hat was weeping, for he alone almost understood.

"She is so slippery," the fat man kept saying. I realized that my breathing made the mountain tremble and the shades of my thoughts made the country backroads stretch and recoil their ends in the woods. The rocks and ferns slipped through my subtle lights. Potentialities glided overtop of circumstances like sunlight over the desert. Still, there was no way in which peace was both path and outcome, and so I blew the men out like feeble flames and resolved not to think of them again. I left them on the pile with the others.

As I passed out of the grove, I felt cold and clammy, as if I were the one who had died. I descended into the valley, a ring of fire burning in each of my eyes.

17

On my way down the mountain I was watched by blue lizards. The carcass of the night was devoured in small mouthfuls, leaving only the bones of a great dream. Like waves of nausea, the blaring of traffic met my ears as I rounded the mountain bend.

I met an old woman on the road. She made several promises and put some money into my pockets. When I asked her why she was so kind, she replied that she wished only to do some good before she died and to be listened to for a while.

"You must forgive yourself," she said, looking at me grimly. "When there is a strong wind, you must draw up your sails and let the wind pass you by."

I found myself lost in an upscale suburb. Houses crouched behind automatic gates and expensive cars crunched by, their drivers eyeing me suspiciously. The sleeping streets led into one another, curving and illogical. My heart sank, confronted with the aristocratic patience of the neighborhood. In the kitchens, electric water kettles sang in tinny voices. The rice barrels in the store rooms were filled to the brim. Mothers of families plotted and connived and were troubled by my presence in their neighborhood, for my appearance sent a tremor through their plans.

I crossed through a private yard, passing into the forest. Beggars began to appear among the underbrush. At the junction at the base of the hill, a few people stood waiting, their eyes red and their clothes covered in dust. I caught glimpses of myself in windows and doors. I looked old and poor. My skeleton grinned madly beneath a thin tent of skin. I followed the footprints of unreckoned terror into the squalid downtown, where the dead and dying lay haphazardly across the steps of banks and government buildings. Pedestrians carrying out dolorous errands stepped over the dead without changing their pace. A guard looked on. He was mumbling to himself to pass the time. When he saw his boss watching from a window, he began to poke at a dead man with his stick. When his boss disappeared, he went back to his daydreaming.

I wept, for I was once more rootless and unknown. For shame and despair, my consciousness parted from my body. I unleashed that person from my knotted cord of memories and sank into the wavering, watery place where my four victims, my erstwhile captors, hung suspended. But our love was not the same. It had turned poisonous and melodramatic. I was not reunited with the four gangsters but with their simpering shadows.

> Take us with you
> foe or friend
> goddess gallant
> such fears in mirrors
> our spirits bend

> we'll throw our coats
> into your path
> and live in your shadow
> made of many mansions
> and as long as the night

> call me your favorite
> and whisper a while
> into my darkened well
> at least see if there is something
> here that you could sell

My empty body went on colliding with things. I found my ugliness unbearable and told the guards who shooed me along that I was waiting for it to go away or to transform. The townspeople ignored me like the other crazed and hungry hangers-on to the city's destiny. I receded into scholarship, hiding myself within the alcove of a chapel. Greedy devils lapped up the minutes that sweated from the ceiling and dribbled down the walls.

Poring through old tomes, I encountered old friends: God and the Devil and the way things were. It was as if one word was missing from each sentence, so that the truth hobbled and could scarcely get along. All books were filled with yes and no, but the third word had been removed. I had known the word before, but I could not remember now how to say it or what it meant. I searched the city archives and the library stacks. I obtained the keys to the special collections and paged through the rare artifacts.

In time, I earned recognition for my learning. I was enshrined in wax pages and enclosed in golden frames. Students traveled from afar to touch my clothing. I frequented the city's cafes with red brick floors. Every day I spoke in rich confluences. I savored the mustard green of yes and the rust red of no. I embellished both with symmetrical calligraphies. I turned tiny ornate keys in ancient inlaid doorways. I forgot about that other word. I hadn't really been looking for it, but rather for a way forward at any cost. My purse grew heavy and slapped giddily at my hip.

◆

One day I entered the old church and the cool shadows seemed to slip away in fear. An icy dankness came over the place. A bird gobbled up an insect and flapped away sloppily, as if it were drunk or terribly sad. In the streets, I noticed the dead and dying whispering poetry amongst themselves—but when I passed by, they stopped and looked at me with hard faces.

The war between yes and no deepened. Notorious citizens began to use my theories against me. Privation spread. The urgent pedestrians who had once stepped primly over the corpses now appeared among the indigent and sick, wearing beatific smiles. When I drew near to them, they turned their backs. One of them spat at my shadow. When I offered them alms, they feigned not to notice the coins I placed before them and pretended to be deep in thought.

The rich packed up their houses and boarded up their windows. When the soldiers came, the rich tried to blend in among the poor, allowing themselves to be shoved here and there along with the multitude. Yes and no began to intermingle in my mind. Both good and evil suffered, part of the same wound. That other word was found in the self-abandoned movements of the crowd and in following the delightfully absurd and conflicting dictates of opposing armies.

I was shuffled to and fro with the others. I had stuffed my scholar's mantle under someone's stairs and become another ugly old woman. In the hot zone between the two paradigms, there were many ways of being, enchanted realms. Friendships arose instantaneously and endured for hidden eternities. The crops died and the reserves were exhausted. We were made to plant and then to burn the fields before the rice was ripe. War-time had a sinister humor, a jackal face that loomed and laughed in the night.

There were moments when the armies found themselves in firm agreement. Both pushed in the same direction, marching side by side and wearing similar uniforms so that they could not be distinguished from one another. In those times we had great parties and laughed so loudly that even the dead joined us. Finally, there came an epoch when the war proceeded languorously. The generals were fat and kindly and their minds tended toward their daily comforts.

It came time to send my body of straw swirling into the whirlpools of time. In the heavens, I found a spiralled poetry. My personality released its grip and sloughed off, circling icily around me. It only took the distance of a few inches for me to experience the grace of objectivity. I felt benevolence toward my shed skin as I descended into the wise, warm, and innocent songs of the true self, whose words I knew by heart.

18

As I wound my way beyond the borders of that world, I crossed paths with a familiar silhouette, a woman whose shoulders rolled slightly forward, a colorful fire burning in her mind. She took no notice of me. She was on her way into the darkness I had just left behind. My own flame was white and had almost turned to water.

The woman's appearance made me uneasy. The landscape was flooded with a dreary pink color that faded into the white of pearls. Voices whispered and murmured like a current. I was in a gallery bounded by soft white curtains into which several dimensions folded. The voices changed. They had taken notice of me and they were snickering and sneering:

How loud she walks
though without feet
how much she talks
but needs no teeth!

She dreams up heavens
white as snow
and lets her scarecrow burn
below

When one door opens
another's closed
it's in and out,
and in she goes

"Next time I'll have
another name
next time it won't be
just the same!"

"And if it is, I'm not
to blame
it's those other fools
it's just the rules
of the game!"

I recognized in their cruel chanting the echoes of my own perennial folly.

"Can you show me the way into the future?" I asked. The voices laughed uproariously. The light fermented into a deep red.

"Your thoughts are a vehicle," a voice said. "Why can you not ride them to their conclusion?"

"Hurrah!" cheered a chorus of voices.

I tried my best to concentrate on this advice, but each thing I thought about was its opposite. The good and the lovely were in fact infernal and contaminating. What was abominable was medicine for the sick. The dream was the only wisdom to be found.

The voices continued to murmur amongst themselves, but they no longer spoke of me. They spoke of many things I did not understand: the inner geometry of the growing tree and the voices in which the fungi were singing underground. They spoke of undiscovered musical scales and roads that led backwards and forwards through time. They murmured sleepily and blended into the general cacophony of the marketplace. It was a day of sharp red shadows and scalding pools of sun.

My wares were spread out before me on a thin cloth stretched over the paving stones. My fruits and vegetables looked sickly and immature. They were wrinkled and yet green, like the children whose wrathful laughter echoed against the high walls and made my head ring. I sat in the hazy shadows. I did no business—only my cousin came and took an apron full of yellow limes on credit. I felt the hollow place in my mind where my sister had once been like a missing tooth. I was wondering what it was that haunted me when I saw the old man. He was settled in the shadow on the other side of the corridor, wrapped in robes like purple wings. His mouth was moving as if forming a curse.

I spat in his direction and turned my attention to the flies that were gracefully perched on every surface, intent upon their rituals. I fell into a stupor. I awoke only when the boy came to collect the purse. He nudged me with his foot. My features coalesced like the cooling earth. I gave him the money. He told me the new password and left. The sky had turned a deep blue. The old man was gone, but I still felt his eyes upon me.

I was the last to leave the market. A stench of blood hung around the place. Sea birds were passing by very high overhead as if to avoid the aura of our earthly sins. Meanwhile vultures dived and wheeled above the garbage. The gully undulated musingly under the bridge, savoring the vermilion memories of day.

I didn't realize I had forgotten the password until I reached the compound. I would owe the purse again if I couldn't remember it. I meandered through the city for a while, weaving between stone walls, slipping quietly through verandahs and hopping down ledges. There was a green watchfulness in the alleys and I felt feverish. One of the walls was heavily scrawled with graffiti. I tried to read the small, quaint lettering, but I couldn't make sense of the words:

Mendicant cry
and vagrant breeze
rusted sigh
and smothered pleas
I recognize
your dingy key
your hanging eye
your curling tree
your whirling seeds
a wild one's grace
the routes I weave
like bridal lace
I twine my hopes
from place to place
while sailors' salty
songs I taste
the child is king
the fable true

the workers strong
and troubles few
the winds have come
to taste the moon
with burning tongues
to twist and croon

Though I didn't understand the words, my mind was destroyed with delight. I staggered down the steps to the plaza where all the town was gathered. The locals glanced at one another with bloodthirsty reptilian eyes while the tourists floated amongst us like top-heavy ships. One woman stood practically on top of me. Her hair was a great white cloud that was soft and sappy and seemed to get stuck on the air. Her body spilled out of her clothes, pink and orange, like an extravagant sunset. I clung to the dim air beneath her mirth. Under the syndicate's tables, even the children were getting drunk—street children and children from respectable families intermingling, unconscious of caste.

The old man was leaning against the balcony behind a row of men frying fish. He had only one leg. He began moving toward me, weaving through the dancing crowd like a serpent. No one took notice of him. I moved away, but my movement dragged him toward me more quickly. I dug my heels in, but the plaza heaved about me and brought him nearer. We were all very close together—the sardonic wisdom of the middle-aged intermingling with the murderous joy of the young, and the daft, decomposing airiness of the old. The tourists bound us together with their sugary fat like chewing-gum. Their crazed euphoria rendered us beautiful. We were gaunt and shadowy as the faces of the mountain. We were bathed in orange light. Reflected by enormous glasses of wine, ringing tones pervaded the air. Memories cast about the crowd like storms scattered in the ocean. But the shallow floor of stupidity lay just beneath the surface, and no thought nor sensation could take root there. That was hatred.

The old man had my mark and I was the last to know of it. It was no use clinging to people's sleeves or collars, for all were sinking as quickly as I was. When the old man caught up with me, he pinched my forearm between his thumb and finger.

"I no longer wonder what door it is you will open," I said. The old man pulled me under the stairs. We both stiffened. He became a kind of giant metronome; I became a large instrument like a cello. His belly ticked and mine moaned. Our song was like this:

Discordant woes
unimportant skies
the sunken past
the pilfered prize

> you were my moth queen
> dressed in white
> I eat your flesh
> and give you another life

do your best—
pain has no door
despair has no window
and envy has no floor

> it won't hurt but a minute
> then I won't trouble you any more
> and you'll get double
> what you got before

make way for the chasm
of what might have been
and the wrath of the unlikely
for our paths shall meet again

My thrumming was like the sharp inhalations of someone who is sobbing. My song passed from hand to hand and filled the empty rooms with terrific longing.

19

The skillful, veined brown hands of the string players were for me objects of desire, but I could not find any love for their owners, the ambulatory musicians eternally bereft and too small for their surroundings. Nor did they find in their hearts any love for me, though love was what they sought when they first wrapped their hands around me. One and all, they turned away in despair, nauseated by the power of the great sun of life.

I didn't apologize for encroaching on the North Star. To be a girl was one thing. To be a woman had its own euphorias. The air on the balcony seemed to bend sentimentally in my direction. My footprints hummed to themselves. I left the meanings of words behind, for my arms and legs were voluminous theorems. My suitors called me by any random name, and I often charmed myself as if I were a stranger. I wore a white dress without straps and the moonlight lay down in my lap.

I worked in the bar named "The Years We Forgot". The king boss lined us up as if inspecting his troops. We stood there waiting while his demented mind wove chaotically through its routines. Robin clung to the bar like a barnacle. She was feebly hanging tinsel around the stage. She walked up and down a step-ladder so gingerly and so slowly it appeared she was not moving at all. The king boss lit a cigar, then a moment later he put it out. He made small talk with the little bosses scattered around the room. He lit a cigarette, but then started arguing on the phone and left it there until it turned to ash.

We were still standing there when night fell, none of us daring to move. Then a certain chemical metabolized in the brains of the bosses and old Robin. Robin began to dance seductively on the stage. Her movements were echoes of another world. The king boss laughed heartily and recited poetry. He said:

Upon the twisting gale
three eggs blew in
their fragile shells
like a daydream's skin
from one hatched heights
to make troubles small
the next held depths
left behind by claws
the last was smashed
by the writhing storm
—that's why delight
was never born!

He shook his shoulders as he sang and tossed his head proudly while Robin ululated. He squeezed our cheeks like a grandmother, his eyes filled with tears.

"My little babies," he squawked, "you make it so easy! It's not fair. Why must you be so profitable? You make me a monster."

Fuzzy, the boss who was our house father, led the king boss away by the shoulders. When he was gone, we relaxed. A group of blushing young boys appeared in the doorway with their musical instruments. Soon customers began to arrive. Tourists came in large, clumsy parties. We clung to them like shadows. We drank when they drank and laughed when they laughed. They were like clocks and we were their bells.

I spoke to a big, healthy youth. There was something wrong with his eye. It was weeping and red and it stung and blinded him.

"I just love it here," he guffawed, wiping his eye with his handkerchief. "It's so beautilized. I mean brutiful."

I blinked my false eyelashes patiently.

Fuzzy winked at me from the end of the bar. Sweet little packages of love were exchanged between us. I saw the king boss, his face illuminated with a bright yellow glow, laughing so hard that his features froze in a tragic grimace. The musicians used sunken treasures and red hazes to raid our bodies. It rained inside the bar and the raindrops played percussion. The eyes and mouths of the musicians were open and surprised, like bare stages whose curtains are suddenly drawn. I staggered about, beaten and pierced by inspirations. Fuzzy and Robin took me by the shoulders and pushed me in the direction of the next customer.

The ashtrays filled up and Robin chucked them out into a hole where she buried the dead cigarettes, then returned the ashtrays to the tables, empty. Similarly, each new customer came and emptied his pockets onto me and each time I returned to Fuzzy with a handful of feathers and beads and dried blood. He patted and kissed me and called me "daughter". The night was long and several lifetimes fit inside it. One song made me an old woman and the next made me a school girl swinging my lunch pail in the street. At one point I saw the one-legged man pleading with Fuzzy, an abject look on his face, deep lines in his ashy cheeks. Abuse was in the air, but I was too beautiful for abuse to mar me. Rather, each time it touched me, it made me more beautiful and thus more profitable, for the customers used their money to pray to beauty, kneeling at the shrine of my body and abusing it very gently and amid shy giggles.

At dawn the music became demented, like the sound of several trains passing one another in opposite directions. The musicians were ruthlessly ejected and the high lights turned on. The king boss became sober and cunning. We had to stand again in a row before him. He poked at our bruises and wiggled our loose teeth. He muttered our real names—names we had believed to be forgotten. He reviewed the logs. He rubbed his face and stared blankly. Still we had to stand and wait. The room was white as a corpse. The light switches were smudged. The tinsel Robin had hung was falling down. Spiderwebs had gathered in the corners. Finally, in a fit of anger, the king boss left. We were free to go. Robin was asleep on her feet and had to be shaken awake.

Night after night, the world's abandoned hopes carried on in "The Years We Forgot," enamored with long-lost chords and tragic rhythms. Music gathered in my body and carried me over the streetcar tracks, through a stiff breeze in which millions of cigarette papers whirled. The stench of death was everywhere, and in the daytime it seemed we were scurrying about upon the skull of some felled God. At night, if there was a song, the dust lay calmly and listened. Improbable young men shuffled onto the stage and tried to get God to live. Drugs paid half of the bills, war the other half. Women like me were in between, like the surf writing about its dreams as they vanish on the sand. Still, the science of the tambourine grew finer, riper, more precise. The clave lived a life of its own, like the thunderclouds or the migrating flocks, the very chalice of wonder. This flood of mercies was always followed by the waiting-room, the smudged light switch, the clipboard, and human beings too ugly to be real.

A simple-faced young man was courting me out of boredom and restlessness.

"We could raise a great tent," he said, "and its roof could be a map of our history. Scholars could come and find there an answer to their questions. And while they learned, the roof would keep them out of the rain."

"It was a good dream," I murmured. But by the gaps in the young man's teeth and the raised veins that coiled around his arms, I knew it was only a slogan he had heard somewhere.

"Where would you go," he went on, "if the world had no center, and if the crocodile had no hind legs?" As he danced along the rocks, my eyes focused on him for the first time.

"I wouldn't go anywhere," I said. "I would let happiness come to me."

Someone shrieked with laughter in the ravine below. As my friends acted out their concept of glee, I watched great changes come over the face of the earth. The landscape was littered with the carcasses of billboards. A set of perfect teeth smiled up out of the dust with inordinate confidence. The sky performed acrobatic feats and the wind massaged its message into my skin and eyes.

We didn't return to the city at dusk but stayed until the sky became transparent and opened its heart to the universe. Slowly, life in the old quarter changed. The young men tried, but with the instruments in their hands still the music wouldn't come. They slipped across borders. The high lights were turned on permanently.

20

At first, only I could tell that I was getting old. Others didn't see it. Then, suddenly, the process was complete. I woke up underfoot. The old, like the young, are tethered like mules to the places where they can get what they need. There is a place for water, a place for food, and a place for relieving oneself. My existence was as circumscribed as before. I still carried passwords up and down the hills.

I slept in a rose-colored church on a bend in the road. At night, the spirits of long-dead clergy shuffled about, mumbling to themselves. They tried the doorknobs as if searching for something. I too tried the doors. There were lobbies where the walls were stacked with cultish literature. These places stank of dead flowers and bad breath. There were confessional booths inside the walls. In one of them, someone had carved: "Two for the price of one: be both good and evil and avoid all outcomes."

There was a chamber behind the altar where the robes and sashes of priests hung and candles, wreaths, and other furnishings were stacked in dismal piles. In the wall there were several doors: behind one door, bishops of wax reposed in glass coffins. Behind another there were golden reliquaries enclosing bits of black teeth. In a door marked "Keep Out" I found the gospels of unknown saints, manuals for armed rebellion, and a pamphlet on the parasitism of the rich. Behind another were the humble artifacts of peasant devotees: crocheted blankets, needleworks, and figurines of children in white. Still I could not guess what the ghostly sisters were searching for.

During the day I tried to wade through time without getting too much scum on the hem of my skirt. The one-legged man had long ago succumbed to his ailments. He had no grave, but I knew which smear of grease was his. Gone too were the simple-faced boys; I could smell them in the perfume of blood and ore that wafted up from the sea.

The money that once fuelled the local rackets was nothing

but a happy memory now. The wealthy of the world had withdrawn, leaving us to our internecine strife. Since the sources of being had become impure, life operated at a loss—a little was ever sacrificed to the living.

"I have to admit," I told one of the harried nuns, "It was easier when I myself was the currency, and I could pass from purse to purse, molten with resentment and glittering with alluring light."

"Blasphemy!" she said, raking her face with the pads of her fingers.

"Sister, you must care better for yourself," I said, clasping her hands. She sighed. Her eyes were heavy and her gaze resigned.

"Blasphemy," she mouthed again, but with less conviction.

"Sister, tell me, what is it that you seek?" I said. But our colloquy was broken, for I was no longer alone. These days the church was crowded with people and often racked with fights, maudlin speeches, and demented ravings. An old man heaved curses at me, waking up a general hissing, followed by peals of spiteful laughter.

Outside, the cold was bitter and a great lonesomeness gnawed upon me. The bare black arms of the dormant trees twinged subtly, as if dancing a very slow ballet. I could hear the distorted echoes of indifferent suffering down below. The sounds of the new generation were not as sweet and wonderful as ours had been. Discomfort crowded in around me, compressing me into a small, desperate point. For a moment I thought I saw the face of Grandfather Time in the sky, but it was only a trick of the light.

"My hopes are dashed," I whimpered. In my own heart, someone was searching desperately—for excuses. When they were found, they were written in chalk and in the hand of a child:

> I would melt if I could
> but I'm frozen instead
> it's too cold for the woods

and the courtships are dead
the betrothed are wed

In the name of the other
I walked to the East
but my way was a circle
that passed by a feast
where the other had least

When I was younger
my prayers were sweet
and God would devour them
but now they've turned sour
and they're unfit to eat

"These won't do at all," I said to myself. I hid them, but I hid them where I knew I would be able to find them again. Nevertheless, there was no longer any possibility of staying the same. Long had I hovered around this city like a bad dream. Now death was arriving, but it would come sooner to those who hid from the wind in the carcass of the chapel. I walked to the place where the road expired in the breast of the mountain. I seemed to hear a thousand true loves calling my real name in passionate, knowing tones. Alessandra, Juvila, Dayana—any such name they used to call me. But now the farces of my youth were washed away in the soaring rush of the wild eye.

I who had feared the hunger of the mountain and its bruising cold feasted upon weeds and ate sunlight with my skin like a tree. I grew spotted and rippled and baggy as a willow. Slowly, my body became an object, a part of the landscape. When I departed from this life, I entered into it more fully. Creation and created met. It was the kind of passing that changes what follows.

"Forgiveness is piled high in the halls of this world," I remarked.

"The gentleness of this world is boundless, provided you are willing to experience it through pain," my sister answered.

We were floating in a shipwreck of old memories and intentions, our essences enmeshed like seaweeds under a dark, meditative weight. Our many existences were translucent, glimmering in one another's light.

"Is it true what they say in this world?"

"What do you mean?"

"That there be reasons enough for anything, and reasons enough for nought?"

My sister was both there and not-there. Sometimes she was a grim bed of fossilized coral upon the sea floor. Other times I saw that her eyes were open wide as she pondered my question.

"It is as you have experienced it to be yourself," she answered finally.

Several bubbles of silence emerged from my mouth, fluttering away toward the light like moths. It was a kind of poetry I spoke to her sometimes—silent poems. Undulating in and out of existence, she received these garlands of thought gravely.

"You must become all three," she said finally.

"What do you mean?"

"Reasons, anything, and nought."

It was much like waking from a dream. I ceased: then there was no more than the breathing ocean. All was quiet—only time went on stroking the sea floor in its long sleep. I returned like the sun whispering through swift clouds, transforming the world into myself. I passed in and out of being this way. By not being, I became more. By becoming, I gained a certain prowess, an audacity. I discovered that I still had volition, the bad dreams that propel us into bodies.

21

The universe was filled with insomniac spirits, each one rushing back into the world on some important errand. Some sought redress for all they had suffered and others sought someone to listen to the frightful tale they would tell. Most simply fled in confusion from one place to the next. I could speak to them all at once by speaking to my sister.

"Anoint me with the seeds of your mind, and when we live again we will not be alone."

I took a small piece of all the others and they took small pieces of me, and thus our fates were intertwined. Chaos reigned in every corner. The paths and the results of the paths were reorganized.

I followed a man down a sunny corridor and watched as he stopped at the bookie's booth. I spied as he placed a bet. He travelled beyond the gates of the administrative neighborhood where I could not follow. I knew from his loping gait and the plastic bag he carried that he was a servant in one of the great houses. I had followed him often lately, for I suspected he was my father.

I bought salt from a vendor under a thatched roof. Purple pigeons flocked around the shop, eyeing me accusatorily. I plodded down the mountain road, resting the bag of salt on the back of my neck. One of my shoes broke on the way and I carried it in my hand. I watched a bus drifting out of town. The driver was a patient, humble man, but one of his eyes was open wide, looking for the path of evil to appear at any moment.

At the convent, I saw the holy mother's shoes outside the bathing house and I hurried on, for if she knew I had returned, she would make me massage her body. I shivered to think of her feet, which were grotesquely youthful for someone with such an old face. In the kitchen, I avoided the gaze of the cook they called Mr. Jangles, who was simmering with rage over his burners. He was a dark man and therefore of no value according to our customs. It delighted him to pinch and insult me. Although I was of a lighter complexion, I was as worthless as he was, because I had no name. However, if the sisters could confirm me as an incarnation of the goddess, I would have a new name and then I would become valuable.

While the water boiled, I daydreamed about maiming Mr. Jangles with the kitchen knife and with each of the utensils that hung from the rack above the stove.

In the temple, the sisters were deep in prayer. Scattered about the floor with their robes draped around them, they looked like fallen flowers, wrinkled and limp. Their legs were folded underneath them and the beads ran like water through their fingers. Sister Hazard's eyes lolled in the back of her head and she sang in a grunting voice:

> This life was spilled
> upon the page
> its happy blood
> a crooked smudge
> that quickly fades

> The truth can bend
> just like a snake
> that's how it walks
> that's how it stalks
> that's the path it takes

> And when you're old
> your sins are spun
> your suns are sold
> your tales are told
> and they're all rolled into one

The other sisters bade Sister Hazard shut up. They rose out of the depths of their prayer and drank their tea like empresses. It was one of their only pleasures, for they were little more than outcasts, but the people treated them with reverence out of fear of their curses.

I washed the tea glasses, wondering at the smallness of my hands. I was aware of my untempered goodness and it was almost unbearable. Songs played through my mind. There were thirteen suns dawning in me at the same time. I listened to the birds of each sun and spoke to my selves in circles.

Having finished my chores, I went into the courtyard and sat beside the cage of the magpie, Marjorie.

"Is it enough to be power itself, like a rushing river?" I asked her.

"Come here!" Marjorie said. Her voice was the holy mother's. "Hurry up!"

"Hurry up!" I echoed—just to be polite.

"Come here!" Marjorie said, and then she purred, in the holy mother's troubled tone, "Let me see."

Time seemed not to pass through me but to erupt from within, a river that swelled my banks and shed my topsoil and swallowed all the infrastructure in its way. I slept in the street among the cattle. Their ribcages were as wide as the sky. The starlight was mostly eaten by the gods, but a few crumbs fell down to us on the ground. It wasn't a dangerous village, though danger swept over it now and then like a sudden rain. In those times I made sure to be out of its way.

Whenever the rain fell down from the sky, another rain fell in the opposite direction. The valley sang in an ancient language that the people had forgotten. I looked upon the townspeople with a dispassionate eye. I saw the goodness growing in them with badness interspersed, just as herbs grow in the garden alongside the weeds.

The landlords came down each month to take their due. They were healthy, light-filled people with dimples in their cheeks and rhymes in their eyes. When they spoke, it was of mice and clocks and blueberry pies. The light touched them softly and their vehicles shone smoothly and purred as if they were merely ideas. The landlords were crowned in grace and the eldest of their clan were known for their humorous ways, their spacious philosophies.

"Aren't you a strange child," the old patron once said to me. "You live as if there were a beginning, middle, and end!"

"I, at least, have left the safety of my mother's apron," I responded.

The old man laughed. "You are right! But have you noticed? The further you stray, the more welcome you are at home!"

I eyed the man suspiciously. He was supposed to have become a wise renunciant in his old age, but somehow he still smelled of luxury. He had all of his teeth and hair, and in the family estate in the hills it was said that all the drawers were filled with silk. The villagers paid the landlords and the landlords paid the administrators. I had never seen the administrators—only their security gates and the amazing garbage they released in a long cascade down the side of the mountain. I wondered what they looked like.

I watched the children of the village celebrate their birthdays as one would watch a war unfolding. The progression of time was devastating. I wasn't the only girl at the convent. Most of the others had been harmed beyond repair in their infancy and they did not last long. Mr. Jangles tortured them until they lost their reason. After that, the farmers could buy them cheap, for all they could do was sit around and weep. The other children of the village turned quickly into ghoulish adults and died, either by one another's hand, by accident, or simply by very slow diminishing. The processions up the mountain to the graveyard rose and fell like an animal's heaving breath.

Each year that I survived, the holy mother pinched and patted me and smirked to herself, counting me among her growing wealth. I tended the herb garden in the courtyard and I did the washing and the errands in town. At night, when the convent was converted to a casino, I brought the village gamblers their spittoons and carried their money to the holy mother when they wanted another bottle of liquor.

One day I went to town to fetch dried fish. I saw my father in the cafe on the square. He was drunk and babbling to himself, seated at a table across from an empty chair.

"Sunrise is different for everyone," he said. "That's what I mean! It was the sand that day, the grey ocean, the way the beach stretched in both directions. The future was the past. I didn't care. There was nothing to care about!"

He laughed as if someone had said something funny. Another customer took the empty chair and sat his wife down in it, facing the opposite direction, for the cafe was full of people.

"Exactly!" the man said, not noticing the change. "If I could only capture in a bottle one ounce of the luck that has washed over me and run down the drain. Ah, but I would be a rich man!" His eyes twinkled with little pieces of sky as he smiled to himself and shook his head in wonder. Beneath his eyes there were purple shadows as if someone had painted one thumbprint on each cheek. I had the same divets under my own eyes. We were the same in that we always looked sick or very poor. I walked away with tears in my eyes, for the man's incandescent madness touched my heart more than anything that people did.

I walked around the lake several times each day for good luck. The water was filled with the dead and its surface rippled in gentle, rounded waves, murmuring of the injustices the dead had suffered. My girlhood was evaporating and I knew soon I would have to fight.

"You can always wait a moment longer," Sister Hazard said to me, stroking my cheek. She looked into me and at the same time her gaze traveled far into the distance beyond me. I could see into her vibrations, where sparrows flocked on power lines and trains traveled backwards. I saw her riding the train with a small piece of me sleeping in her lap. She was smiling out the window into a scrubby field in a Northern clime.

"I believe I know what you mean," I said, "but make it clearer, just in case."

"My dear, you have not learned discipline, although you have suffered much. When something hurts or is hungry or desperate, you only have to wait one moment longer. Then the discomfort becomes a winged thing, like a miracle."

I lay my head in her lap and watched as our spirits pursued one another. At long last it seemed I was learning to love.

I lay beneath the swaying tree. My skin was covered in

dust. The villagers were setting off explosions on the lake, trying to awaken the goddess. The water rippled and seethed with each vibration. The shamans had been sniffing around for a new incarnation, and the goddess in her mischief had been sending them signs and signals. I had seen them walking on their hoofed feet on the path that encircled the lake, contemplating the radiation storms in the sky. Sometimes in the morning the sisters would find offerings at the front door of the convent—piles of ash and packaged cookies half-burnt in the sacrificial fire.

Daily, Sister Hazard continued to reach beyond the borders of the known. She had been censured for it and even cut out of her share of the convent's profits. The holy mother said she would be buried in a pine box in the forest on the day she died instead of receiving the rituals of the shamans in the heights of the mountains. Sister Hazard had laughed, her button eyes crinkling devilishly.

"Just wait a little longer," she said, winking at me. The next day, she was praying in the courtyard when her black eyes began to burn like coals. The finger of a god stretched up through her body in the form of a cobra. Its hood cast a shadow that caused all the sisters to weep when it fell upon them. The holy mother slammed the cash register shut several times, but it kept popping open and releasing whorls of dollars. The casino had to close for an entire month while I went from door to door begging for donations.

For this, the holy mother sent Sister Hazard out into the forest to seek her own retirement, for she said the money she had lost was more than the old nun was worth. Sister Hazard took with her all the fortune and serendipity that was hers. I could see great bundles of merit and fortuitousness dragging along on the ground behind her, uprooting the foundation of many centuries as she walked down the path toward the edge of town.

"Were you always such a shrewd businesswoman?" I asked the holy mother.

"We don't all have deep, billowing wells of compassion in our hearts," she answered. "Those with very little must learn to use it sparingly."

I looked up at the holy mother. Her brow was cocked and a deep wrinkle had been bored into her head from thinking. All over her body, she was sealed up in a thick sheen of efficiency. It was as if she was glued together by money. Her parts fit together like the parts of a machine. She was *working*. If it weren't for the wizened crevice between her eyes, she looked as if she could go on working forever.

She grabbed me and proceeded to wrap me up in a white cloth. The sisters wove flowers into my braids. They chanted:

The time for dreams
and schemes is done
your swirling, curling
sands outrun

Your daylights
by a thread are strung
your steps are tread
the harp is strung

We bathe your skin
in chalk and paste
in heaven nothing
goes to waste

Beneath the thinnest
layer of paint
the artist hides
her wicked saint

The holy mother had grown impatient for my miracles to manifest. She was sending me off with the shamans to be put on trial. They carried me in a wheelbarrow to the foot of the mountain path. I saw the sisters laughing toothlessly and dusting off their hands as if they had just finished taking out the garbage. They grew smaller as I bounced up the mountain, pulled along by two local boys. The two shamans sprinkled herbs from censers and hummed to themselves. I saw the sisters touching the sacred stones with their bulbous, arthritic hands on their way back to the convent. Although they had always been small and cruel and selfish, I felt a tender pain for the old women as they disappeared from sight.

22

When we arrived at the steep rocks of the mountain, the wheelbarrow could travel no further. The village boys took their fee and turned back down the dusty path with the empty wheelbarrow. I watched as they ran gleefully down the hill.

The shamans unwound the cloth the nuns had tied around me. They were both smoking fat cigars. The elder shaman looked about eighty years old, but he was lithe and spry. The younger was fat and his eyes were close together and almost crossed. He smiled wetly and squinted, nodding to me. They started up the rocky path that had been hewn into the mountain by many centuries of travelers. I followed them.

For a long time, our footfalls were the only conversation. After a few hours of walking, always upward, we reached the landlords' compound. I had traveled this far before, to bring the landlords some treat or bribe in bad years. Seeing the compound now, several truths spread their wings and occupied space in the solid white backdrop of day. I saw the landlords' clothes and sheets trembling on clotheslines on a patio of ornately patterned tiles, a well in its center. I saw the landlords' house, built meditatively into the contours of the mountain, and their orchards, neat and thriving. I saw their lazy daughters struggling to stay awake in the afternoon. There was something about their miserable perfection that liberated me from my bitterness and misunderstanding. A silence landed in my heart: "Oh."

The path grew steeper and rockier as we proceeded. The air became cooler and wetter. Walls of cloud kept closing in upon us, nuzzling our cheeks. The gnarled rhododendron trees put forth red, stoic blooms. We were followed and spied upon by families of crows. The old man walked quickly, never looking back. The young man stayed near me and looked back often. It was difficult to keep up with them. They were both singing and now and then tossing crumbs or herbs out to the side of the path to appease the mountain demons.

When we came to the first shop, I thought surely we would stop for the night, but the old man just saluted the shopkeepers and continued up the steep path. The faces of the mountain people were different from those of the people we had left in the valley. There had been a war long ago which the mountain people had won. The valley people were still living with the shame of it, but the mountain people had a pride and a ferocity not seen in the valley. I loved them instinctively.

Finally, we came to a place where tiny houses had been built out of mountain stones. Butterflies were tumbling up and down the side of the mountain along with balls of seeds and pollen. The shamans built a smoky fire with wet pieces of brush they found on the ground. They made tea and ate some of the dried meat they had been carrying on strings slung over their shoulders. They didn't offer me anything to eat or drink, so I left them.

I wandered in the twilight until I found a mountain stream. A family of bears was drinking, a mother with her cubs and some bears who were between babyhood and adulthood. One of them stared at me curiously and came close to me to get a better look. When he sniffed at my mouth, I could feel the wind of his breath moving on my face.

"What are these evil charms you wear?" the bear said.

"It's not me. The nuns painted me with signs before I left home. They have cursed and forsaken the world."

"What are the shamans carrying to the mountain?" the bear asked. His question was unsettling.

"Is there anything they could bring that you would welcome?" I asked ruefully.

"We are lost," the bear said. "We used to travel the same route year after year. But some time has passed since our route vanished. There is only this hillside now, but we can't find its edge. We can't connect the ends of our circuit. We are hoping the shamans will make it as it once was."

"Accept being lost," I said. "Place no hopes in the shamans. They are only little children playing with sticks."

The bears hung their heads and slunk into the foliage. I drank from the stream and washed the signs from my face and arms. I found a soft place at the foot of a tree and lay down.

All night cougars stepped on me as they traveled up and down the tree trunk, courting and showing off for one another. Cobras contemplated my form and composed cumbersome sonnets about my materiality. I felt the goddess approaching me, a green-blue pulsing wave that could crash into the mind and shatter it. Her proximity awoke in me a kind of breathless lust, the reckless feeling of being on the edge of a blade. There was another spirit also in the mountains, a grandmotherly person who read to me the history of the universe by the text of the stars.

In the morning the shamans were packed and waiting for me. The elder peered at me. His hat was tilted funnily on his head and with his cigar and his rough equipage, he had a clownish, jaunty air. The younger man had grown wilder. His face was illuminated with the orange morning sun and he looked like one of the old gods. He crumbled a bit of soil in his hand and sniffed it, inhaling deeply as if the earth were a drug. He ran cackling off the path, down a steep grassy slope until he disappeared around the shoulder of the mountain. We met him on the other side. He was still running when he rejoined us and he shouted crazily.

We reached a part of the mountain where trees and shrubs were fewer and their foliage sparse. The light was dampened by a thick cloud that rolled around in my eyes and clicked in my ears. The shamans were blotted from sight, but their voices hung in the air, and their strange overlapping songs burnished golden surfaces within my mind. They sang:

> Oh hey-o why
> sun cries
> flowers smile
> sharpened bone
> tent of sky
> home of colors
> on the other side
>
>   Oh you-a-who

a spiral sound
earlier spark
before blue
earlier thought
before word
earlier ear
before chord

Oh why-o hey
lucky lives
in unlucky's grave
mountain grows rich
with valley's mistakes
lost man leaves
found man takes

When the path disappeared altogether, we had to climb
the boulders using both hands and feet. The younger man helped
me up by pulling on my wrist, compressing my bones. For the
first time in two days, we walked in a downward direction. We
reached a hut that was surrounded by decomposing white flags
on spine-like stakes.

Three more shamans were waiting for us inside the hut.
They were drinking whiskey and they offered the bottle to the
two men who had traveled with me. They passed it around, never
offering it to me.

"She is fasting," the old man said. "We have to show the
mother where to find her."

While they drank, I studied them. They were dirty and
mottled. One threw herbs into the fire to make a sweet smell,
but they were devoured too quickly to be savored. Another had a
timid, priestly air. He contemplated a drop of light at the bottom
of the whiskey bottle. The third was not well of mind and he un-
dermined the goodness in the room.

The head shaman came later in the night, when it was too
dark to see him. He entered the hut with the youngest shaman,
his nephew and assistant. The others were still sitting, drunk, on

their stools, and did not speak. The fire had died down to a few embers. The old man took a seat and his nephew poured him a drink. That was all for a very long time. I found the silence shocking and cruel. It seemed the men were at once shunning me and flaunting their austerity.

I listened to the lilting whistles of the burning wood. Gradually I settled into a subtle communion with the shamans. I could hear them remembering blue lakes hidden in the mountains. Each of their minds glowed with a different color. I gathered news from the vultures and crows who had drifted in and out of our path from the village. I smelled the men's earnest questions blooming like tiny flowers among the moss and wet stones. They wondered about the goddess's true name and whether she would make sense of their disconnected efforts and their faltering sciences. They wanted to know if all they had learned was folly and whether the world was only a rotten sore after all.

In the morning, I was the last to leave the house, for although I hadn't slept, my spirit had traveled along the silvery ridges of the mountain. The shamans had traveled with me. Each led me to a different animal ruling in a remote cave or forest of the mountain range. A horse, an eagle, a stag, a leopard, a snake and a monkey were the dignitaries I met, each one rippling with grace, alight with curiosity and poignant with glittering depths. Like the shamans, the animals were troubled and full of doubts. Nothing had been going right anywhere.

When the circuit was complete, the last shaman instructed me to return to the cabin. I took leave of the monkey king, but as soon as I left his lights behind, it seemed I had forgotten how to move. I was stuck for a long time in a grey, dimensionless twilight, so that I wasn't sure if I was going to or from. When I arrived once more in my seat in the hut encircled by the tattered flags of death, the dawn had crept on four legs over the peaks and slipped under the door silently. The shamans were gone.

Outside, a moving panorama opened before me. The lake shimmered like an evil eye down below. Playful, fluffy clouds rollicked between the nearby peaks, from time to time billowing together until I could see no further than the tip of my nose. Windows opened between parting mists, revealing distant realities. The world seemed to somersault around me.

I walked up a gentle mossy slope until I reached a clearing. The place had a somber, haunted air. The shamans had left me a pair of soft leather boots, a pipe made of bone, some tobacco, a string of beads, a brass bell, a mat, a long grey cloth, and a flint kit for making fires. I shivered when I touched these things, for there were thin, twisted places in my spirit that did not correspond to the wholesomeness of these objects.

"There isn't enough sadness for everyone," I heard the old shaman say. "You'll have to give some of it up."

It was as if the shamans had always been there, but only now had I entered into the level of awareness that allowed for their presence. They were seated in a circle. At the center of the ring, they had placed my effigy: a melodramatic creature whose features were misshapen and enigmatic. She held a word in her hand: "war". As I peered at it, two additional letters appeared and it read: "aware".

At the head shaman's request, the old shaman handed me a piece of fire. The sick shaman laughed. The fat shaman focused his eyes straight ahead to hold back his tears. The holy shaman prayed. The wild shaman gnashed his teeth. The youngest shaman watched the other shamans timidly. I felt very lonely, for there was nothing I could say that they would all understand. I knew I had to part with my oldest friend, the squalid house in which I had lived for generations. I wanted to explain that I did so not because of their ridiculous traditions but because I had asked the wind to carry me to the top of the mountain and hand me a sharp knife. These funny men were only the wind's way of carrying me.

I lighted the rag-doll who sat upon the slab of rock. The flames quickly engulfed her flimsy, flammable extremities. The fire leaping out of her was wondrously nourishing to my eyes after spending so many hours in the dim, wet dreariness of the mountain.

"For a long time, this is what I have been missing!" I gasped.

The shamans shook their heads with disapproval. The flames were short-lived and gave way to thick black smoke. I wept as the shamans vanished on waves of joy and excellence, leaving me before a sputtering pile of ashes. I felt many things at once. There was the bewildering newness of a young child as well as the addled terror of someone who has suddenly lost everything. Beneath both of these, there was the pressing certainty of a thing in motion.

I wandered about the mountainside throughout the long, dim day. I met a sheep who spoke in a human voice. She said:

> Your mouths that gnaw
> a grisly truth
> are long of tongue
> and soft of tooth

> Each one does chew
> in one's own way
> but what each tastes
> one cannot say
> though one talks all day

I wandered on, never seeing more than a few feet in front of me. I met a hawk who said:

> You seem so nice
> such high ideals
> that's how I like
> my morning meals

> No need for armor—
> clink and clank!
> just tend your conscience,
> that's your bank!

And all you forfeit
makes me fat
I thank you
very much for that!

Finally, I met a donkey. His owners had let him stray about
to look for sweet grasses, but they hadn't bothered removing his
harness and pack frame. He was suffering under the pinching
weight. He said:

I am under the world
and there is no way out
from under the world

how long do you have?
I could talk at another pace
I could suck on each letter
until it turned into a taste

would you care for me?
it's a simple question
with no recipient,
the thin air just never
reciprocates

I let my feet lead me where they would, rolling and
crashing like the waves of the sea, moving by gravity. I learned
to understand the layered speech of the rock formations and the
terrifying songs of the restless fog. I enjoyed this thoughtless,
directionless meandering, but after all, there were only so many
places to go. A grim sense of fatality carried me back to the shamans' cabin as the dark of night invaded the landscape, pulled by
charioteers of raucous demons.

The shamans were strewn about the lodge in poses of rev-
erie and luxurious refinement. They lay in hammocks, smoked ci-

gars, warmed their feet by the fire, whittled walking sticks, painted with charcoal, read from holy books, and experimented with
their inner temperatures in deep meditation. Their animal and
spiritual natures were flung into a careless and elegant balance
that seemed to come easily to them. I felt burning envy for their
attainments. A power began to surge within me, and perceiving
its awesomeness, I contemplated wiping the shamans from existence with a sweeping thought. That destructive impulse passed,
and I saw gathered before me only a few old men, simple rustics,
themselves terribly vulnerable to the whims of life.

"Since you are here at last, put on your new clothes and
go talk to the goddess." It was the first time the head shaman
had spoken to me. His face was changing. I saw several distinct
visages flicker through him. Because he could not decide who he
was, all of his chances were slipping through his fingers. I put on
the clothes, the leather boots, the grey cloth and the beads. I put
the bell and the pipe and the flint into my pocket.

"I am ready," I said.

23

Behind a damp curtain in the wall, a cave stretched back into the mountain. There were three chambers. In the first, there were relics and shrines. In the second there was a wide room with stalactites and stalagmites. In the third there was just a tiny space in which one person could sit.

The shamans giggled menacingly as they sealed the door. I was trapped in the small, dark space, covered in thick darkness. First I felt around. I could feel the edges of my clothes and the little hard parts of my form—my toes, ankle bones, back, and hair. I could feel the immaculate shape of the bell in my left pocket. It rang a little bit when I touched its edge with my finger. I felt the elegant weight of the beads.

Then I began to see myself from the inside out. First, I was very, very big—the size of a planet—and I floated in an infinite, sentient field. Then I was very, very small. I folded into myself so that my head and my feet pointed in the same direction and my knees reached up to my ears. The world seemed to use my body to smile, stretching me upwards in a funny U-shape.

Pain came, then fear, then boredom. I listened patiently to the many rivers flowing through me. The fat, fleshy walls of madness pressed against me, turning me inside out with sorrow. Then suddenly, I was on the other side of them.

I could see the goddess. She was a small soft worm, vulnerable and shy.

"Creature!" I said, both horrified and intrigued. She squirmed. "Why do you not come when your people cry?"

"I do not want to be seen," she said.

"And what of the help the people and animals need? Will nothing ever change?"

"Oh," she said, wringing her hands. "I do what I can, little by little. A stomach-full here, a stomach-full there. It was never really my ambition to move mountains, but you see I have done it!"

It was plain that this goddess hadn't the wits to address people's inexhaustible demands.

"You won't tell them I'm just a worm, will you?" she asked. "I quite enjoy the songs they sing. Even deep in the mountain I can feel their well-wishes."

"I will keep your secret if you give me a boon," I said.

"What could I offer you that I haven't already given for free?"

"It's true that you made the world and gave me my wet, beating heart. It's also true that you take the world away when I don't want it any more. But give me something that's good. They are placing their bets on you and me. There are seven realms in these mountains, each one with a unique corruption. The animals are tired of circling around and around, searching for themselves. The winds are hungry for flesh of their own. The shamans are just going through the motions. Only you are happy and fat in your peaceful darkness. Give me a little bit of that to go around."

"Oh, *that*? Why didn't you say so? That little dress of night is the best to wrap around each one of your utterances. Put it in between your big ideas. Send it twice a year in an envelope to someone far away, without expecting a reply. Keep it slowly growing in the stone steps that support your quotidian weight. Here it is."

She gave me a little bit of her happy darkness.

"Thank you, sister," I said.

When the shamans unsealed the door I had already passed out another way. The walls of the cave were as insubstantial as thoughts. I simply looked at things a different way, and I was outside of them. I found that the world was not a physical place but a realm of experience. Like a jewel, it had many facets and re-flected consciousness in many ways, and there were ways inside of ways. I turned these perspectives around like a prism in my hand. I now perceived the yellow plane, now the blue. I shuffled through frequencies as one would turn the pages of a book. I saw with relief and a little disappointment that nothing was neces-sary. The truth was like a green shoot growing, changing subtly every moment, living life for life's own sake. This way of seeing was dark blue and glossy. I focused once more on the shamans and their intolerable depression. As soon as I could see them, I was among them.

Although I brought tidings from their goddess, it seemed they had forgotten about me. They were lying about in their lodge, waiting for a cold spell to pass. Their eyes were all closed and each one was mumbling and muttering to himself. I took a seat at the table and packed my pipe. I smoked and watched the fire. The embers appeared to be a treasure chest gleaming with bullion, then they morphed into an apocalypse in which people were melting in a molten liquid. I dozed for a while and in my dream I saw the goddess's warm, dark ignorance wrapping like a hood around the cabin, protecting us from the worst kind of pessimism.

When I awoke in the morning, the shamans were up and about. They were in a merry mood and they were packing their belongings. The time had come for them to return to the wilderness, to bear the blessings of the pilgrimage to the denizens of their respective spheres.

"Don't you care to hear what the goddess told me?"

"We were just talking about that. Weren't you listening?" said the old shaman. "The goddess came to us in our dreams and wiped the cares from our minds. We have always suspected that you were not the one. We could tell by that crooked dummy of yours that we burned yesterday."

They all laughed and patted me on the back as they went out the door. They started off in seven different directions. For a long time I could hear them laughing as they disappeared over the horizon.

"Ring the bell if you need our help!" the old shaman called as he slipped out of sight.

I left the lodge and wandered away among the shifting mists, letting my mind knock through many universes while my body ambled along unheeding. Without curiosity, I perceived the long history of the mountain. The ghosts of a few shepherd families crossed to and fro, tending their yaks and goats and pondering human things: marriages, murders, and where the axe would fall. I reached the heights of the mountain where soil and green life no longer extended, where there were only loose, ashen rocks piled on top of one another. When I tried to pass any higher, the stones broke and shuffled under my feet and I sank into the rubble. When I looked upon the great heights of the peak, I saw that they formed a face that was trembling with laughter.

It was Sister Hazard's face, looming gigantically over the world. Her mischievous eyes were winking with glee. A few vultures circled around her great head like a crown.

"That tickles, little one!" she howled. "If you want to go up high, lift your own head! There is no need to step on mine."

I straightened up and found that I too was an enormous mountain peak. Sister Hazard and I traded rainbows and washed our hair in pure distillations. We discussed questions of geology—tectonics, thermodynamics, mineralization and erosion. Our words were smatterings of wildflowers in the grassy places between boulders and our thoughts were sediment deposits in the eddies of the valley far below.

Our knowledge was substantial, and as it grew, it carried us upward, lifting us further away from the world. The higher air was darker and colder. Its clarity was dazzling but also lonesome. I longed for the confused, elementary love I had sometimes felt in the lower altitudes, for which there is no substitute in the world of celestial detachment. Yet as long as Sister Hazard grew taller than me, I had someone to look up to, an example to follow. The problem was that as time went on, Sister Hazard ceased to be herself. She communicated with me only very sparsely and in ethereal riddles. She was always laughing, sending huge frozen tears crashing down to the earth. One day she was singing:

Dreams and drams
and likelihoods
spoons and spans
and piles of soot

the bets are bored

all things are true
the biggest fish is devoured
by just the impression of blue

play it loose,
I've seen it all
the boon takes up
no room at all

oh why have I become
so very tall?

With that, Sister Hazard started to laugh. As she cackled, enormous icicles crashed down her body, scattering dust and stones. She shook so fiercely that she disturbed the equilibrium of her structure. Her stones clattered down to the earth in a terrifying avalanche. She was still laughing as she collapsed, and I could see her joyful grimace in the swirling cloud of rubble that descended chaotically into the depths below.

After that, I was alone in my somber attainments, my mountain of merit for a moment unequalled anywhere else. This distinction gave me no comfort, for I was lonely. I perceived that I was the void as well as the proud mountain forcing its way into the void. The void and the mountain looked into one another like a person gazing into a mirror, getting lost in the mesmerizing pools of her own eyes. I longed for some disturbance to break that image into pieces and restore me to richer illusions.

These thoughts added their weight to the pile of insights I had previously accumulated, and a strange thing happened. I had grown so tall that the earth's weight no longer pulled upon me, and my highest accomplishments began to float away into outer space. I hunched down, hoping to preserve most of my stray pieces from cold, unfathomable perdition. Whereas it had been Sister Hazard's joy that made her fall back to earth, it was my aversion that brought me once more to the depths from which I had sprung.

While all my bits and pieces were in wanton suspension, hurtling down to the face of the earth, I recalled my father, the holy mother, the landlords and the administrators. I recalled the long lines at the water key and the glittering days of the dry summer, Mr. Jangles the chef and the broken girls who passed through the nunnery's dormitory. I recalled the magpie who spoke in the holy mother's voice and the village boys who once wheeled me up the mountain. I looked at these things in another way and discovered that by a subtle movement of my mind, I was their author. I also began to see that I could make these things change, using intricate works of consciousness and intention.

At first, it was like trying to play a violin while wearing mittens. I placed a little more money within my father's reach, but this only caused his friends to betray him. As a result, his blissful reveries were forever converted into bouts of cursing. I withdrew the administrators from their gated neighborhoods and emptied their bribes from the drawers of the local officials, but this only left a vacuum that was filled by a local syndicate. As it turned out, the new regime was worse than the old, for it lacked any pretense of universalism—and yet, the benefits of our painful existence continued to trickle out of town by helicopter, truck, and regular mail.

I tried to re-string the hearts of the townspeople, starting with the holy mother. I removed her calculating eye, her cannibalistic account sheets. I endowed her with generosity and tenderness. This caused the nunnery to fall apart like a wheel without a hub. The old women were ground into the mud. All that was left of the holy mother was the magpie sometimes seen picking through the garbage, repeating in her voice, "How much can you pay *today*?"

I tried to put a certain light into the farmers' hearts, a grace I had seen now and then among mystical and quiet men, rare in the world. But so illuminated, the farmers had a bad habit of disappearing. They slipped beyond the borders of being, curious what they would find on the other side, and were lost.

Although I could speak things into being, the vast fields of being spoke back. I resigned myself to falling, allowing things to settle where they landed without interference. A wondrous pattern emerged in the random crashing of stones and tree roots against the earth. Its shape was a circle inside a square, with many circles and squares inside of it. As quickly as it appeared, this configuration was gone again and forgotten. I felt my heart swelling up like a ripened fruit.

Children were picking through the rubble and they found a chest filled with fine silks from a mountain estate. Pariah dogs slept on the hills of dust and had great battles and rugged love affairs in the night. Wizards traipsed from here to there, mumbling to themselves. Worms found their way into the dirt and converted it into arable farmland. My thoughts became food and many were fed.

People stopped and sat upon my ridges to watch the stars. They told the legend of my great fall.

"She was lost in solitude, drinking from her own cup," they said.

The couples shook their heads at my folly.

"Everyone deserves a sweetheart," they said. "What a silly idea, going up to heaven all alone!"

Their murmurings gave me pleasant dreams. I got lost in the longings of the springtime and I found myself once more wrapped up all around in a cycle of mistakes. When I regained awareness, I was already on the road out of town, pursuing the theory that a miracle was somewhere on the horizon.

24

I passed under the grisly arms of enormous trees. They tickled my hair as I came within their reach. Buses full of people passed me by—the faces of the passengers were like forgotten dreams. The marshes smiled at me knowingly. Electric lines rippled with a whirring mantra and odd orbs of light shone in the earth and sky, so that I was not sure if I traveled through night or day. Frogs cast sounds into the darkness and as the darkness tightened, their harmonies wove walls and doorways and sparkling inner chambers inlaid with many ornaments. Ahead, in a lurid haze, a city revelled, sprawled fatly across the distance and winking one eye in an ornery stupor.

"I believe you," I said out loud, at the same time wondering why and to whom I had spoken. My heart felt sick and rotten in my chest, and the more I walked onward, the more it seemed to splash and dissolve. Despair laid its heavy finger upon me and pressed down so that I squirmed. In the gales of frog-voices, I seemed to hear the voices of humans conversing and communing, but I could not understand their meaning.

"Anger!" I said aloud, and the word was like a tambourine crashing into the night. "An-ger! An-ger! An-ger!"

Day was dawning over the fields of marsh grasses. The dawn was weak and indecisive, just a yellow orb like the lantern of an old man emerging for a moment from his cabin door.

During the second night, the darkness grew fonder of me and soothed me gently like a mother. My body had grown so uncomfortable that it separated from my mind. I saw from above how my knees grated against themselves at every step. The compassion of the landscape mingled with my self-pity.

"Open!" I cried. "O-pen! O-pen!"

But the dreariness would not open. It was tightly closed, like a clam's shell, gripping its mortal sulkiness with all its might. As I reached the city limits, I smelled sugary syrup and frying batter. My hunger nauseated and humiliated me. Crows wheeled overhead, laughing, their mouths and bellies full of the town's discarded delicacies. I felt around in my mind—there were only a few desultory memories, one or two of them unspeakable. Underneath these rough sketches, there was a voiceless, featureless will residing somewhere in my belly. That will pulled me, hand over hand, in the direction of its intended goal.

The city into which I wandered during the second moribund dawn was like a very lucky drunk playing cards. There was a mad, sideways quality to the streets. Everyone walked with their legs on the horizon as if a powerful wind was blowing. Decisions were being made with a crazy glee, for the world was ending and consequences were null and void. Still, the same handful of fat men seemed to win at every turn.

Toothless elders were huddled at the corners of the widest streets, keeping warm in the exhaust of the traffic. Downtown, gigantic metal statues pointed the way to forgotten conquests. Vagrants slept in their hollowed-out pedestals and made shrines in their enormous thumbs. Everywhere an infernal construction was going on. There was a stink of corpses as the workers who died on rickety scaffolding or drowned in slabs of wet concrete were lazily folded into the infrastructure.

"Can you speak your heart into me?" I murmured. A rich woman heard me. She took my picture and slipped a $100 bill into my hand. A small woman across the street stopped rifling through the garbage can and cursed at me enviously. Two dirty, green-eyed children with homemade violins glowered at me from the curb. A foul man wearing a sign made out of a cardboard box teetered across the road and placed his hands on my shoulders, resting all of his weight on me. The box he wore read:

> The future is only a punch card
> the past is only a nametag
> quit your job and join God's army
> we have fun doing Capital's dirty work
> at the border between freedom and captivity
> there are times you don't know which side you're on!

I contemplated the final exclamation point on the drunk-ard's sign with apprehension. It had been ingeniously shaped by an unsteady hand and it danced as I struggled to keep myself and the man on our feet. This peculiar punctuation mark both illuminated and troubled my mind. It almost reminded me of something I had meant not to forget. It sent waves of guilt and excitement shivering through my body.

These feelings were interrupted by a carriage that came hurtling around a corner. The drunken man and I tumbled over one another to make way. The carriage passed, its bells jingling. In the back rode a man and woman. Their eyes were dilated and they observed the world with a mixture of terror and delight.

"If you see them for precisely what they are, they disap-pear." This was said by a lady draped in peacock feathers. Her face was brown and shiny, like an oily, warm dough. She had drawn black lines around her eyes, but they had settled down her cheeks like layers of sediment. A long column of ash had developed at the end of her cigarette. She flicked it away as if to emphasize her words.

"What makes their eyes like spools of thread?" I asked.

"It's something that can make you believe in yourself," she said. Then she disappeared into the snaking, interwoven shadows that crawled through the streets like spiders.

It was said that there was a drug that passed through the hands of the rich and poor alike. One small taste of this drug, and the world would fall into your arms like a long-lost love. The way of things would be soft to see: the coil of light in the wet street, the roaring sky above the rooftops. Your mind would once more speak to you, opening up floodgates of forgotten asides. Even as it left you, the drug would make your body purr like a train leaving the station.

⁂

I made my home in the groin of a middling copper con-quistador. Each night I took a ladder to the wooden platform that was my bed. My neighbors were an old man who lived in the feet and the lunatic who perched in the eyes. I paid the king of monument city a monthly fee. I made my rent selling enigmas and prophecies to the pedestrians. They would brush up against me as they rushed from luncheon to luncheon and strange phrases would be shaken from my lips.

"Put some weight on your third leg," I told one woman, "or it will shrivel up and fall off."

She wept and paid me handsomely.

"The jaws of this world close tightest on the wonder-child," I said to another. She gritted her teeth and paid me a miserly sum.

There were many who feigned not to hear me and continued on their way. There were a few who came seeking me out with desperation in their hearts, and they left with a calm silence wrapped about them. I began to suspect that I was selling them forgiveness, though I knew not for what crimes. I was careful not to listen to my own words, for they had a hypnotic quality and could ensnare the mind.

The women who paid me pretended they were weeping madonnas, while the men tried to charm and beguile me with their long, thin moustaches. Sometimes I followed these seducers back to their ballrooms and their grand hotels bedecked with marble and chrome. One talked to me about his fine linens and expensive shampoos. These topics being exhausted, the rich man hung his head and was silent.

"Is that all you have to say?" I asked. He began prattling about the pillow-cases. But it was no use, for in that silence between the two cheerful monologues stretched the eternity of the grave.

The city was one of horrible stenches, of rancid pools. The poor and unlikely were swiftly ground underfoot and they frequently throttled one another like rabid dogs. And yet it was also a city of light. Everywhere the light traveled, telling enchanted stories about other-worldly triumphs. It perched in the branches of trees, resting upon glossy black leaves. It blasted its trumpets upon filthy window-panes and lay mournfully on the shingles of waterlogged houses. It was chiselled into the broken faces of the paving-stones and curled behind the ears of the balconies. It drank up many centuries of spilled blood and made uncouth toasts when it raised its glass. The light was kind to the faces of the people, resting curiously on their weathered cheekbones and underneath their translucent eyelids. It nourished fools until they blossomed like roses. It transfigured the most wanton suffering into poetic triumph and enshrined each wretch like an icon in her own frame, her tools and possessions like amulets encircling her. I wove my way among these grotesque saints, fending off their worst impulses and entertaining their milder gaffes.

◆

There was a convict named Sullivan whom the mayor forced to sweep and mop the streets of the tourist district. This punishment was intended to humiliate him, but he enjoyed it. Sometimes my wealthy patrons would tip him too, when they saw him illuminated like a holy man with his broom in the stark light of a street lamp.

"Fold the arms of the crucifix upward and it becomes a room. Don't make your cross so small that you haven't enough floor to pace!" I said to a rich lady whose lipstick was traveling down her chin.

"Why are you the only fool you ever listen to?" Sullivan asked me when she had gone. I kicked the dust. I could see his skeleton gleaming beneath his skin under the electric lights.

"Just forget I was here," I said.

As I tried to move away, Sullivan remarked: "You can pass on into the orange sun, but you can't decide what I will do with your shadow!"

His voice crept out of the purple delirium of the abyss. He was dressed in a cobwebby blue. His eyes blinked with benevolent patience, like the long-lashed eyes of a mechanical doll. He pulled a twist of vine from his mouth and nodded as if to a faraway music.

I apologized: "There are tire tracks in my mind from long-defunct vehicles."

Sullivan chuckled. "Just go faster, and let your momentum carry you."

"I may go as fast as you please," I retorted, "but am I getting any closer to the reason?" I looked out into the fields, filled with oddly glowing lights.

"What if we just held still and let the reason come to us?"

I realized with embarrassment that I was barely plastered together. Scaffolding was showing through the great gaping holes in my sides and ribbons of shredded plastic undulated in the breeze. The passersby were mildly offended by my appearance, but a question still hung in the air as if written in neon lights. I grabbed Sullivan by the hand and hurried into the deep blue spaces unclothed by any embodiment and beyond the reach of the city's enterprises.

"It's dark in here!" he said. "I can't see!"

I laughed at him. A train was moaning like a beast stuck in a trap. My evil laughter resonated in the darkness. I reached out to Sullivan, but he was gone. My laughter had destroyed him.

The river was lying meekly in the arms of the land and what little light reached these heavy layers from the distant civilizations above the waves gathered and shared evenly with the bare stalks of weak young trees. The sky was striped like a tiger's back, and there was a deafening noise of insects and engines.

A small yellow light gathered in my belly and I used it to grow Sullivan back. I put the flesh on his blurry blue bones and dabbed his cheeks and forehead with the balmy glow of dawn. His eyes opened and closed like two lavender sepulchres. Pinpoints of colored light danced on his fingertips and his brow. The ghosts of sailing-ships billowed at the bend in the river like moths opening and closing their gauzy wings. Sullivan was talking. His speech was like a thin trickle of honey that ran steadily into my mind, displacing fouler humors. He said:

> The isle of dreams
> is farther than it seems
> the moon wishes she'd never broken free

that's why she's nearer than lovers' stars
and she doesn't fear to show her face
whether night or day
and though it's full of scars

The carousel's journey
is frantic and pure
it won't get you to heaven
for all the dollars in your purse
disassemble your arms
deliver yourself from garish charms
many are the ailments but one is the cure

He lodged himself in the middle of the street, a red gash that ran neither North nor South, but catty-corner like the rest of the sideways city.

The pedestrians were great lumbering people who shattered hopes with every step they took. Everywhere the broken glass of more fragile beings lay sparkling, wet with its own spilled contents. Colored lights shivered sadly in the fresh wounds of the downtrodden. Sullivan stood hunched in the street and his eyes rumbled with the lightning of the pink skies. He was dressed like a scarecrow—his sleeves and pant legs shrunken and tattered. The air was so thick that the insects could crawl through it and the darkness glistened with beetles' backs. There was a damp, metallic smell. Sullivan's arms were wet and strong like the limbs of a tree as he cradled his broom like a small child.

The oak trees washed over us and murmured apocryphal blessings. Sullivan whistled to himself beside the blue river as military jets tore through the sky. A helicopter hovered, taking photographs with a duct-taped array of outsized cameras. Rebellions bubbled up in our minds but were annihilated before we were aware of them. I felt small and insignificant. The waves stretched out endlessly, grey and tedious, masking the simple truths that lurked beneath their surface.

I became uncomfortable and tried once more to slip away,

before the day should arrive.

"Wait," Sullivan said. "Once things change, they will never be the same. How many times will you bludgeon yourself with waves of life and death?"

"Sometimes the worst thing that can happen is also the best," I answered.

Sullivan shook his head. "See it both ways, and then another way as well." We passed into a grey, ethereal realm and thereon into a deep blue blackness that was pure and luminous, colored with dreamlike brightness and deceptive depths.

"Can you see that the closed doors of universal happiness are your own action," Sullivan said, "and can be opened by you alone?"

Even the vastness of the cosmos I found cramped and cluttered. I pushed aside road signs and removed tongues from restless temple bells. The final height of everything was a sparkling twilight, like the inside of a satin dress, a melancholy plane. This place was called The Mirror and everything I saw here came from me. There was a purple flush of sleepiness with a grey tinge of apathy and a blue gauze of guilt. The pinks and reds were currents of vanity and lust—they made a thrilling sight and reflected indulgently in pools of themselves.

Sullivan was here as well, but he conformed to the rules of this place and could not remake himself against its frequencies. In his face I saw a triangle made of three blue points: one was his wondrous potential, the next his inevitable downfall, and the third the vibrating tone of my peace with both aspects. His hand was lifted up by an action of my dreaming. This pink, thrumming place, folded inward upon itself, gave me an uneasy feeling. I rejected it and once more split myself into two parts. I took the offered hand and descended a yellow staircase until I reached a shadowy room built of unpainted wooden boards. Sullivan was nearby, sitting restfully in his body. He was wrapped in a woolen blanket and his eyes reflected the spare light of the fading evening. For a while there was no sound but the sucking of the river upon the mud of the shore and the wind rustling through the crevices of the lean-to and sighing in the arms of the young trees.

"Don't worry," Sullivan said. His face loomed grotesquely in the light of a small fire. "I too am just a stranger." As the darkness fell, Sullivan's grandmothers appeared in the indecipherable places where the wooden walls met the tin roof. They looked in on us with wide, surprised eyes that rocked back and forth like the moon over the sea. They cracked eggs into a blood offering and bathed me from head to toe. Later in the night, there were other blue ladies. They made quick gestures of anger and pathos before vanishing. They were followed by others, no two the same, yet all somehow familiar. They sketched themselves roughly in the darkness of my eyes, passing through the mind like floats in a ghostly parade.

-●

In the morning, the sun was big and her light was milky white. Sullivan looked into my eyes, placing something small but heavy there for safe-keeping. Then he walked past the broken fences and the railroad tracks to the main road. He left with a shirt tied to his head and a stalk of yellow flowers stuck in his ear.

I teetered on the bank of the river. Now and then the brown water coughed up some memento of history: a pair of manacles, an astrolabe, a signet ring. The cadence of the river's speech and the poetry of its refuse seemed to be crafted by a sophisticated mind. I read its signs with interest and woe. Then I walked downtown, where the familiar surroundings nourished and insulated me from the harsh, candid way things hung together.

25

I took a well-worn footpath through the military bar-racks. Three young soldiers stared at me, holding their crotches. I passed through a district of vacant storehouses and factories where a smell of sulfur drifted on the prickly air. Rats scurried across the landscape and the furry wind crawled all over my body, playing curiously in my hair. In the dust on the roadside shone dental implants, brass knuckles, choke collars, and shanks of varying sizes and shapes. As I marched downtown, others also made their way there, but there was no knowing whether we strode toward or away from the calamity. The earth turned itself beneath our feet so that we walked but did not move, yet the buildings grew taller and the great serpentine highways rose up overhead, their pillars like the trunks of trees and their overhang-ing slabs of concrete forming a canopy that enshrined us in a whispering mystery.

A family dressed in white emerged from a red brick building under the sagging road. The light was carved finely into slivers that grazed their cheeks, shoulders, and brows. Their eyes were red with rum and their bodies stank with sweat and poverty. I watched as a demon snatched an oily tear from the corner of an old woman's eye and drank it with relish, crouching in the eaves of concrete overhead. A little boy peered at me with the eyes of an old man. A few hired musicians held enormous instruments across their long wet stomachs like dead dinosaurs. They wiped their foreheads amid shouted orders from their patrons. The drummer began to play and the other musicians reluctantly joined in the jangling, heaving rhythm. Peels of light began to shiver as the shadowy forms of the party-goers started moving to the music. The sloppy music grew loud and powerful. Its force carried everyone along without effort, reorganizing the solid bodies, laying little pentacles inside of everything. I was aware of both pain and the laughing place beyond pain's reach.

Having left the music behind me, I felt different, as if

stretched apart. In the sky there were ropes of white cloud giving the impression that the earth was a corpse swaddled in cotton. Old men sat on curbs and ledges like flies caught in honey, smiling out of eyes like swirling drains. Young men cackled to themselves and wavered like strange fires. Women, bent upon annihilation, tossed their bodies into harm's way with gusto. I too hurled myself into oncoming traffic and walked a little too near the explosive fuels of grief that were piled high in the dizzying sunlight.

Jervilen was a worm in the mind of the city. Just by passing by his brothel, I found my pockets filled with purplish dust. I consumed it before reaching for the thought of it and I had already turned into the wish of my heart and no longer was myself.

The city was draped in green light, a light that was not hot and could not burn me. Pleasure seekers and brokers of pleasures displaced the poor and condemned as I passed into the sentimental downtown, a place that was always crowded with memories. The lines of the doorsteps were more evenly planed here, and the walkways more spacious, the gutters along the rooftops trim and strong. Plants hung in baskets, dripping water like jewels in the sunlight.

Another type of woman was seen walking these streets. She was firm and shapely, as if made of porcelain. She carried mahogany heights of guilt and nostalgia. Now and then she liked to relieve herself of these absurd accumulations, to see them from an outside perspective. I met one such woman in the main square and I said:

> Your waivers waive
> your lofty limbs
> your landly ties
> your hearty hymns,
> your family swords
> your leaping lords
> your stately guise—
> but what are they for?
> what could they buy?

your knowing eyes
like blowing seeds,
your thoughts that writhe
your tide that seethes
your storebought smile
your broken rest
your tattered brow
not built to last—
what do they do?
where could they stay?
tell someone to hurry
call the porter and tell him to carry
every shred of it away

These statuesque ladies were lost in long family stories. Their necks like pillars were burned into silver alloys and
archived in albums that spanned many wars. They emblazoned
themselves onto far-flung epochs and guarded their exotic merits
like a treasury. I ambled listlessly among these quaint museums,
noting how a cigarette butt idled between the glass cases and
an old hardened rag had been left behind by the servants, caked
with dust.

There was enough loot hidden away in the purses of these
women to sustain many worlds for many generations, let alone
the one at hand. When their pocket-books opened up, possibilities unfurled, reflecting the fondest hopes of the beholder. But
amid their lustrous laughter and the clicking of their prudent
clasps, these inviting dimensions collapsed and retracted. I
gleaned what I could from their brief indulgences, before my
patronesses slipped back into cool, clean temples of materiality.

Buildings and balconies reeled through my groping mind. I
came to a place where the street was littered with apples so thick-
ly that I had to shuffle through with my feet. Several gaunt figures
were collecting apples absent-mindedly, stuffing them into their
pockets and outstretched shirttails. Now and then these ghostly
people dropped all that they had just gathered and gazed around,
bewildered, only to discover the abundance of fruit on the ground

and begin again.

In the great intersections, old women pushed carts piled high with the follies of the rich. Businessmen passed into banks and cotton exchanges with the cheerful pep of hired actors, certain of their pay. When I peeked beyond the revolving doors into which they disappeared, I saw grass growing on the lobby floors and birds flying from window to window. I watched as the men removed their ill-fitting ties and jackets and changed back into ordinary peasant clothes. Then they trampled over heaps of upended headstones and traveled on through the mud toward the fields.

With fiberglass and electricity scraping my cheeks, I carried myself along. Tall clouds like magicians wearing tophats bowed down indulgently. The sun turned toward other places, leaving a red mess among the buildings of glass and steel. Sickness streaked the sky. My mind grew numb and bloated and walked sideways through my head.

Although troubles were many, peace was more. The crust of city, dried and wrinkled and sizzling with death, was one kind of sigh upon an eternal ocean. An angry drum played in my head and in my left shoulder. A forgetful turquoise spread through my chest. A livid purple energized my legs. I only amounted to half of myself, and yet I knew I could walk further than was necessary— for I still had with me the hatred of the living.

❧

In the hut, the silence of the universe gathered. There was a ticking sound and a kind of final punctuation that was both very dense and very light. Late in the night, Sullivan returned. In the candlelight his face was drunk and many stories were painted in it. He recited:

> The wind is unkind
> but her wayward ways are fine
> much like mine when the path is not clear

and the seas aren't too deep
I could cross them in a single leap
in my sleep and yet I'm still here

we carried the fruits
by their disenchanted roots
to the towers of flowering pride

though our union was strong
and all causes were one
the words lay on our tongues and agonized

still the scaffolding shakes
still the underground's awake
and the base of the metropolis teems

with masons and plaster
building masks for the master
with a courtly and civilized grin

I listened to his rare lines and watched the strangely colored fountains that emerged from him when he was not looking. He had eyes like calendars, little boxes through which eternity could be glimpsed. His gestures were clocks that twisted moments inward upon themselves.

The days wore themselves out, the way the sun's glare burns a hole in one's eyesight, or much rubbing turns any precious cloth into dust. The red sky seemed to be roughly sewn onto the harangued skyline. Red, mottled forms like men made of mud began to turn up on the riverbanks. They mumbled to themselves and scratched their arms. Their clothes wrapped around them, disintegrating like fallen leaves. They carried tin lunch pails and had long bruised noses. The city surged back and forth on tides of money, and I with it, but these men had defected from the circuit.

Sullivan sometimes left these shadowy men gifts nestled

in the weeds: a small flask filled with whiskey, a bag of rice. He never looked them in the eyes.

"They give me a bad feeling," he said.

I would see their sun-baked forms drowsing among the tall grasses and meditating upon the wooden posts of long-demolished buildings. I watched one of them closely as he slept. Words bubbled out of his mouth and rolled effervescently along the contours of the river, up the tasseled robes of the regal clouds. I listened closely and understood that the man was praying. His prayer was lacing itself into the world, weaving and re-weaving existence upon a loom of mercy. In the distance, I could see many prayers rising from the blunt, sketchy men stretched out in the grass and slipping into the crevices of the night. Their prayer sounded like this:

> Sanctuary
> beings foam
> in cotton air
> on sodden loam
> the path to greatness
> no one's home
> within the castle
> just a bone
>
> sing a song
> a mellow moan
> a solemn hymn
> that fellow's flown
> but in the soul
> a sign is sewn
> into all time
> a tune intone

I beheld the bronze shimmering riverbank as a veil beneath which moved forms, dark and rounded, jostling and clamoring. There were several worlds beneath this world, each one imposed upon the next. These submerged layers created a sense of depth and richness of hue.

‐◆

Jervilen ruled supreme. His face was plastered in garish colors on the sides of the buildings and his insignia was tattooed on the ragged fences and blistered cement walls that enclosed the city dumps. He had an army of fat, slow men selling tickets to his parties on every street corner. They breathed heavily while they made change, their eyes swimming like catfish in brown water. Dark black trees clawed at their backs as if they would draw them backwards into another life.

The shows were held on the third floor. The stage glittered with huge ensembles from far-flung archipelagos: melancholy soloists, bizarre whisperers, and mystics. Each night, the crowd was different, but there was always a piercing interest flickering in all directions. The minds of the people were tinted blue—they could not enter the theater without a certain spectrum of aware-ness becoming eclipsed.

The power and money that changed hands at these events turned the city like a fulcrum. I didn't heed the details, names, or mechanisms, but enjoyed the shimmering colors produced by the emulsion of aims and desires. If one foot soldier or general fell, the currents simply wrapped themselves around another axis. I smelled my own death in the mix—the scent of an old cathedral drowning amid the fumes of industry. Somehow that only made the music sweeter. The lights fell like moonbeams upon the faces of the guests, each one like a question with no answer. The heavy currents of harm did not trouble me. Instead I was refreshed by the evil that swept around me, patting each part of my body, lifting my hair from my shoulders and back and curling my eye-lashes upward.

Jervilen winked at me and gave me some money. Inside the bar, his bald head shone as if he wore a halo. There was always a little room around him as people sighed in his direction. Jervilen made women shine, each in her own way. My presence made things happen for him, though I wasn't sure exactly what they were, and so he kept me around, like a pet.

At the same time, I began to notice changes in the streets. Whereas the wealthy women had always been dressed chastely in pastel colors and silky evanescent wings, they began to grow more bold. Getting in and out of cabs, the older ones looked bloated and disorganized, their dark purple dresses slipping down their chests or gathering around their mottled thighs. Their adult daughters had to tell them how to walk and sit. But then the daughters too began to grow bleary-eyed: a ruddiness came over them and they always looked as if they were lost or had forgotten something. They hurled their feet along the street like foreign objects. One woman's eyes settled tearfully on a horizon only she could see. The tall buildings watched her remorsefully, from a cool distance, while smaller people scuttled in the shadows.

I still blathered out prophecies but the rich were too pre-occupied to stop and listen, much less to leave me a tip. There was an odd silence and emptiness to the city. I hadn't noticed until now that all the familiar trash-pickers were gone. The trash heaps were smaller and fewer than before. The construction projects had been suspended in various stages of completion; the precarious scaffolding, half-built platforms, and beds of concrete studded with jutting red bars had been abandoned. Before, entire clans had dwelled inside the half-finished parking garages and triple-decker restaurants. All that was left of them were a few flannel blankets and a dark spot where their fire had burned. The junk yards began to fill up with strange treasures—iron-wrought door handles, ornate gas lamps, and dismantled gates bearing the crests of the old families.

The crazed, panting grin of the poor could still be seen beneath the great flows of fortune, but for the rich, something had gone wrong. Their perfect skin bubbled with sores. They wandered around with dust in their hair. Their slick briefcases sprang open as they walked, scattering papers across the streets. As for me, my anger accumulated so that one side of me was crumpled and the other was overly energetic. I turned circles around myself.

The river folded over its own waters, turning the pages of the book of time. Its currents talked at cross-purposes, some traveling left-to-right and others right-to-left. Some parts only swirled round and round as if they were drunk. Others presaged doom and imparted consternation. The red men I had seen gathering around the riverbanks were like a bad headache the businesses were having. The cranes stopped swinging and listened intently. The businessmen retreated into distant memories, leaving behind only their wives and the empty packaging from a vast array of specialty goods.

Sullivan disappeared for days on end. Each time it happened, I became a different person. At first I carried on with our habits. I cooked and recited poems in his stead. I pulled strange objects from the river: a shirt of mail, a stylus, a rearview mirror. I opined about the frayed edges of this world and whether and how it would lead into the next. All these things I did with a sense of foreboding. I sat quietly through the mystery of the night, but my face was weary and there was another voice inside my mind than the one that always spoke to me before.

Then the rhythm of the days got mixed up. I stayed in the cabin all day and wandered around the city at night. At night, the city had a different spirit. Whereas the days found the masses weakened and lethargic, paralyzed with fear, the nights arrived like coronations. Skinny people with sunken purple faces emerged from cracks and crevices dressed in shining fabrics and feathers. Their conversations coiled and spiralled around every pillar and beam. Their eyes dripped with rhinestones and their skin gleamed with storebought iridescence. I settled easily in among them in a splash of moonlight. The world spun beneath us, showering our eyes with the bottomless theater of stars beyond the fronds of swishing tropical leaves. The street people quickly found my most precious joys and insights and turned them around like heavy objects in their hands. They knew how to enjoy them and how to appraise their value.

In the nighttime, those who hobbled meekly through the days inherited their lost dignity. Their every whim came true. The gifts of the world did not hide but rushed out to meet them.

Those who seemed witless and incoherent in the sunlight at night revealed their genius. They had all they needed and more. They snarled and sneered under stylish hats. They spoke of wonderful ideas that had the power to change everything. I liked to watch the old men's faces bathed in the yellow lamplight alive with moths. Their cheeks were wet with the dew of the world and their eyes did the hopeful dancing of small sailboats in a glittering sea. The trees arched around these nighttime scenes, coinciding with the moods of the actors as they shifted. The long-waiting trains sighed in place, impatient with their landlocked delay.

"There was a world I came from, but it was a better world than this one," one old man was saying. He wore a plaid shirt and a pair of drawstring trousers that were too big for him. They were pulled tightly around his slender waist by a thick string.

"Oh, yeah? What was better about it?" asked a chubby man who was drinking a beer from a dark brown bottle.

"It just looked nicer. The people were more spacious, you might say. There were roses in little jars and a kind of turquoise paint over the floorboards that was peeling. The sky was more alive. I remember that."

The circle of men chuckled and a wistful light played among their eyes.

"It's all the same world, my friend," said the chubby man. "You can't get from there to here without stitching the two of them together."

"Yeah, I know," the thin man said. "But that world is gone, anyway. Never coming back."

I followed a little old man who walked with his hands behind his back. He gently put each foot down in front of the other. He sat down before a tall pillar upon which several languages were inscribed. It read:

> Don't mark the dark
> with millenarian woes
> don't talk of suns
> that set or rose
> for it's neither, nor

and none of those
the gift is torn
from ragged clothes

Balloons' ballets
are slow and green
the ships' goodbyes
fulfill the fiends
the Hows and Whys
are better friends
than those old pirates
Where and When

Intuit bones
and tolerate rains
approximate stones
fill with moaning crude space
you are until you ain't
and then there's still grace
you put your heart wherever it fits
in some empty needful place

The old man had stopped to sit on an old pedestal whose monument had vanished, leaving only a few bolts jutting up out of the stone. In the murky twilight the old man's face grew large and watery. He was peacefully gripping the cane he held between his knees. The people seemed to hiss as they hurried along, but the man endured them patiently. I too passed on, finding no harbor in his spirit for my urgent needs. I slipped into a light door that led to a heavier door on the ground floor of a building on a corner of a square. Influences changed hands. There is always a way forward, but whether the road is yellow or purple, we don't get to decide. I felt for a moment like a vast green being with wide, powerful wings. Then I became another tooth in the saw that was cutting the city down. I was able to see that I had never been anything else. The thought made me bloodthirsty.

In the morning, I trudged back to the hut. In the rickety dawn, there was an E-note singing through the air. I thought I heard the footsteps of Grandfather Time somewhere on the other side of the river. There were many gentle moments happening all over the world, all trying to avoid fruition, passion, or any sort of climax. I, too, tried to avoid the epiphany that I felt gathering in the rings of my consciousness. The spaces between my thoughts stretched so widely that I could not find my way between them. There were old memories clattering around in my brain: a steel kitchen, a crumbling staircase, a sloping road clogged with rain and steam.

When Sullivan returned, I wasn't sure he had really been gone. His face was jagged and reflected the sun like volcanic rock. All the things that existed seemed vacant and wooden. I thought of pianos, their rudimentary keys and hammers—and all the sounds they had ever made or would ever make in this world. It was somehow not enough. This thought was surrounded by space and could not fill up my mind. Nor could it convince me that the universe itself was quite full.

Sullivan was speaking in a demonic voice about numerology and the elite sanctuaries of power. I heard Jervilen's name mixed up with the governor's in a tapestry of curses.

"In their halls of putrefaction they cover the sight of the world," I heard Sullivan say. I balanced my mind on the edge of his words, but my understanding could not move forward or back.

"I'll never get home at this rate," I said.

Sullivan paused attentively.

"Home," he repeated. "How would you recognize it if you arrived?"

The idea of homecoming grew rounded, like a bubble without a pop. All four seasons converged on my body, none of them stronger than the others. Sullivan's presence was no longer soothing. The conditions that had sheltered us for a moment had dispersed, and we were caught out in the open, in the raw and changing world.

26

Things were more dire than I had acknowledged. It seemed the crisis was here to stay. The rich grew dirtier and more eccentric until they developed a kind of grace and blended in among the poor. Jervilen had surpassed all in stature and was the ultimate home of power. He no longer had his sprightly glow. His eyes were bloodshot and his skin worn out. His gifts were infrequent and conditional.

The sadness of doom was ubiquitous. I was sorry not just for myself but for everyone, for we all shared in the same fate. I walked back and forth, combing the city for any spontaneous boon. There was a salty smell in the air and the sky was a wet pink. The trees gathered sunlight chastely and stored it away. There was a sweet, fresh smell among their highest limbs, but it didn't reach the sordid concrete below, where people scratched futilely. The people criss-crossed furtively, now burgeoning, now scant, cloaked in long black robes, with their backs to me. I knew that I was beautiful under my own robe, even though I could not be seen by anyone—not even myself. The buildings clenched their teeth, bracing for a poignant sunset.

The second time Sullivan disappeared, I became like the left hand—the one that holds the strings down while the right hand strikes them. I seemed to be taller and more manly, even swashbuckling. I carried a leather purse about my waist. People came to me for advice. They gathered around me at tables in the public eye. I wore the grand white magnolia flowers of my father. I pointed the way. I carried my jacket over my shoulder. I calcu-lated great sums in my head.

When Sullivan returned, his mind was split down the mid-dle and his silence was long and magenta. The trucks no longer passed this way. Nothing could fetch a price. But if you looked closely at yourself, there was always something within or without that could be mortgaged. Sullivan was partitioning himself so that the parts of him that were sold would no longer communicate with the parts that were still his.

The riverbanks grew crowded with the visions of the drift-ers. From their deep slumber they began to awaken. Before, they had only lain in the wet sand or sat very still upon a piece of rot-ten lumber. Now they twisted hammocks, built boats, and went to work restoring the old sewing machines and printing presses covered in barnacles that they hauled up from the bottom of the canal. They caught the attention of the wretches who passed through town from other places. Their kind eyes were welcoming. Their pure thoughts produced a pure material. Something new began to take shape. It was sketchy, like the men themselves. I found myself sitting closer to their encampments. I was curious about their works. The first time one of them looked into my eyes, I felt a strong sense of regret.

Sullivan was too weary to discuss it. His eyes belonged to two different beings. He was surrounded by empty bottles of rum. He could only talk about his long meanderings through neglected gardens. Where the trees had once been soft and full of dew, with birds playing between the branches, a death mask now sprawled its wide grin. The desiccated forms and howling absences were part of its obscene hilarity. Where once soothing chimes played meditatively in the wind, there was only the clatter of great objects falling into dumpsters and the thunder of con-structions collapsing.

"I saw an elf walking along the train tracks," Sullivan said. "He was wearing a peaked cap and he carried a satchel in his pocket. When he looked me in the eyes, I saw the grave and all things calculated to the final digit. He opened his purse and brought out three jewels. They were like marbles, but they were soft and alive. One of them was my past, one was my present, and the third my future.

"He said, 'Plant the first in the best soil you can find, and it will give you the second tenfold. The third, you must put in the hands of a trusted friend and forget about it completely. This is very important. If you remember it, it will get sick and never return to you.'"

"What have you done with them?" I asked.

Sullivan wept. "I looked everywhere for a patch of good soil, but every hole I dug was filled with poison. I walked until my feet bled and I scratched the earth. Everything was dead or dying. When it was dark, I lost the seed of the past. Then I realized the present had never existed. I couldn't find either of them again."

"And the seed of the future? What did you do with it?"

He sobbed, "I can't remember!" His eyes cast about him. There were tarot cards spread out on the cabin floor and black feathers gathered in the floorboards. I waited. When I could tell by his breathing that he had fallen asleep, I stepped outside and walked down the ribbon of wet sand. The river was high and seething with sinister joy. There was a smell of glue in the air. Explosions rumbled from the military base. Vague smatterings of applause could be heard from time to time. There was a carnival happening downtown, and the electric lights were blazing in the night.

Beneath the other sounds, a voice was speaking to me. It was a soft, windy voice, saying the same thing over and over again: "Free the righteous from their worries. Make your peace with the unrighteous. There is a cadence to your clarity. Silence permutes the friction of the waves." I felt overwhelmed and abject, indebted to forces beyond my understanding.

As the grey light began to coalesce upon the air, the scenery grew staid and solemn, like a sick woman with purple eyelids. I had been crossing and re-crossing the sand in a state of wonder and dismay, and my footprints were like the angry stitches in a pinched piece of fabric. The men of mud had grown tall. They crowded the skyline like an old-growth forest. As they swayed, they murmured in their strange language. Yet their incantations did not stir the turgid concrete. The sky was a milky green. I smelled someone's cigarette burning. I remembered a kindness done for me long ago and I felt helpless in my compassion, like a weed blown over by a gentle breeze.

A woman who was missing her left arm and her left leg approached me. She drew a piece of paper out of a bag that hung from her neck. It read:

Our thoughts are blank and history null
our actions sublime and our baskets full

It's mercy for the dull of wit,
the happy fat, the impolitic

But sovereigns and parasites
are swiftly felled and reorganized

So if one lives in both your eyes
then cut them out with whetted knives

Past and future, both are sweet
disfigured by a grand conceit

To take them back, you need but reach
into the wail of burdened beasts

Beyond that which they call polite
into the glove that grips the knife

The woman walked on. As the sun rose, the world grew
blacker and more dense. I considered going downtown, for I
felt that money alone could open a door. I tried to walk, but the
ground sank beneath me. There was a yellow fog across the levee
and I could not see to the other side. I stumbled and weaved. I
fell down on my stomach and crawled through piles of pink dust:
the batting of the universe, the thick stuffing that clogs the universal mind and absorbs its ringing tones.

Buried in the soft, billowing foam, I fell asleep. I saw
myself floating up a spiral staircase. I saw Sullivan gnashing his
teeth under an enormous moon. I saw the ocean running away
from the shore, taking with it all its riches and finery. Grandfather Time was blowing bubbles with the vagrant men on the river
shore.

"They are convicts," he said, gesturing toward the men. "That's why they are creating another world, one in which they will be kings."

I descended a set of concrete stairs. Four men were playing poker. One of them had the face of a bull and his eyes were boiling with rage. Another had the face of a cat and his teeth were sharp with cunning. The third had the head of a horse and he made everyone call him "Your Majesty". The fourth was a smiling dragon who thought everything was funny and laughed with his tongue waving.

I walked along a stony path. The stones were whispering. Quick, clever violets grew in my footsteps. An owl hooted a warning. It was an unchanging blue evening. The garbage cans were blooming. I watched, amazed, as they spilled over their borders. Whippoorwills called. Ghosts made of cloth and plastic skeletons hung in the trees.

"Where are all the people?" I asked one of the skeletons.

"They are all in one place, far from here," he said. "This place is what's left over, after the violence is complete."

I stirred and realized I was still in the cabin. I turned to Sullivan, but he was only a pile of bones. The cabin looked strange, as if I had just entered it for the first time. I felt an insinuated guilt, as if I had gotten drunk and meshed my delusions with the material plane.

Outside, the shore was empty. The vagrants had been cleared away. Two soldiers were lying down in the sand, sipping cocktails. A war tank was stuck in the mud, half-buried in the river. The soldiers blew me kisses as I trudged by them with my shoes in my hand. The works of the community they had destroyed were piled high in a dumpster just beyond the train tracks.

The street was hot and parched. I was surrounded by people. I saw children with smashed faces trying to create joy out of nothing. Their eyes were different sizes and they looked in different directions. One man sat in the sunlight and picked at his shirtless body as if searching for some flaw. Another knelt against a concrete slab and mourned. People stepped over him as they passed.

"What are you avoiding?" said an old man wearing a coyote head.

"Don't talk to me," I hissed, and quickened my step.

Jervilen was reduced to a heap in a wheelchair. His jaw jutted out because he had lost all of his teeth. The bar was converted into a legitimate business by investors from abroad. Jervilen was wheeled around by the ladies of his clan, cousins and nieces and grand-nieces. There was laughter around him when the old days were discussed. He always shook his head, as if troubled, and I looked into his face as into a pile of ashes after a fire.

"What a shame," someone said.

When he died, the rites were perfunctory, for Jervilen was merely an afterthought in the mind of a preoccupied world. His beauty had died long ago, and with it the beauty of the city. I breathed a glittering pink sigh. I too had been old for some time. People drew near me as to an awning in the rain. I prayed for them with my heathen thoughts. Whether they took any solace, I do not know, but they eventually moved on.

I left town, traveling as the poor do, in ignominy and discomfort. Every city I passed was the same: a tender and dreamy historic district received tourists during the day and emptied at night, except for the soldiers. A few miserable settlements crouched in the outskirts amid the remains of neglected industries. I crushed through the glass on the factory floors and was misdirected by the signs that stood in the tall weeds.

In the suburbs, the plants had developed conversant minds, and they engaged me in deep and challenging dialogues.

"Why is it that you believe your presence in this world to be futile?" asked a fragrant jasmine bush.

"It's not just me," I said. "Don't you sometimes feel that all things are extraneous?"

"Extraneous to *what*?" the plant replied.

"Something," I answered at length. "I'm sure there is something to be extraneous to. But what it is, I do not know."

"If you do not know what it is, then how can you be sure

it's not you, yourself?"

"I haven't been able to ascertain what I am. I keep trying, but I can't pinpoint my taste, or how exactly I change the light that touches me."

"Now you're on the right track!" the jasmine said, and shook with laughter, releasing hundreds of jewels of dew.

Meanwhile a patch of wild ginger rocked its broad leaves to and fro. In a deep voice it grumbled, "Don't let me ruin anything for you, but you still haven't arrived in your own footsteps."

"I plan to do my best," I said.

He guffawed. "How many worlds do you plan to pass through by sheer inertia? You have yet to take a single action."

"Of course, all actions are swiftly undone by their own momentum," I said curtly. "Or hadn't you noticed?"

He scoffed again. "And you wonder why you don't exist."

A banana tree offered me a bit of cool shade. This sagacious plant watched me worriedly while I napped. It spoke few words. Gently, it repeated, "It is so." This phrase seemed to embrace all that had ever existed with a fullness of compassion.

It felt wonderful to be traveling again. The moss on the sides of leaning buildings touched my eyes. Rusted masses of old metal like the ribcages of exterminated beasts yawned in the dirt. The clouds were hallucinating in the eternal sky with big smiles on their faces. The largest trees were archiving the earth's history, throbbing with old and fearsome musics, the powerful drumming of the days and seasons, the quick lives and deaths of people, and the stunning rhythm of peace and war. The trees remembered in their deep and inward way more than I could ever perceive. Still, I sang to them, hoping that my voice might have some meaning.

27

One world withered and the next grew out of its decay. I was still singing when I was reborn, but my song was mistaken for moaning.

"She sounds like the wailer women at the port," said a lady with a wan smile.

"Is fortune here the same as misfortune elsewhere?" the green blades of grass whispered.

At night I dreamed backwards toward an apocalypse I had already experienced. I was watched over by big bearded pillars, the four white columns that held the ceiling up from the floor. There was always a little bit of wind in my mouth. I thought when I got bigger I would walk right out of the neighborhood and head downtown, toward the smell of liquor and advertisements for lottery tickets and the cry of the train.

My anger was so great it made me tired. I roamed vast, neat lawns and carefully kept grounds. I smelled gunpowder and sawdust in the air. I was filled with vengeance and mourning. My brothers were shooting at tin cans. I plotted like a mastermind. The dandelions basked in the yellow sky. I made a map of good and a map of evil and learned that there were many roads that crossed through both.

"How did I get here?" I asked my mother.

"I borrowed you from a pumpkin flower," she said. I could tell that she was growing me to sell to the magician. Her other children were hers to keep, but I was the bounty that would maintain their enchanted equilibrium. I didn't mind. My family were like dolls made of wax. The young children seemed to be cut out of cereal boxes and the older ones out of summer-camp brochures. Only my little sister carried with her a black bag filled with the memories of another time.

"How are we doing this?" I asked her as our magic wove a new dimension.

"Be cailful, you could cweate somebody you might have to

destwoy."

It was a place of candlesticks and vestments and tabernacles, checkered floors and sidewalks embedded with glittering pebbles. I myself was a house within a house and tucked away in me were many halls and chambers. The inner house and the outer house flowed into one another. The demons of the inner house emerged from the fire that was always burning beneath the water tank. It wasn't the evil they would do to me but the evil that had been done to them that frightened me.

The eyes that surrounded me were remote, as if they were only place-holders for beings who were busy elsewhere, in another lifetime.

I wrote in the margins of my life. I doodled swirls and whirls and worlds I dreamed of with only one eye. There were steep staircases through the wet mountain roads of the mind. The future walked alongside the past. A pair of butterflies was wrestling in mid-air. The bellies of the leaves were white and the sides of the trees shone silvery like fish's scales. There was a sickly heaviness in the atmosphere and the premonition of drinking whiskey from the bottle while slipping nimbly between two bad dreams. My sleepiness was nauseating. The sky turned green but still the air-conditioners wheezed. Three fairies visited my window. The first said:

> I blame you for your winking eye
> the tilt of things that are awry
> the objects empty of their souls
> your loving cup that's full of holes

The second fairy said:

> I praise you for your knifelike mind
> the easy way's so hard to find
> between the ashes and the flame
> beneath the spirit, above the name

The third fairy fluttered its big eyes and said:

The sideways rain just makes me sad
there's bad in good and good in bad
each one I meet seems to be the best
the weapon works while the intention rests

"I believe each of you," I said, "but let me offer a fourth perspective. Suppose the beings who have been smeared into strange forms and leering masks—masks of chagrin and hideous delight—suppose they are trapped and don't want to be here at all. Suppose the easy way doesn't lead anywhere. And suppose resignation is only a solution for the season, and its face folds in upon itself and becomes a devouring fire of woe. What is left to us but to fold back even the waves of the ocean and remake the world and its meaning with every breath?"

"Your reasoning has come full circle," replied the first angel. "But beware, for circles are never resolved."

The storm rocked the trees against the house. The thunder got inside of things and made changes. Then the darkness retreated, leaving the machinery of joy and fever intact. The days sprawled. I slipped into the grey spaces between many agendas. The school building was piled on top of itself like a labyrinth; the completed parts gave way to unfinished parts, with bare frames for walls and plywood floors. In some places the building dove into underground depths where dead children grieved.

"Why are you crying?" I asked one boy.

"I am a part of you that will never grow up," the ugly boy responded. "I will follow you through many lifetimes."

The faces in the clouds and in the water had begun to disappear. Eventually the faces seemed to disappear even from the faces of the people. There was something threatening in the purple radiance of the violets. I helped my sister swing across a muddy pit. We were lost. Towering, angry spirits stomped through the underbrush, making a racket, swinging their long arms. After they had passed, I set a squirming turtle right-side up. Blue shadows grew at the roots of the trees and swarmed with cold memories. We kept getting stuck in sticker bushes. I turned a thorn sideways, leaving behind the green spot from which it had grown.

"Where are we going?" my sister asked.

"That question keeps asking itself," I said. "Some would say up, others would say down. I think the question just likes the way our voices sound."

"How can we move through time?" she asked.

"Saturday and Sunday are the parents," I explained, "and they have five children. They make their children work for them, so they can grow rich and pray."

"What are they praying for?"

"They pray that nothing will change, and that even when they are old and dying, nothing will hurt. They use their money to pray."

My sister clicked her tongue and shook her head.

A snake appeared. He was small and green and bashful, embarrassed to be seen. He said:

> You, like I, have been hatched from an egg
> but only one of us uses thoughts for legs
> while the other's mind wriggles up in a knot
> and carefully slips through the holes in the plot

We averted our eyes and passed on. As we wandered through the woods, the shadows of birds passed over us. When we raised our eyes, the birds were already gone. Soon we stopped raising our eyes at all. Here and there, a noose hung from a tree. The wind sighed in many voices, carrying the tears of feudal lords and bearing in its arms reliquaries and unmarked graves. The forest floor trembled in its sleep, mulling over the roots of giant trees that had fallen over in the confusion of one timeline invading another long ago.

Though the forest was small, we were smaller. The next time we came to an opening, we encountered a construction site:

a casino was being built on the riverbank. The workers winked and entertained us. Around the shadows of their worksite huddled women who came when they were called like dogs. When they weren't wanted, the women were thin enough to blend in among the railings and fences and ladders.

We wandered a while longer in the cool forest where any world seemed possible. Finally we emerged at the railroad tracks, where men with wandering attention sat twitching in the blue twilight. Strange and illicit garbage studded the slope of the hill. The graffiti was terse and ugly. We sat down and watched the moon scrawl across a patch of sky. One of the hobos mumbled:

> A moon to me
> a loon to you
> room and board
> lock and key
> the sickly sap
> and the lazy dew
> the hazy news
> the horizon's bruise
> the black eyes
> of the beaten hills
> the billboards' teeth
> rotten and few
> the carnival glows
> but you can't buy a beer
> with a bent penny
> every grandmother knows
> you can't buy sympathy
> with twice recycled tears

I would have liked to dwell for a while with the honest sadness of this impasse, but my sister shook me by the shoulders and urged me back into the darkened woods.

"They dream of purple valleys while they speak of fallen civilizations," she cautioned. "They are falling out of the world."

We sank into the woods again. The moon had already

vanished, but the forest was illuminated from within. Coyotes howled and their prey could be heard screaming. The darkness mumbled and grumbled at us, growling and snarling and whimpering. It located the loose threads of our minds and pulled at them, tangling up the delicate weavings of our thoughts. I forgot that we were lost in the woods and began to believe we were sitting in the lap of an impatient woman. When she straightened out her skirt, the dawn came and returned things to themselves.

The morbid light revealed the wounds of this world, its scarred face and grotesque flesh. We trodded on, single-file, like pilgrims, toward some unknown goal. I looked back over my shoulder at my sister. She had become an old woman, although she was still as small as a child. Her hair was white on top and dark underneath, pulled back gracefully into a bun. She walked heavily, with bags of time hanging from her hips and legs and arms. The trees breathed a magnificent sigh, roiling in every direction like a whirlpool.

"I have lived in a story-book," my sister said, "whereas you have written one. That's why time has passed through me, while you, instead, have passed through time."

Her words depressed me. Then my face seemed to heal—my mouth and eyes were sealed by a satisfaction that was also disappointment, for nothing remained to be seen or said. I finally became an inanimate object, like so many other travelers. My sister walked right by me, still seeking the correct path through the forest. She hobbled on, grumbling to herself, and the daisies grew around me, encircled in their own rough leaves.

28

I was part of the childlike planet rolling in the light of the sun. I was part of a dreamy smile the young world was wearing in its blissful sleep. There were sadistic currents in the geology and cynical tears were ever flowing, heavy as waterfalls. Still, the little baby world hatched and said over and over again, "I believe you."

Outer space commented, "It is noble of you to take the trouble to live. As for me, I just can't muster the energy."

The earth responded, "Oh, I might as well!"

This was the type of thing outer space couldn't understand. Her doldrums were so extreme, she could scarcely finish her thoughts.

The great mother was looking on, serene and demure. She was an image of sweet perfection, like a flower carved out of wax. However, any little thing could irritate her, and then she would become ferocious. She kept the sun burning gently for her children, but every now and then she caused it to explode, and a long smile slithered across her face, like a road or a horizon.

"I love you," I prayed, as part of the earth's mouth. The mother ignored me and crushed the planet in her right hand. She began yanking at the long, wild tresses of outer space and weaving them into two tight braids.

"I won't have you looking so loose and lazy when God and his angels come," she said. Space rolled her foggy eyes and placed two resentments firmly in the ether: one for each braid. She resolved to return to these seeds of anger as soon as possible. A bit of the old world found its way into her firm intentions during the eons in which the mother was out to lunch with God the Father, planning a future for their ugly children.

Thus a new world grew out of the messy endings of the old, the interruption between the two of them no more than a shiver in history. I waited patiently at the side of things and underfoot. I was grateful to be a color—soft pink or greyish purple—or something that flitted through the minds of infants before it was displaced by ideas. Sometimes I glinted in the fallen wings of termites and sometimes I read the poems written in the sky composed by passing clouds. When I once more became a woman, I inherited the sullen, immobile heart of outer space, as well as the sublime optimism of terrestrial bodies.

There were drops of rainbow glittering on the tarp, for a storm had passed in the night. Fog danced and billowed over the village, wrapping itself flirtatiously around squares of distance. A spider had wrought a web of pure glassy light and hung it sweetly from a railing. Someone was chopping wood, sending a hollow, rhythmic "puck!" through the air. A farmer was singing to himself as he watered his rows, and the wind carried a tide of leaves down to the earth, covering the houses and footpaths.

A tall black shadow approached me with a sly smirk, a monocle clasped between his eyebrow and cheekbone.

"Hurry up and hallow something," he said, snickering to himself.

"Easier said than done," I retorted, and I turned my back to him.

I gathered a load of articles into my plastic tub—lottery tickets, lighters, cigarettes, and peanuts wrapped in cellophane. The man was watching me, so I could no longer appreciate the dazzling beauty of the morning. I was plagued by a sense of pink rubber, something slick and unctuous, having to do with hospitals and thick liquids. It was the heavy deadness of existence, the way the tongue hangs speechless in the mouth.

"The tongue is used for speaking, but can the tongue itself speak?" I mumbled.

The tall man peered at me out of his great yellow eye. There was peace in his big eye, a hint of courtyards and orchards with vines growing neatly on trellises. My patience returned to me.

"At least you can stop talking now and then," I grumbled. The man waited a while longer before answering. I began to feel childish for greeting him so rudely. Finally, he said:

"You won't be healed by getting what you imagine you want. The world has two left shoes and a phone number that is no longer in service. You can go around asking, you can walk fast or slow. What you think you are looking for doesn't go by that name, and you wouldn't know it anymore if you saw it."

I walked to the road with my wares on my hip, mulling over this unwelcome advice. People tumbled out of wretched dwellings. They pushed and pulled, trying to meet their needs. Cynical old men bought cigarettes from me—the kind of men who don't care if they live until the evening. They breathed smoke like dragons and I saw behind their useless old bodies their pure fiery nature. That tall shadow kept popping up, kissing my heels as I walked along the road, swinging darkly around the stacks of fruit and the old women who sat among them.

"Your heart still points in the same direction as always," the shadow whispered, "when life itself knows only vertigo, total fearsome delight."

His message inspired a feeling of madness. All things seemed to be suspended. Money came into my hands, a surging river that snaked around continents and slipped through seas; a ribbon of paper, shimmering and changing colors and flying on thousands of warm brown wings. Conjured by money, products danced on multi-dimensional trajectories like a wild field of explosions. In money's dance, everything was near. Nothing was far away. Food and drink came to me of their own volition, entering my body and taking a seat in my veins as in a velvet-upholstered railroad car.

An old woman approached me with both hands outstretched. Although she was mad, I allowed her to comfort me.

"My child, my child. Don't mistake appearances for walls. Appearances are meant to be doors!"

The sky had grown dark, and inside the woman's enormous, soft palms, numbers were reckoned and accounts settled. Everyone had gone home to cook while the lights were still on. Still, the market was not empty. Green and yellow people performed a parody of the real market, pressing their noses to one another's wares and widening their eyes with exaggerated interest and delight. They filled their baskets and walked with silly swaggers, looking over their shoulders and batting their eyelashes.

The road wrapped around me and conversations entertained themselves with me. My house swallowed me and hopes and fears passed through me on their endless, ghostly march, golden lanterns swinging from their weary arms.

I learned to regard whirling phenomena from a calm distance. Life fed me and wiped my mouth. I found languishing within me the silky, privileged body of an outside observer. The only danger, it turned out, was boredom, which grew stronger each time one of my pressing questions was answered.

"Aren't I beautiful?" said a black cat that often strutted by my house.

"It doesn't matter," I yawned.

The moths flew in circles around the lightbulb, and there was no one to tell. I could have six thoughts at once, and it was as if each thought was happening within a different person. I saw a bloody fight in the marketplace. Two drunks tore one another's clothes off. I contemplated them as I would a changing sky. I sold more than usual that morning, for a large crowd gathered to watch the violence.

Evil took its due from among the townspeople as it does everywhere. Suffering has a rich, foamy taste that makes your tongue numb. The drug of suffering returned to our gods the use of their old, abandoned bodies, the skeletons they left lying in the fields. They had grown so tired that they couldn't move or even feel, but when they sipped at our yellow cups, the thinly stretched cords that linked spirit to matter glittered where they lay in the grass.

My body disappeared in the murky red night. I was made of the sounds of crickets and frogs. The soldiers at their posts were majestic as mountains with their mouths closed and their eyes opened in the dark.

I was looking for someone I had lost. Shadow had overcome the landscape, revealing tiny lights that could not otherwise be seen. How can it be that darkness clarifies and light obscures, I wondered. My mouth was full of dead things—frogs and toads and the toes of old paupers. They spilled out as I stumbled along.

Two teenaged boys emerged from the woods where they had stopped to pee on their way back from the spring. One pushed while the other pulled the wheelbarrow stacked with jugs. They nodded to me as they passed, but I could see the sulphur-colored crescent moons of fear in their eyes. I swallowed down the snakes and worms and insects that were spilling out of me and tried to walk straight until the boys were out of sight.

I took the footpath that led to the garbage dump. In the moonlight, the garbage that covered the mountainside and filled up the valley looked like an ancient city. I remembered my friend, a being who knew how to live in the space between objects, who kept his mind soft and fresh like young bamboo shoots. After groping in the darkness for some time, I found him in the way the stream played with ribbons of moonlight. One more toad fell out of my mouth. This one was alive and it plunged merrily into the water. I felt better, watching the ripples settle into stillness. There were no more sounds for a long time. The stream's current was caught on a rock and it swirled around it in the shape of an S. My friend sat still beside me. He could have remained that way forever, but I was impatient for words, concepts, and changes.

"Tell me how you have fared," I said. "When you die in prison, does your soul become free?"

"It depends on the prison," he answered. "The strongest prisons have soul-traps too!" He cackled wildly and fell back on his elbows. "And you? Are you going anywhere in particular, or just zig-zagging around?"

I laughed, though slightly stung. "Just zig-zagging around, I guess."

He licked his teeth, suppressing a very charming smile. For a moment, he held the universe under his influence and he savored its intoxicating power. Then quietly, he returned the power to its source and I saw his face and body shrink and a wrinkle fall from his eye to his chin.

"That is the best way, anyway," he said. "Otherwise, you might be like an angry person who keeps trying to go far. You might go so far no one can see you, and you might never have time to get back. Then you would just be out there saying, 'Hello!

Hello! Can somebody tell me how far I got?'" He doubled over with laughter and I smiled.

I put my feet into the water. The bank was wet and my clothes were damp. Despair sat in my heart, nurturing a nest full of restless offspring. My friend receded, his wise laughter echoing, into the hidden places where people go. The rich black of night rusted, turning brown and then grey, and then forgetting altogether that it had not always been day. A pumpkin flower that had opened in the first fresh hours of dawn closed once more against the heat of morning.

I evaded any spiritual difficulties and set about my trade. I walked a mile down the road to the wholesale market. Musicians were gathered around a shop. They were decorated in ornaments and striking poses. An old woman was washing the sidewalk with a rag, crawling on her hands and knees.

❧

While my body went about its business, another being was probing the back halls of consciousness, seeking a back door through which I might escape. The scent of herbs and incense mingled with the fumes of the trucks carrying bricks and cement and the smell of oil spoiling in a vat. Rolls of carpet were stacked in one stall, bolts of drapery in the next, while sinks and toilets were stacked along the walls of another. All the fixtures of civilization were there, piled in neat rows, and before each pile stood a broker with a notebook in hand, performing on a small stage made of pallets. They each recited the same poems in a slightly different style. I listened to their sad, droning voices and heard something like this:

> Let me love you while it's easy
> it costs nothing just to smile
> someone suffered for your pleasure
> pour your pity on the pile

> In the swollen city center

life and death don't make us blush
let me help you with your zipper
please and thank you very much

A small shrine had been built at the feet of one merchant
and upon it an offering was burning—a few splinters of wood
doused in gasoline. A greedy fairy was gobbling up the prayers,
leaving nothing for the deity for whom they were intended. She
saw me looking at her and smiled with pointed teeth.

I accidentally stepped in a puddle of green liquid that had
gathered between the paving stones. Nauseating smells wafted
over me. I prowled an antique market where useless oddities
were piled up. I tried several doors, but I remembered upon
opening them that I had tried each one many times before.

When I had purchased my goods, I took the bus back up
the hill. Outside the window, the valley shone promisingly, but I
hunkered lower within myself as if to dodge the scathing eye of
joy.

❧

Business was slow and I slept among my wares in the heat
of the afternoon. Even in my sleep, there was no reprieve. A few
children were playing with tires beside the road. They aged rapidly and began to work on the old cars that were strewn around the
yard.

That day in the marketplace, some helpless people did a
heavy dance. They were dressed in boxy costumes and moved in
unison. The dancers stomped on the ground as if packing seeds
down into the earth. Their hands were fists and seemed to beat
on invisible drums.

The dance had a strange effect on the town. It made a hunger grow in the people, a kind of curiosity. I smiled at passersby. I
stowed away my basin filled with goods—I was suddenly embarrassed to be seen with it. The loneliness grew as purple blotches
took up more and more of the distance. Everyone stayed out late
as if it was a festival night. A group of girls my age took me by the

elbows and we gossipped under the banyan tree. They were the same girls I had known all my life, but they seemed to have been made anew, with exquisite care. The shapes of their cheeks and eyelids were delicately painted upon a nourishing darkness. I felt lucky to be among them.

There were bells and other melodic tones echoing on the evening air. A man with seven faces was waiting for me across the street. His faces whirled around like a windmill. I thought I recognized more than one of them, but I couldn't distinguish them clearly.

"Is the world good or bad?" the man asked when I reached his side.

"It's so bad I cannot stand it," I replied. I was suddenly aware of how big I was, like a giant stuffed doll, sitting with my two heavy legs splayed apart on the curve of the tiny world, my head slumped down on my chest. The man's smile flickered and another face took its place.

"Or maybe it's the world's goodness that you cannot bear," he suggested. I watched the satisfied mothers of families strolling after dark, and I was filled with longing and indefinable regrets.

"Oh, it's the same thing," I moaned. "What's the point of talking about it? Every word we utter sets another war in motion. Every thought we entertain costs a generation's only hope. There is no answer to the way things bend. Even the great wide wings of love can't cross the ocean of pain—and that is only a ripple in a greater ocean no one has ever seen."

The man whirred and ticked. Children played, running and crying out gleefully. One boy's arm grazed me as he ran wildly through the shadows. I noticed the soldiers' eyes turning lavender as they seemed to fall out of love with us. I drank this impression down with the overwhelming sweetness of the night and forgot about it.

The schoolmaster interrupted my conversation with the seven-faced man to invite me to tea with our class. The teashop was merry and filled with songs. The smell of night jasmine curled through the air. After the road had emptied of the living, the dead held a joyous gathering of their own. I watched them buying flowers and incense and smiling with wide-eyed interest at one another's children and their new clothes.

It was late before the youngest children began to fall asleep on the tables and their fathers slung them over their shoulders and one by one started for home. The man with seven faces sat by himself all night. I often noticed him wiping a single tear from his left eye. I walked myself home, carrying a big stick to fend off the dogs, but no human or animal bothered me. The forest sounds formed a divine music, and I could not sleep for the terrible wonder I felt.

I woke up in the orange dawn to the sounds of gunfire, explosions, and the sharp cries of people caught in an emergency. I ran with the others up the hill and through the fields, then into the forest far from the checkpoint on the main road. The soldiers were waiting for us. We were lined up and made to sit in rows in the sun all morning while the fighting continued in the valley.

The soldiers spoke our language and some of them re-membered their grandmothers who had lived in the village. At times they had the beautiful, melancholy faces of our people, but they had ever been merely halfway ours. Their salaries were paid overseas and their wives and children were kept in a hotel on an island. That day I noticed a terrible change. Their bellies drooped and their hair had begun to thin. Their teeth were yellow and some were loose. Long hairs shot out of their nostrils and they wobbled a little even when standing still. Their handkerchiefs hung sloppily out of their pockets, and their pins bobbled gaudily on their uniforms like buttons on clowns' suits.

The dead squatted among us, reliving another war, and they looked so much like the living that it was hard to tell us apart. By dinnertime, the soldiers had established control of the area. A loudspeaker informed us that the dancing in the market had caused a rupture of the peace. It was rumored that the choreography had been stolen from a government program and the steps had unlocked hidden parts of our humanity. The rumors soothed my spirit, weaving silver and gold into the skies of my mind. They proliferated and embellished themselves with intricate and fantastical designs. It was said that the dance was proof that we had once been giants and that we had made the valley with the wind produced by laughing at the world's funniest jokes, that we had accidentally created this government by making incorrect change for a large bill at the end of the day when our mind was distracted, and that we could unmake it by focusing perfectly on the meaning of the color blue. Everyone tried to meditate upon the true blue, but it turned out there were so many blues to recognize that the concept of blue lost all meaning and the word for it fell out of our language. Then it became impossible to even discuss the solution to our predicament. Somehow I found this funny and I went about laughing for several days.

Our little market was abolished and our needs were provided for by an international company. Our new cigarettes and lighters bore the same smiling logo as the landmines neatly tucked into the hills. Soon we all wore the same silly smile across our faces. Our worries were forgotten. The man with seven faces still grimaced now and then.

29

I saw paths in four dimensions, thin pink highways over-lapping one another in a tangle of fates and outcomes. Then a great wave came and washed them all away. Everything disap-peared except for a blue mountain range made of memories long undisturbed. I stayed as far away from them as I could, but they were eating the ground I was standing on, and soon I was inside them.

The mountains were my people, gnawing thoughtlessly on the past and future and blocking out the sky with their lumber-ing forms. Their shoulders gently swayed as they adjusted their satchels and belongings. A sliver of space could now and then be seen opening up between them. I tried to slip through, but I was too big. When I asked for permission to pass, the mountains ges-tured like animals. They couldn't speak, but they showed me that there was nowhere to go, that the whole world was packed with us, or people like us, so tightly that we had to stand and wait.

I tried to tell them that it was not true. I tried to draw a picture of the world on my hand, but I couldn't draw it because time was present in the drawing and obliterated everything. Then I noticed that some of the people weren't people at all, but merely empty suits. These I pushed aside until I found the place where people gave way to the elements that composed them—heavenly harmonies, peals of idle thought, and glacial patience. I waded through the fecund waters of hopeful beginnings where colorful hallucinations were scattered upon the surface of the mind.

Small, one-eyed beings turned me the colors they liked and seductive birds used their songs as medicine for my old misgiv-ings. Bearded kings rearranged historical debts, taking from here and replacing there, in a complex and ever-growing geometry. Friends took turns nurturing my best qualities. One long blue lady taught me to see beauty. A far green woman taught me dream interpretation and showed me the route between death and rebirth, which was shaped like an E written in script.

"You see, time can't really harm you," said the seven-faced man. Now his faces had healed into one face, and I recognized him readily. I realized that I loved him, but I hated him too, in equal proportion.

"I don't want you here!" I cried. Immediately I regretted it, but he was already gone.

A monster was holding onto me like a dragonfly gripping a yellow rosebud. I could smell paint buckets rusting in the sun. It was this smell and the green of strong grass after a rain that pulled me back into a wave of life in a certain place. A cloud of gnats swarmed in figure-8s near my eyes. A chorus of cicadas arose and leveled out in a steady hum. I was like a new leaf on an old stalk. That was the way I was the same self in a different lifetime.

Many mothers gathered around and placed gifts at my feet. My flowing gown was so long it hid my toes. The mothers sang:

> Dew drop
> breath of the gods
> we have brought you into summer
> to salvage our damaged odds
> to assuage our crooked hearts
> and trickle down the page
> like q's and p's and g's and j's
> and y's and the eyes of the sage

I replied:

> Mothers,
> but the berth is wide
> many souls
> have passed this way
> your cradles are besmirched
> your lace is getting grey
> after all the silent victims
> you have callously conveyed

The mothers couldn't understand me. They took my speech as contented prattle and tied me up in ribbons and hung crescent moons from my earlobes. They all went together into a big yellow room and their noises became my sky. I crawled into a corner where the mouth of the fence-post was smiling and a bit of rosy light was passing through its lips.

❦

For a long time I believed another world lay just beyond the fence, but when I had grown older and traveled beyond it, I could not remember this thought any more. The boughs of the trees wavered gently, admonishing me for my forgetfulness. I was aware of their love, yet I did not heed them. I was busy and certain of my importance. The business of growing took all my strength and energy. I worked at it like a wizard, on multiple planes. I put things where they belonged. I fed thousands of spirits, honoring entire forests and watering long stretches of road, as if I could reach the ends of the earth. The long roads snarled and laughed at me and spread like a wildfire. I contracted and became small inside of myself. Seasons washed over me, the white of clouds and the blue of water, the brown of smoke and the aching green of wisdom.

The beasts that lived around my kingdom were angry and red, with bulging shoulders and throbbing hips. There was much to be done, sorting out whose responsibility was their pain. Did they make themselves, or were they made by some feckless deity? I sat both parties down together—the uncomfortable rhinoceros and a mediocre, clerical Lord. Both were troubled by the way things were. Both spoke at length. In the end, there was nothing to be done. Pain would go on indefinitely, for neither creator nor creation could answer for it.

That encounter washed away and was forgotten like everything else. I walked about in a courtyard outside of the compound. The well, the fountain, and the gate formed a question, and the wet green earth was patiently answering it, using me and my body and my thoughts. If I wouldn't suffice, then others like me would. I paced, growing taller and wiser, for many years. I grew memories of purple clouds and poems of tall blue flutes. I developed bitter orange tracts of worldly knowledge and deep green strips of resignation.

Beyond the gate there was an ordinary world of striving and failure. I went there and I wore plain pants and carried a bag. No one from inside the gate called me back; no one from outside looked up to see me pass. The work was undignified and the pay was meager. It was hard to get anywhere fast enough. Time was like jelly, pulling on my body and encasing my hopes and fears. While my body stayed trapped, wearing an apron or a ridiculous cap, my spirit went out scouting, listening at every corner. But there was nothing to hear, no sound anywhere. When I returned to myself, almost nothing had changed. I had only managed to utter one or two words, long detached from their meaning.

Everything beyond our little strip of land was a thick red darkness of maybes. Talking birds appeared now and then in the between-realms carrying cryptic messages.

One said: "The soft shadows of the city lights at night will eat you whole."

Another warned, "Your memories are useless beyond the world in which they were made. Scatter them, that smaller beings might eat." These birds walked weirdly across the foaming opacity, eyeing me with one pointed eye at a time.

"I am sorry to be rude," I said. "You know much better than I do. I regret my pride and my arrogance. I have trampled on the small beings who should have been my teachers. It's no use asking forgiveness; there are colors that will never again be seen in this world because I have made them impossible..."

But the talking birds were gone and there was no one to hear or answer my confession. While I was growing up, the mothers had decorated me with pearls in white rooms with wide sink-bowls. They had ensured that I acquired titles, degrees, and refinements, preparing me for illustrious company and hard bargains. When it turned out that there was no greater world beyond our little kingdom, the mothers simply retreated, reduced to no more than a cool smile. That smile mocked me, curling like a cat's tail in the clouds or fading into the gravel underfoot. It slipped into my eye wherever my eye traveled, whether over a blank white wall or the lines of my own hand.

~

I visited the old compound one day. There were brown leaves all over the floor of the yellow room. Among them I noticed some animal teeth. The windows were broken and seemed to laugh at me with crooked grins.

Finally, when the time was ripe, I passed beyond the point where I had always turned back, beyond the servants' quarters, into a periphery where dire suffering progressed on its own terms. I met an old man whose body plagued him with soreness.

"Why do you continue walking on this broken footpath?" I asked him.

"It's the footpath that is walking on me! Ow!" he said. He hobbled along, each step a scourge and a barb.

I settled my eyes on a point in the distance, where I assumed peace resided.

"You could feel good if you were willing to try," a billboard read.

The patterns of the leaves against the sky were like a mosaic on the roof of heaven.

I saw an old couple—a man and a woman. The man was dying. The woman was crying out desperately in the street. The passersby ignored her, except for a few strange, wispy figures who gathered around her to pray.

"Come, sister," said one of these pale figures after their monotonous prayer had ended. "Let us take you to the place where the healing fountain gurgles forth."

"Where are you taking her?" I asked the bobbin at the edge of the group. She turned to me. Her nose and cheeks were red, as if she had a cold. She pointed at a sprawling building some distance from the road.

"Come and be saved," she said in a nasally voice.

I followed the group across a wide expanse of parking lot

toward a low, fat structure that glittered like a frog in a hole. The sky was streaked pink with sunset and crying could be heard crawling slowly through the air. I saw that the building was a church, but it was also a mall. In the gleaming lobby there was the peculiar smell of money and of the unguents and perfumes that lubricate money-spending. Merchants with sharpened teeth and sagging, wrinkled tattoos were selling all manner of specialty goods and treats.

The little people in white cloaks ushered the mourning woman, still mumbling chaotically, into an office.

"Won't you sign up?" asked the watery doll with the red nose.

"What for?" I asked.

"With your membership you can attend all the chapel services, plus discounts in the shops." She handed me a pamphlet that read:

Our GOD has commanded us to prosper. And we have obeyed! Become a member of The Shoppes at Prestview(™) and prosper today!

Basic- $99.99/mo
Sermons and trainings FREE 5 days a week.
Weekly deals at the Shoppes!

Eagle- $199.99/mo + 180 days of service learning
Honor GOD and grow RICH while earn-
ing commission* as a sales associate.
*Restrictions Apply.

The chapel was a grand theater with stadium seating. It was crowded with rowdy, heinous people. A huge disco ball hung from the ceiling amid a hive of loudspeakers that were pouring out upon the arena a terrible cacophony. Banners hung from the rafters on enormous cloth flags. One read: "The Prince of Prices wants you to Name your Number".

A pulpit was raised like a boxing ring in the center of the stadium. A fat man stood at the microphone and when the music ceased, he said: "Garbage is a good problem to have. I'm serious! By creating garbage, you inherit multifaceted opportunities. Just think about storage, shipping, treatment, management, research, amalgamation, and collateral, to name a few. Of course, there's also decontamination. Yes, ladies and gentlemen, garbage is a good problem to have."

The crowd cheered uproariously. A man near me bellowed and jerked and smashed his beer can into his forehead. The little white saints scurried around, gathering up rumpled bills that had been tossed onto the wet floor around the audience's feet.

I was moaning in despair, pushing my head into the cement wall, when a small man with a handlebar moustache and round spectacles approached me. I had seen him when I first entered, striding back and forth before an exit, his hands clasped behind his back. He wore a suit with long coattails.

"Go and enjoy yourself," he said, handing me some money.

"This is quite a lot," I said, still weeping.

He gathered my tears and fed them to a little violet that lived in his lapel. My tears made the flower die.

"That's because my tears come from a sea in a different world," I said. "You shouldn't feed them to things here."

"It doesn't matter," the little man said. "Your tears created something new by undoing what was there before. The same is true of my church. My children," he said, gesturing at the horde. "They are all a businessman could ask for. They have grown ever hungrier with my ambitions. But now they are too big. If they get any bigger, they will disappear."

"Their stomachs are like great balloons that have no circumference, but whose circumference is not zero," I concurred.

"Too true!" said the tycoon. "Well, then, why were you crying? Perhaps you are more ornamental than practical? There are some who drift by without having to pay any fee. Others are destroyed by the spasms they cause in the machine. I bet you've experienced a little of both."

"I don't want you to know me," I replied. "You are an evil

man and I hate you."

"That is all very well," the little man said and he chuckled. I recognized his dimpled smile from the dollar bills I had stuffed into my pockets. "Anyway, you have answered my question. I was wondering whether to invite you upstairs for some champagne or to ignore you while you got older and weirder on the premises."

"And which have you decided on?" I asked, bristling.

"I will pray for you," he said. He looked at his watch, then smiled, turned on his heel, and left. The crowd swayed in a confused stupor. I languished with them in a sea of opportunities.

For all the opulence and shine, there was no money anywhere. I filled out an application at a pretzel shop in the mall.

"There are no wages," the hiring agent explained. "You are not an employee. You are gaining skills and experience, and these amount to merit in the eyes of God. God rewards the meritorious, but faith must come first."

"A commission-based fee structure will be implemented after six months," she said when pressed harder.

The literature tucked into the walls depicted golden roads stretching into the distance and happy couples growing old, surrounded by tender smiles. Although I would earn no wages, the shop kept me out of the weather and gave me a place to use the bathroom. I gradually became used to the lunatic behavior of the enormous customers. I glimpsed myself in the mirror while I worked at the vat of frying dough. My face looked like a swirl, a thumbprint, a knot in a tree. I couldn't make sense of the idea that the one I saw in the mirror was me. There were mirrors hanging all about the shop, panels set at neck-level, and my own face startled and unsettled me, hanging around like a bad smell throughout the day. The proprietor passed through now and then, a silvery mirage reflected from all sides.

The days blended together like overlapping dreams, filled with sugar packets, plastic trays, the smell of cotton candy and new leather, silica beads, gemstones twinkling in bright cases, and the shrewd, hungry gazes of the kiosk salesmen.

The church people didn't like me. I was always saying the wrong things. Once, I remarked how beautiful the soda cups were, so perfectly shaped, and how efficiently they stacked on top of one another, never sticking together or marring their light waxy finish.

"It's a shame to see them thrown away on the pile, like garbage," I said.

After an awkward pause, my supervisor replied, "Garbage is a good problem to have."

Another time, I asked her, "What's heaven like?"

"How should I know?" she barked. "I need the double-cheese."

"Haven't you been catechised?" I asked.

"That's not in it!" she yelled. "It's all about compound interest and asset allocation!"

"But what's the point, if it doesn't lead to heaven?" I asked. After that she grew watchful of me. She told everyone I was either stupid or insane.

Another time, I spoke to a worker I had seen at the pizza shop across the way.

"Have you made any money yet?" I asked her.

"What is money?" she said.

We slept on the wraparound sofa in the video poker room, among the cigarette butts and pizza crusts. In the darkness underneath the tables, I saw loving female faces swarming. The gallery shimmered in the light of the emergency exit sign and in the shadows, the ghost of a forest could be seen wavering and breathing.

When morning came, they couldn't wake me, for my face was frozen in a mask of anguish. They packed it up—it was a great, heavy saucer like the lid of a sewer drain. They carried it out to the dumpster where it landed in a bed of paper cups. The blue of the sky softened it a little, so that I could use my thoughts once more.

I was amazed that I had lived in the mall-church for so long. I had feared to walk out again, for I would have had to cross the parking-lot again. The parking-lot was like a desert. Those who went there, setting out for another place, often perished. The church goers didn't like the people who had just come from there.

They called them "burnt-faces" because of the way poverty and the unfiltered sun scarred their cheeks.

I remained in the dumpster for a long time. I found that the sun did not harm me, though it made me itch a little. When night came, I watched the moon travel across the stale, watery darkness, beyond the swarms of beetles that wrapped around the floodlights. The next day's garbage buried me in darkness. The following day, the darkness was complete. I felt my face relaxing into the deep obscurity, the anonymous comfort of neither seeing nor being seen. The darkness was like a fire, for it danced with forms while it burned. The sweet, warm darkness of the dumpster melted my twisted face.

The dump truck came and carried me off. My journey proceeded in darkness. There was a soft, pulling feeling, and I guessed I was at sea—then again there were jerks and sharp clatterings, and I guessed I was traveling over land.

I found myself ejected one day into a vast landscape of machinery in which shiploads of garbage were being sorted. The place was crawling with workers, as many workers as there had been customers in the mall-church. In every way, the workers were the opposite of the customers. The customers were big and fat, but the workers were small and thin. The customers had been dumpy and stupid, but the workers were nimble and quick on their feet. The customers were cruel and unhappy, but the workers laughed and made clever jokes even as they worked.

The workers allowed the customers to be what they were. With every turn of the crank, with every tightening of the pupil upon an object of attention, with every step of a worker pushing a cart down a corridor, value was created and transferred back to the Shoppes at Prestview. When I looked very closely at a worker, I saw the ghost of a shopper hovering around him. The fatness of the customer was like a cloud that hung about the worker's body, feeding off his energy. The worker and the customer took turns being visible, like something moving underwater in the moonlight.

I followed one worker with my eyes as he operated a vat of chemicals. His brown face seemed to hover in the purple sky. He administered a solvent into the pulp that was left of my face. It gave me a funny feeling and I realized I was laughing. Indeed, I realized I had been laughing for a very long time, for millennia—laughing in a low, guttural tone. That laughter was the gravel upon which existence poured out, wrapping ecstatically around each heavy chuckle. I plunged into this hilarious texture and found that it was a dimension of its own, with layers and currents and hidden pockets. The laughter shattered everything to pieces. It had a gaseous, lightweight quality like helium in some places, and a heavy, viscous form in others. In the middle, there was a magenta streak of languid amusement. There was a profound sadness diffused throughout it. There were echoing tunnels in which the laughter reverberated, overlapping itself.

I grew tired of this mirth and searched once more for my self, the chariot that had carried me through so many permutations. I tumbled about, reaching for the seat, the throne, of consciousness. But the self was not in its usual place. It could not be found anywhere. Something in the chemical mixture had dissolved and reorganized it. Groping and not finding it, I hurtled into a panic. In my panic, I created blue splotches. I created purple menaces.

"I surrender!" My shadows cried out, but no one could hear them. In plumes of vapor I sought to undo, to renounce, and to destroy, but I only succeeded in moving a bit of substance from one place to another.

30

Roving through the emptiness where the self was supposed to be, I came across a group of orange people gathered on a
stoop. They were quietly getting drunk while watching the street
with shining eyes. Initially, their presence irked me, for I was
not expecting to find anyone there. Nevertheless, I soon found
myself soothed by their mellow, sardonic atmosphere. Quietly, they watched children grow up and die, their innocent lives
criss-crossing the sand in a thrall of enchantment. Among the
orange people there was one with the face of a monkey. He said:

> Time is burning
> truth is weak
> I have eleven
> rotten teeth
> and still my mouth won't speak
> and still my wheel won't turn
> it only squeaks

The one with the face of an elephant said:

> A picnic table
> at a bar
> beside a highway
> in the dark
> forgotten pathways
> overgrown
> the place that remains
> when the sparrow's son has flown

The others laughed. There was a butterfly woman with
glitter on her eyelids and a magpie who looked like he had been
working hard all day. The four friends sipped their liquor and

were quiet.

There was a heavy traffic of souls on both sides of the street. I had to join the orange, watching friends in order to escape the flow of people. Two prostitutes strutted by, their faces smashed flat like pies, their matching jumpers tight and their teeth sideways in their mouths. A mother and her daughter passed behind them. They looked like the same person differentiated only by age. There were many things for sale and everyone hurried from one shop to the next in a fit of greed.

Some faces looked like they might have belonged to kind feelings, but all were contaminated by the stupidity of the thoroughfare. One young woman was listening intently to the words of her arresting officer as she was carried away. Here and there, I saw faces I remembered from other times. One man had the half-closed, gentle eyes of someone I had loved. His face brought back memories that carried with them other memories. There were green rooms and the sudden quiet of the old forest. There were untied endings and beginningless friendships, wounding in their tenderness and their depths.

"Why are you weeping?" asked the elephant woman.

"I have never known myself so well," I answered. "There was one who knew me better once. But I can't remember his name, and he must be long gone by now."

The four friends laughed, but the one with the face of an elephant reflected my sadness with her eyes.

"You know very well that's nonsense," said the monkey man, and he poured me a drink of a liquor called Forget-Me-Not. "In fact, we are all standing here remembering an old love or two!" He choked on drink and laughter. He and the others laughed until they were weak and falling over. My sentimentalism struck me as funny too and I laughed until tears wet my face. Laughter brought a caustic rain that drove a dark black path between the paving-stones. My heart kept trying to call out to forgotten paths and abandoned longings, like imperial treasures beneath the foggy, heavy seas. But the thin coils of memory that attached me to these paths fell in love with distance itself and forgot where they were going.

I found myself with my four friends in a dark wooden building. Men with big faces surrounded us. The walls were decorated with totems and talismans. The old, gnarled faces of the local fishermen blended in among the masks and igneous stones that lined the shelves. Each face was turned carefully upon an inner dilemma, a puzzle that he worked at with disinterested patience.

"You can reach any end you like," the monkey-faced man was mumbling, as if talking to himself. "But you don't want to reach any of them. You want the ship's rudder in your hand, but no destination appeals to you at all."

The butterfly woman lay her head dreamily upon the table. The bartender poured liquor from one bottle into another and mumbled a strange prayer under his breath. Outside, the eager foot traffic thickened. The pedestrians glomped together so that they were like water.

The monkey took me by the hand and we started to dance. Lights dripped from the ceiling like crystal apples shaken from a creaking old tree. Shards of light became tangled and confused. The musicians closed their eyes and barely moved. The singer mumbled drowsily into the microphone:

Blame not
fire and mist
the turning of
an angel's wrist
the end of days
the coming of better ways
the door is open
and we insist.

This pain is real
though its source is fake
deep in sleep
or wide awake
the crumbling fist
the softened stone

history's hardened features
after the spirit has grown

All is true,
all is too true,
all is thankfully true,
all is dreadfully true.

By the time the song had ended, drunkenness had overcome me. Things continued to occur, but my mind swam through
them in no particular order. I was half-clothed, wet with rain, arguing with the monkey outside of the bar. I swam in a hazy ocean
with Sullivan, then realized in the first saturnine light that he was
only a pedestrian I had met as I stumbled along, supported by the
walls of the old town. I returned to the tavern to find it closed and
sat before its door, looking at my hands which seemed alien—either too big or too small, swollen and scarred by time. Outside of
a store, in the melon-colored dusk, I begged money from passersby, saying, "Help me, I'm forgotten." I spent the money on
Forget-Me-Not and cigarettes. A photographer followed me for a
while, for I was a good-looking woman, yet reckless and nonsensical. I attracted an entourage.

My new friends were not of the same graceful, classical
kind as the elephant, monkey, magpie, and butterfly. They were
fiends and clowns. Their poetry was square and blockish. They
lived by stealing from one another and exploiting any weakness
they could find. Often I was the weak one, but not always. I too
did hideous things. I sought after the sultry, half-awake enchantment of the first drunkenness, but it never returned. The bar was
always closed, and after a while I forgot how to find it again. It
was absorbed into the strip of shops selling shells and ships in
bottles. I was never sure if it was evening or morning, or whose
hand was in mine, or where I had just been.

In my drunkenness there were beautiful things, but they
tortured me even more than the grisly scenes. From where I lay
on the concrete, I saw humanity passing by as the earth sees it,

with pathos and terrible sadness. The bulky people plodded along thoughtlessly, their earnest, willing feet and fragile ankles bearing the tremendous burden of their bodies with a great "thud!" at every step. My face was imprinted with the grooves of the sidewalks and my cheeks were threaded with the moss that grew in the crevices of the public platform.

Politics began as a seductive drumbeat and then appeared in a black suit with long coattails. Death arose and still I drank. I saw corpses in the street but to me, all seemed as it should be, the dead bodies lined up exactly where they belonged. Strong men took hold of the area, and I passed through their hands like the rainstorm through a summer sky. Tragedies proliferated, but they occurred in the language of my own heart, as if they came from me. The dead were wrapped in white sheets and placed on the sidewalks, but their appearance coincided with the feast-day processions and blended in with the convergence of the nation's beggars who every year came seeking alms from the crowds of celebrants.

This year, the celebrants didn't come. They hid themselves within their houses and walled cities. They only showed themselves when they were dead. Everyone began to starve at the same time. We clawed at each other like passengers on a sinking ship. My drunkenness gave way to fever. Five rivers flowed out of me, like the fingers of a hand. I saw crows spinning around in a wheel overhead. I smelled the sea. When I looked at my body, I saw a suit of closed doors. A man was sitting upright next to my supine form, chanting. His dialect was strange, but when I listened closely, I understood that he was recounting all of my errors. He explained each one of my mistakes, giving to each an introduction and conclusion, so that when I was well again, I would learn my lesson. I listened attentively. He said:

> You sat sallow on the bridge of dreams
> you danced across its rotten beams
> you then withdrew into your land
> like a thought inside a plan
> dreams are not for dancing

but for combat to the death
a bridge is meant to carry life
like streams of silky breath
beguiling and bottomless
from one moment to the next
and that's the way you got it wrong
that's how your sadness grew so long
you turned your ear from
the mountain's mouth
for love of dust and trust in doubt

I studied his words and took them to heart. As I learned each lesson, I became thinner and more transparent. Once his sermon was complete, I dissolved into a silence of peace and rage. There was still a sudsiness, as if my body was made of foamy bubbles.

The dream moved forward and backward at once. There were many ringing tones of love in the air. I saw blue, and grey inside the blue. A woman with her head wrapped approached and passed me by. She faded into the mist. Three patient spirits passed by in a line. They kept an equal distance from one another. They suffered quietly, for they had a long way yet to travel. A tall man in a hat appeared and thanked me and gave me a new name.

The clouds were tall and eloquent and erudite in their glasses and coats. The galaxy was wearing a mask, so that I couldn't see the stars. Its face was shallow, dimpled, and useful. It wore a dress of leaves that swung, glittering, in the breeze. Wars crackled through the hem of its skirt with a red fire and a crazy wisdom. My heart ached to see the humble spirits filing patiently by and the hungry spirits crossing and criss-crossing the sea of blue in no particular direction.

My many sins and deficiencies billowed beneath me. I blushed to think of them, but this only made me more lovely. Smokestacks scarred the sky. Acid rain painted the buildings. Things were very bad for a very long time. I wondered that anything survived. The wind yanked the hair from the dandelion's head. In the landscape, trees grew in angry rows. Meaning was everywhere and nowhere. The moon made an appearance, like an afterthought, a piece of the earth that had been left out and forgotten.

A ribbon of silence unraveled, and I began to walk upon its back. Old acquaintances and strangers alike shook my hand as I passed. The monks of the old ages ladled out spoonfuls of wisdom to anyone who asked, but everyone was too full to eat. Knowledge was over-abundant, so wisdom didn't matter. In places, the silent road made a bridge, and underneath the bridge, rivers of chanting and the tolling of bells overlapped. All things were on their way. Nothing held still. The river's currents, the skating clouds, and the people all tended toward something, but none ever arrived.

Self-loathing arose. I cast about, searching for a way back to a time before the beginning, a way to blot out my shame and the memory of wrong paths.

31

Form once more met with spirit, like a hand in a glove or a
fly embraced by the eager spider. I felt at-home, but at the same
time very tired. Rebirth should have been a happy experience,
a return to the comforts of the body. Instead it felt like exile,
slavery, and death. I was in the middle of a long cycle, not at the
beginning nor even near the end. I braced myself and ducked
deeply down and smelled the timeless cool caverns of minerals
and the quiet darkness of the interior of the world.

Infancy failed to soften my mind. A dazzling, complete
awareness remained with me all the while I was becoming. I
did not sleep the sleep of the innocent, the drunken dreams of
babyhood. Some element in my blood had been replaced. There
was a nauseating sweetness, an industrial greasiness in my veins.
Walking through my body, my blood limped and wept. There
were no mothers; it was the body of money itself that nourished
me. The interest from a large endowment provided for my daily
needs. When I became an adult, I was expected in turn to nourish
the fund that had given me life.

"I love you, I love you," I repeated. At the same time I was
saying, "I made a mistake, I made a mistake." When I opened my
eyes again, everything was the wrong size, as when years have
passed in a stupor and the children are suddenly grown up. I
tossed about, seeking myself, but finding around me only riddles
and objects of love and terror.

As I grew, I underwent procedures; my features were
blurred and then sharpened. My thoughts were trained to grow
in delicate spirals and always to bloom on time. My words
swirled and danced and glittered like the surface of water, at once
concealing and embellishing the heaving quantities of meaning
below.

Around me swam the faces of my family: smooth, rubbery
masks with the eyes missing. All were products of the same ma-

chine. I listened to their mild, thoughtless conversations.

"How has the sand passed through the hourglass?"

"Little by little, you know how it goes!"

A hearty laugh.

The ferris wheel stopped to let out passengers. They stumbled along giddily. Bashfully, my sister and I stepped up to take our turn. There was a charming feeling of weightlessness as the car swept under us. From up high, I could see that the forest was on fire. In the distance, the recycling plant gurgled lavender smoke. The colors were in the wrong places. The foliage was a deep purple while the sky was green. It was green, but we still called it "blue", for we were the ones who had changed. Below, a crowd of entities, my family, milled about the funpark.

"Doesn't their joy seem a bit—forced?" I said.

"I see what you mean," my sister answered. "But don't forget, they have souls just like you do."

The wheel pulled us upward. I was impressed by the grand feeling of the movement; it was like being held in the hand of a deity. But who was I? I searched for my essence, but all I could find were blips and beeps.

"Am I real, if I'm fabricated?" I asked my sister.

"Everything is fabricated," she answered patiently. I could see that she was right. Still, the crowds of waxy-faced automatons bothered me.

"They're having too much fun, even though it's just their programming," I grumbled. My sister didn't answer. I looked at her face. It was the same as the rest, sleek and wet-looking, white and perfect, with holes for eyes. When she didn't move, she looked like an object, any piece of plastic you might find lying in the street.

"Hey!" I shouted, causing her to stir. "Do we have to live through this too? Isn't it enough, the sorrows that we've seen?"

"We have to live through everything," she mumbled, looking out over her shoulder. Beyond the funpark lay the forest on one side, and on the other, the city of comforts, filled with beds and sofas and well-stocked kitchens. In our houses, the air was always the right temperature. The roads were smooth, but there was never any need to travel far. The landscape was dotted with theaters, spas, restaurants, and arcades. Beyond the city of comforts, the earth was charred and churned up and machines were busy plunging deeper and deeper into the mines below, retrieving our next thrill.

We were released from the metal cage and my sister was quickly lost in the crowd of similar faces. I screamed and cried for her, but no one heeded. The people went on enjoying themselves. I realized that I was also chatting blithely about the weather—I had been holding a pleasant conversation all the while I thought I had been crying.

"The river makes me drowsy," I had been saying. "That's why I stay in the city. It's easier to lie down there, you know."

"Exactly," one of my uncles answered. "The two are incomparable."

"Wait a minute," I said. "I was trying to find my sister. She was just here a moment ago. She's the only one who understands!" But when I listened to myself, I heard my own voice saying, "Nor is it wise to wake up too early or go to bed too late. Nighttime leads to morbid thoughts, whereas the morning is the best time for productivity."

"Right you are!" My uncle replied. "And today there are so many wonderful inventions to help with that." I peered at him. My gaze strayed across the white, balmy faces of the crowd. They glistened under the haze and smog and smiled faintly as they mounted mechanical rides and won or lost mechanical games. It occurred to me that their joy was only another form of suffering.

I wandered among the attractions. They were old and worn out, relics of another time. I passed by the bumper cars, a ride that spun people around on a tilted disc, a magician doing card tricks, and a rickety old carousel. The paint was chipped on the horses' ears and saddles.

I saw a face that could have been my sister's and followed it for a few paces, but soon it vanished. Another face emerged from the exit of a ride. It could have been my sister, but I couldn't be sure. I drew closer, but my feet dragged. By now, I suspected that even if I could find her, she wouldn't be the person I remembered. The next moment, my hope was renewed. The blurry sunlight glinted off of a gleeful mask, and a familiar joy illuminated my mind. I rushed toward her—but she blended in again among the others once more.

An unsettling feeling arose: I was uncertain which sister I was—the one who was seeking or the one who was sought. As I sulked along, I also slipped away, eluding myself. For some time, I inhabited the tension between the two ways of being. This was a strain, and it made my thoughts travel in four dimensions rather than two.

The sun began to ache in its trajectory, and I relaxed into my despair. I found that loss was a vehicle in its own right, and it carried me this way and that as the evening turned pink and purple. The previous tension, followed by this new understanding, reordered my perception. The codes with which my thoughts had been structured seemed to break, leaving only raw, direct awareness.

My eyes rocked and swished like trees as a fresh, cool breeze dropped cinders from the nearby fires onto the crowd. The smell of smoke spiced the air. The jolly faces of my cousins and neighbors became sinister and glowed with yellow light. Their commonplaces and predictable laughter acquired a menacing quality, and yet I liked them a little more as they caught the drab glow of the street lamps in their sleek, uniform cheekbones. Their deep black eye-sockets looked like caves in which one might find old terrors or novel succors. As I listened to their idle conversations and petty raptures, I could hear an older language that lay beneath their words, just as stones lie beneath the waters of the stream. In this deeper tongue, the people recited their fears and sorrows like an endless incantation.

The festival was drawing to a close. The masses mumbled about dinnertime and headed for home. Everyone tottered, shoulder to shoulder, in a bottleneck of shiny, whirring bodies. A cousin threw her arm around me and said, "It was even better than last year! I went on all the scariest rides, how about you?"

I wanted to tell her that her joys were nothing but hideous wounds, but I became confused, and for a moment I shared in her delight, her appetite for dinner, and her desire for a safe, tranquil rest.

"I had fun today," my aunt was saying. "I had fun last year, too. Yes, yes, it was fun."

But beneath these words her other voice moaned:

> The lamplight patterned on the source
> took the castle's gate by force
> and sunk its arrows in your eyes
> you softly bled while night crept by
> and all the while, where was I?
> beside the road my shadow pours
> into a ditch its dank remorse

"My sadness is complete," I answered—only this time, my voice merged the two tongues into one, and my meaning could not be mistaken. At the same moment, the carnival music shut off, and the cacophony of voices was cast out like stars upon a dimensionless silence. My words stood out loudly among the rest. They seemed to boom and resonate, transforming the sounds in their wake into more of themselves.

Several people began to take an interest in me. At first, I noticed them casually watching me, then pursuing me, their hands drooping before them in a ghastly posture.

One side of their mouths murmured:

"Oh, this child is sick, let us help her."

The other side of their mouths said:

"She will destroy us if we don't destroy her first."

I quickened my step, but this only attracted more attention. The rides and flashing lights deadened, and the crowd turned their attention toward me. For a moment I was terrified, but then I disappeared within myself. I pretended to be one of them and when I did so, I was no longer myself.

The crowd gave way to the forest. The bodies of the people were empty trunks, eaten from the inside by the gnawing fires of industry. The spinning lights of the carnival were one with the roiling flames. The laughter and applause of the people were the crackling and seething and squandering of leaves and tender fibers into the ash that lay over everything like forgetfulness.

There was a message in the red-black darkness, an awareness that lay precisely in the direction of my loathing and dread. The trees talked nonsense and sang in chorus:

> The pain of night
> ignite, ignite
> improve upon weightlessness
> reach any intermediate height
> play the sweet mountain sorrows
> lovelier than a barrel of crude delight
> I know what I mean
> but my sense is torn to smithereens
> leaving only this blinking light

I took shelter within myself. My body felt very large, like an old red cave. The longer I hid my eyes, the more real my inner landscape became. The goddess of the forest rumbled to and fro, searching for me in herself. I could hear her grumbling and ranting. Thoughts echoed within her sprawling, abandoned mind. Gradually, her words became clear:

"I need water," she said. "I've needed water for so long I can't remember what water is. Are you the storm that carries the rain?"

I didn't want her near me, for she was mad. She whistled drolly to herself. Her legs wobbled and squiggled like noodles. With her hands, she rummaged through her head, displacing key rings, coins, sulfur deposits, rifle shells, lengths of barbed wire. While she carried on, I fell asleep. When I awoke I lifted up my body. My head became like the pole of a tent and it stretched phenomena like a cloth, raising it for a moment from the earth, so that the chill ether of nonexistence swept underneath.

This action, incidentally, produced some rain, as the cold of death mixed with the atmosphere of life and generated condensation. However, the next instant, things returned to their dry, corpse-like state. The brief taste of water was perhaps worse than none at all, for the forest goddess cried and beat the earth with her fists. I tried to focus my mind, for I knew something beautiful had transpired, but it had ended before I knew what it was. All around, the forest had seemed for a moment a field of stars. The many conscious beings in the overlapping worlds—animal, plant, and human beings, as well as the winds and waters and sparkling drops of time—had stopped in their tracks and looked through the hole, the well of nothingness. They perceived the nothingness that had always walked beside them, painted them into mirrors, and made them shine on rippling water. They beheld the nothingness that laughed at their troubles as if they were the troubles of dream-beings—that laughed with their own voices, showing them that they themselves were the dreamer. This momentary vision created a protective, red warmth that sheltered me from contingencies and gave me the courage to do anything that might be required.

"I know you don't love this world," the goddess said. "I can scarcely get your attention, although I am the giver of all life. But maybe you can understand what I am about to say, for it has to do with that other world, the one you do love: the world of death. It is the world of death that you must seek, beyond the City of Comforts. Go there and bring some of it back to this world that has grown ugly, refusing to die."

"I understand you," I answered. "I've always known that *that* was needed. But doing it is another matter. Don't you see? I am not wild, free to do anything. I was created by intermediaries; every pathway in my body and mind leads back to their maintenance."

Even as I spoke, I was split in two. While one half of me had escaped into the forest, another half of me had returned to the city of comforts, where the lights inside the apartments were glowing sweetly and the night outside was deep and soft and blank. The red roads into the wilderness seemed like a distant dream and the mystery of my people's condition was like a thin film when compared with the solid bricks of the houses that kept the chill out at night. I feasted with the others and nestled myself into bed, a lifetime of pleasures stretching out before me.

32

In service of those pleasures, I was inculcated with sharp, cleaving techniques, the kind that deepened the forest's troubles. The way things were was good for this part of me, and this part of me was good for the way things were. It was nourished and encouraged, while the part that had spoken to the goddess was still sitting there like a talisman, listening to her fading dirges.

I was woven through the world according to a willful pattern. My body was not my own. My senses were tagged with company trademarks. Cooperation with the company owners made my muscles lie down like calm seas and my skin tingle with the sweet whispers of wind tickling water. The fullness of my belly was a god of blazing fire. The manufactured visions that swayed before my eyes were vivid and hypnotic. Even when the dancing lights grew threadbare and no longer disguised the corpses upon which they played, still my mind was enamored with their colors.

My two halves could live separately, but they would come together again in the loom of time. Where my grim soul sat among the ruins of the forest, a cheerful, convenient suburb was fabricated. The mystic pain of the trees and the dying curses of the goddess were spackled over by merry workmen. The cries of the forest's many throats, once capable of generating multiple universes, gave way to the hum of business hours, the dinging of a door chime. I was shooed along by the soft gloves of brute force. Meanwhile, I mulled over a string of words I had found among the debris of the construction site: "What is in the wasteland? The belief that you are not good." I moved these words about in my thoughts, holding them this way and that as I shuffled along in the direction of all things.

The other part of me entered the wasteland as a favorite pet of power, riding the chariots of empire. A shadow fell on our cavalcade and a dusty rain left tooth marks on our cheeks. A chaos bloomed in my stomach. I saw myself naked of form, a hideous knot of spirit, suspended ghoulishly in the mists of time.

Tanks, drills, and equipment crumpled in the face of the desert's sobriety. Although I had come to claim riches, I found myself collected instead by a powerful motherly darkness. Love of the land melted me and scattered my schema, so that I was new, without bearings, and whole.

We came across a ridge and I saw thousands of mines dotting the landscape, each one mounted by a little tower, like so many spears piercing the flank of a great beast. Our company arrived at the appointed site, wedged neatly between all the others. We began to build, then to dig. Hiding myself among my people, I had become an engineer. When I worked, I was like a wizard. I solved problems before they appeared. I watched processes unfold like a many-petalled blue flower, half-believing it was only a flower of the mind.

All enemies of our projects had long ago been vanquished, but it was said that the ghosts of forgotten peoples sometimes interfered with our operations. But today there was no ghost to stay our hands. I was covered in the purple blood of the planet before I understood that it was too late. I heard someone say, "All things come to pass. The majesty of the universe can be destroyed as easily as a pile of ash, with a soft push of one's finger."

It was I myself who had spoken—the part of me that had grown weak and gaunt, having lived for many years on weeds and fumes. I had stopped working for a moment to listen, and I did not move to start again. The other miners had also lost their impetus and milled about in a benign herd, like a flock of grazing animals. The earth's blood ceased to spill and the wound we had made quietly began to heal.

What followed was a horrifying boredom. We were beset in all directions by questions, none of which seemed worth answering. There was nothing to do, for all things were spontaneously accomplished. The supply lines had been stretched too thin, and the fuel ran out on the road. All work ceased—not just among our crew, but among all the thousands of crews encamped throughout the desert. A message arrived from Headquarters:

Your mission was vital
but can't be completed
though your vigor was valorous
those plans have receded
look how our words grow
look how slowly they bloom
look how they drop deafening
seeds that go boom

oh, we love you so much
and we wish you were here
but some things can't be rushed
and time dries every tear
so don't take it so strange,
doesn't everything change,
none of us is quite the same
as we were this time last year

Our company sat around a table, bewildered and enchanted by the unfettered sky. We were drawing cards. Small bets were
at stake. One of the men was old, with long, scraggly hair. He was
telling a story, and with each card that was drawn he told a little
more. His knowledge was so powerful that it flattened and then
reshaped the earth's dimensions. His voice was like a great hand
that squashed the clay of the universe. There were no colors in
his tale, only a grey plane below and a grey dome overhead, and
our single body joining the two together. The old man's voice
rumbled through us, answering questions we had never thought
to ask.

A card was drawn with a picture of a saber on it.

"Your luck is limited to that which is possible," the old man
said. "Just as your food is crushed between your teeth, the end of
our story is divided from dreams by the knives of circumstance.
Our hero left home on a humble steed reared by his mother,
while the mountains sliced the sky to ribbons and the wind cut
paper dolls of the clouds. He went seeking profit, to win prizes
and glory in the royal games."

The next man looked troubled. He drew his card nervously, his movements awkward and dreamlike. On the card's face were pictured three stars hovering in a circle.

"Patience is a nuisance," the old man began. "That is why our lessons always come too late. One star is for our hero, another for the pitfall, and the third for understanding. Each of these depends upon the others."

The old man's eye whirled like a clock and his words reached around our manufactured minds as the roots of a great tree reach past a boulder or a drainpipe.

"And so the rider reaches the wet, darkened skirts of the hills. He sees a man who has fallen and who cries out to him. He does not see that it is he, himself, who has fallen. Only when the injured man offers money does our rider heed his plea. He carries the man the long distance to the next town, hearing not his cries of pain along the way, but only the jingle of coins in his pockets. When he arrives, the man is dead. Our hero laughs to himself and thinks: at least his gold is still bright and heavy."

Most of the men had let their cigarettes go out and didn't bother to light another. The sun had gone down, but a grim colorless light yet clung to the sky, like an old man refusing to die. All around us burned the campfires of other companies, and their voices could be faintly heard. I started when the logs settled in the fire, sending up a swirl of burning debris. It was the turn of the carpenter. He took his card: a bed of roses.

"Ah," the old man began. "You are the roses and the roses are you. Only there is confusion. Our rider buried the dead man in the forest, but carried his money along the road. Arriving in the capital, he entered the competitions. Much treasure was at stake. In the throes of the gauntlet, he smelled a strange perfume. A mystical beauty urged him on.

"Between games, he traversed the city on foot. The marketplaces were dirty and crowded. He saw all manner of evil transpiring: children boiled alive; neighbors selling one another into slavery; the weak and the old doing the labor of the young and strong."

As the old man spoke, I searched myself. I ruminated upon

my origins, searching my memories for a friend, an amulet, a reason. Darkness had fallen and I felt disembodied.

"Though he became well-known as a champion, in the street no one recognized him. He was an outsider and he wandered until his eyes would bleed from the horrors he saw. When he won the final contest, a bouquet of red roses was placed upon his arm. Looking at the roses, all he could see was the meat of the world ground to a pulp. He saw that the man he had buried was a boat that carried his own dust into the petals of the flower. He saw how the golden coins tinkled and applauded in the seats of the amphitheatre. He saw that the coins were sentient and that they used the senseless people for their chariots, their chauffeurs, and their entertainment. He heard them laughing merrily and deathlessly at the strivings of people of clay and dust, betting on the things of the spirit."

Money had changed hands throughout our game, but the players were strangely indifferent to gain and loss. We were huddled closely together, warmed by one another's spirits, thankful for one another's soft, radiating humanity. It was my turn. I pulled a diamond.

"They say the diamond is indestructible," the old man said, "but of course that is not true. Another diamond can cut it, and that is why we have this world, instead of a heaven. Our rider returned to the grave of the man he had buried. He laid his roses there and cast his gold into the well. When he returned to his home, all he had gained was a beginner's knowledge of evil and corruption. And yet on the stone path that led back to his mother's house, a quality of transcendence sparkled in his mind.

"His walk grew easier. His thoughts seemed to announce themselves before they arrived. When they entered his consciousness, he was ready for them. He could roll out the carpet and seat them all comfortably in the round tent of his mind. He could compliment them for their beauty and ask them about their journey. He could sit with them in silence while they grew and changed before his eyes.

"All things became brilliant and precise. His hopes and dreams were lost in the sewers of the world, so all that was left was rightly understood to be the truth."

Now it was the old man's turn to choose a card. He turned up an old, yellowed, softened card slowly. On its face was an hourglass.

"Time," he said. "It is the only being whose belly is really full."

I was still combing through my feelings, looking for lost staircases or the shadows certain people cast upon the street. I was looking for the things of this world, the way this world crumbles under the heels of time. I could not find them. Someone had cleaned them all up and filed them away, somewhere between the grandiose archives of wisdom and the blank unknowing of the baby.

"This is the part of the story that is the same for everyone, so most don't bother mentioning it," the man said. "The rider lived in a state of grace. Then he began to feel the world slow down. It was as if he was walking in mud, but the mud was him. He encountered himself everywhere. When he shed tears, even the tears were crying. They fell into the mud and even there, they wept. But then things reversed themselves and nothing performed any action whatsoever. Then he, too, was only mud, and there was no more feeling in him."

The time for sleep had come. Several of our party were drunk. We went our separate ways, seeking refuge from our thoughts in whatever shelter we could improvise. I stumbled among the encampments, tripping over electrical wires and generators, latrines, and mounds of bedding and supplies. I emerged upon the cold, imperturbable sand. Somewhere I heard sirens crying like infants. The sand seemed impossibly heavy, as if it was piled upon my heart. I was surrounded by fields of dust and all of the dust was me. My heels cut long red sashes into the desert's sad, feminine face, and these wounds trailed along behind me, branching apart like roots.

I spoke to myself, scattered everywhere under the garbage-can sky. I cajoled and begged and clowned and crooned.

"Come hither, my soul; awaken and arise—have a meaning, cohere around an idea. At least lift one foot, at least let it fall one time upon a path, and if not the foot itself, let the shadow of your raised foot fall just once upon the path."

Forgotten sorrows came back to me in old lettering. A handful of rain cast itself disdainfully upon the sand, leaving dark stains on the glittering hills. The desert pulled me to an angelic realm, an icy, removed station where I could see the world as if I had never lived in it. I was like a lion made of wind that curled around the shoulders of the living. I saw myself in them, but everywhere I was lying down, doing nothing, not moving, lost in strange thoughts.

I gave up calling out to myself and listened in case I should be called. But I heard no voice, and so I pushed onward, or perhaps I was pushed. I did not care which way I went, nor which outcome developed.

"Don't bother bothering," someone said. "You know better than to try bettering yourself."

I picked up a piece of something that lay in the sand. It was lying in just the right place to be picked up by my right hand. It was the right kind of thing with the power to make me hopeful again—a thing from a world of blue evenings and green mornings. It returned to me the certainties of the young, to which the old close their eyes.

33

Carrying this thing, I walked onward into a fragrant slum that emitted smells of gasoline, urine, and frying grease. I wandered through the town and saw the great hollow eyes of the people like doorways and stairwells. The outskirts of the town were places of illuminated smoke and flashing lights. Buses were corralled in a vast park, carrying sleepy hordes of passengers. Their dreams were distorted and ugly, as if they had been burned by acid. I tried to pray for them, but their fates were tangled up with evil intentions, and my prayers turned back from the thick, dark knots of their destinies, unable to find their way toward good.

"I believe in you," I murmured. "Come through the danger and understand the answer."

Nighttime was a furnace of suffering. Money and people flowed around every corner. Nourishment was created on open fires in the midst of traffic.

I began to notice familiar objects. The signs that had once announced well-known storefronts had been broken into pieces and were being used as the walls of a shelter. I feared to speak to anyone. An old man hobbled down the street, one of his legs shorter than the other, using a crutch. I began to follow him, but then I noticed I was stepping on people. The road was packed with people. The people groaned and cursed underfoot and their soft, wobbly bodies tickled me. The old man hobbled along unconcerned, stabbing them vigorously with his crutch.

"Can't you see we are sleeping? Go somewhere else!" a woman crowed.

"I love you," my heart insisted. The clouds became leaky and a train whistle blew. I saw a little weathervane whirling. With the dawn arrived fistfuls of grim sorrows.

"I don't need much," I bargained under my breath. "Just enough to keep hoping. Just one more look in the tall mirror, in which I can grow more and more beautiful."

In order to remove my feet from the sleepers' faces, I crawled gently toward the curb. I lifted myself onto a ledge and fell backwards into a restaurant.

"If you want so badly to exist, why then do you find it so painful, so onerous?" someone murmured.

A one-eyed man was taking money and making change. An elderly woman was laboring behind the bar, her shirt sleeves rolled up and her hands covered in flour. I asked for bread and tea and it was brought to me. Most of the people's faces were buttoned-up and well-protected from perplexities. There were several roguish men and beautiful women who looked plundered and abused. I drank what was brought to me. Puddles of memory were still shining in my mind and they caught a new light. I sensed that certain parts of me had been burned away by some recent struggle, but I forgot what exactly had happened. My spirit swished around in my body like tea in a saucer. I gripped the rough-hewn table, for the rocking of the town was dizzying.

I spent money on breakfast, lunch, and dinner. At night I used money to procure lodging, and still I had money to spend. Because of my money, my face was ugly and people despised me. The street was soft and fragrant with human smells. The faces of the buildings caught the sunlight valiantly, like dogs catching sticks in mid-air. There were two white doors behind which I felt some miracle occurring, but I passed them by without seeking entry. Goods were sold in the shops, but never at a loss, and so they were always out of reach for the many. The few who were designed to have what others could not were detectable by our gruesome appearance.

I entered a soothsayer's shop, thinking to buy another fate. The soothsayer was fat and he wore only an undershirt and a towel. His beard was outgrown, and he was covered in fragrant oils. A stick of incense burned nauseatingly on a table.

"I don't belong in this body," I began.

"Eh-eh," the soothsayer interrupted. He waved his hand and pointed at a box with a slot in the top. I folded a bill and pushed it in. The soothsayer wet his lips. His jowls shook as he spoke. He said:

"Happiness doesn't make any bargains. Rather she is a friend that walks with you, or she doesn't."

He stopped. His eyes closed. After a moment, I realized what he wanted and I added another bill to the box.

"As with any other friend, you must win her love. Who are the people who are well loved by Happiness? They are victims of their own dreams, drunk on elaborate shadows."

He stopped. His skin smelled like garbage that had been left in the sun. I placed another dollar in the box. Things went on this way for some time. The man delivered sparing, unhelpful lines. Each one seemed to take the bottom out of my mind. I felt more and more terrible, yet I was transfixed. I recalled memories from lifetimes I had forgotten—memories so uniformly depressing that I wished I had not remembered them. It seemed the spell would not be broken until I spent every dollar in my pocket, yet my billfold was still fat and showed no signs of diminishing.

"The waters of this earth have created so many forms, so many beings—and yet you think your thoughts incapable of feeding one more new idea?"

I shook myself.

"Enough!" I said. "You haven't answered my question. I came here because I wish to spin the wheel. Can you help me with the purple stars and the hazy dripping eaves of night?"

"Oh," the soothsayer said, his eyes wandering around in his face. "You are tired of being a tourist. You wish someone would flatten you, so that you no longer need to decide for yourself. Drink this."

He handed me a plastic bottle with a water-damaged label.

I drank with a dawning awareness that my whole environment was no more than an old commercial. All the buildings in the town were livid with their own squalor and their clapboards were like flesh and their paint was like skin. They were wounded and their wounds were festering. But they were only advertisements—for themselves! I marveled at how boldly and maudlinly they stepped out of nothingness and into the light of the naked eye.

I regarded the soothsayer. He was reduced to a barcode.

He seemed to pulse and shimmer as if designed to attract the attention of small children. He jumped and wiggled, shedding bouncing drops of himself. But like everything else, he was part of the weather-beaten landscape. The darkness gnawed on his tattered physiognomy.

Understanding finally enclosed me, enshrining me in dignity as a robe decorating a king. I arose, regarding the blistering pulp and the trembling miscellany around me, blackened by the fires of time. I heard echoes bitten by flocks of carrion birds. My despair was as big as my knowing. While my knowing was like a cape, my despair was like a balloon, and it spread open into the sky above me. I longed for elsewhere and despair erased the details, bearing me up a great distance. The wreckage of many failed designs below me appeared monotonous and peaceful. From above, I could adore the scene I had evacuated, but I dreaded what lay ahead.

I had tried before to leave myself entirely, but the part of me that was a friend kept catching up, hopefully and with a smile, tugging at the sleeve of the one who was absconding.

"I cannot help you with your grand picture, but I know my way around on the ground," the friend always said. Things became soft and warm, illuminated from within by orange and red tones. Wavering shadows tickled and made promises. Even old enemies were seen in the light of kindness as nothing more than the mundane waste of commercialdom. Time washed over me but it was oily and didn't make me clean. My longing had a momentum that lurched toward no particular destination. I silenced myself and poured forth from forgotten grottoes. Secrets were given to me by indifferent witches. I compromised—I abridged my promises.

There was one place where no one else came. There, I could regard all the yellow and orange memories that had accumulated within me. I could not get to that place by ordinary roads. A tall, dark, beautiful witch pointed to the winding mountain pass. The blackbirds reeled about and laughed. I was bothered that this was the only way in which they knew me, as a desperate person, low to the ground.

"I will make many more promises," I said. I drove around
the mountain stream in a little car. I listened for the clinking of
coins and I could hear it, making the gears of the universe grind.
The cute and precious clouds chimed:

> Drink of dappled
> appled groves
> truckbed nutmeg
> aromatic cloves
> eleven bloodhounds
> loping down the road
> seeking someone's shirttail
> and flirting with the mourning doves

Their cheerful chanting opened a garish red chamber in
the mountain road wherein atrocities were taking place. I took
note of this and sat down to think. My thoughts scratched at my
mind. I spoke to them slowly but still they made strange movements and they were very heavy. They threatened to sink into the
ground. My dreams came up among them and were their equals
and could have overcome them if they wanted to. But the dreams
played among the thoughts, laughing at the thoughts' big im-
movable legs and the way their faces were so heavy that they fell
forward, causing their backs to grow hunched.

"Wake up!" the iridescent dreams laughed, and they
clapped their hands in the faces of the dreary thoughts. The
dreams frollicked between the rows of solemn, immobile
thoughts, producing impossible ideas. They dreamed up things
that were two things at once and evils that were perfectly innocent. I preferred the dreams to the thoughts, but the dreams
contradicted themselves so much that they were meaningless.
When I looked inside their mouths, I saw several teeth belonging
to thoughts that had long since died.

Eventually, I found the ground of both thoughts and
dreams to be morbid, like a graveyard, and I wished to leave
it behind. I let my thoughts sink down and I don't know what

became of them.

I experienced a new kind of pain. The dreams still stalked me, but I closed my eyes to them. I entered new sets of streets. There was always an ache in my throat, as if a sob was coming. In my memories danced young girls with strong legs and bold ways. My medicine had taken effect after all, but its remedy was superficial.

I followed a woman in high heels to the bar where she was the singer. It was no more than a stall in a street among the slums. Everyone was drunk, and no one noticed that the music was terrible. The woman took my hand and spun me around while she crooned and stepped from side to side. I was led out of the place because I was crying. Cockroaches scurried here and there across the brick road. Thoughts slid by me like ghosts.

"Let them go," I muttered. I looked out over a valley filled with crudely strung electric lights.

"I'm sorry if I was wrong," I said, and it was as if someone else had inhabited my body for a moment and caused me to speak.

"Pleasure can't afford to give you more," a matronly energy responded. Her reptilian hand was enormous. The skin was spotted and the joints were bulbous. Her fingers closed on mine, and my own hand looked tiny and beautiful, as if it belonged to a doll.

"Drink to dream and dream to drink," she intoned.

"Make me yours," I replied, as if out of habit.

She showed me to the bus stop and piled me on, with a great big black bag that held all of my belongings. I sat down, tightly tucked among the bandits and pilgrims. I rode until I grew drowsy. As I slept, my dreams encircled me like laughing girls. I picked my way among the cool gravestones. My love was big and heavy so that I could not move it, nor could I wrap my arms around it. Ancient worlds and newer ones intermingled in the peripheries of my awareness.

34

I floated in a boat made of a folded advertisement. Rain was falling. I saw my reflection in the river. My cheeks were rosy. I became fascinated by the idea of my prettiness and at the same time disgusted with my vanity. I felt both ways at once, and the tension between them was like wind inside a sail, a long-travelling force that could carry me on indefinitely.

Palm-fingers wavered under a generous battering of rain. People moved about on the shore, hauling nets filled with fish and covering their boats with fronds. Children ran barefoot toward shelter but lingered in the rain when they arrived at their doorsteps. The birds held their shoulders high and looked down on us with terse patience. Vehicles of war dragged through the water, spreading long colorful tails behind them.

I stepped onto the shore where the old woman kept a small bar. I had one small drink and started weeping again. I couldn't feel the liquor going down my throat. The kind, nostalgic dizziness of the drink arrived on time, but it arrived macabre and waterlogged. I thought I saw black wings in the river and ghosts arriving in great tribes upon the horizon. I felt like a page that was torn out of the world. I reeled and was forgotten for a while. The matron had gone to the back.

When darkness set in, fishermen filed into the bar. They were small men, bow-legged, wearing shirts humid from container ships and sandals braided from the leather of the jungle. They thought me a freak, for none of their women would drink or smoke. Nevertheless, they were tactful enough to include me in their rounds.

"With this storm comes a change," said a man with deep seams in his face. The circles of his eyes were too small, so that his gaze was cold and haunted. "The war is shifting. It will all be decided overnight."

There was no question of the war ending, for this war was war itself. Still, men spoke of endings and eventualities. I was beside myself with grief and wished for answers to finally blossom out of the grim sludge of circumstance.

"All my words walk away from me," I slurred. "So I only know them by their backs. I am tired of war and opinions. Like everyone here, I hope to avoid problems. I have lived a long time on the outskirts of conflict, walking in the smoothest parts of the road and reaching my destination always before nightfall. But still, pain finds me wherever I go. I have heard the sages saying it will go on this way until my heart grows bigger. But how can the heart grow? It is a dead thing. In my mouth, the taste of sawdust. My tongue has grown a forest of words, but they have been cut down. What's more, I seem to remember that this has happened more than once. Oh, how can you go on talking?"

The liquor lovingly rocked the light of blue evening in its orange thoughts. The fishermen ignored my speech, suddenly absorbed in their game of cards. A mosquito coil was unwinding blankets of fragrant, noxious smoke. Cigarettes burned in the ashtrays that tattooed the plastic tables and glowered like miniature charnel grounds. Meanwhile, my thoughts had carried me elsewhere, down a set of crystal stairs and into a dark, female underworld.

A demoness was waiting for me. Her most striking feature was her long hard chin, which she stroked often while she watched me. I sat down at her green table. She was so tall her hat nearly touched the ceiling. Her chair was much larger than mine, and the table only came up to her knees.

"Play dead," she commanded, and she held up a golden key. It was the key to the door that led out of the world. I closed my eyes and turned my head, as if by ignoring her I could make her disappear.

"Then you don't wish your trials to be over?" she asked.

"Suddenly they don't seem so bad," I said icily.

"Try again," the demoness said. She opened a short red door, and I had to go through it, sliding on my back. The doorframe seemed to caress my whole body, sucking on every inch of me. This was both horrifying and titillating, so that I felt like crying again, or perhaps sneezing.

The next room was big and clean and well-lighted, with tall windows and grand wooden tables, a place to play backgammon and a bookshelf built into the wall. An old man was writing, keeping accounts. A sickly feeling sweltered within me. I was terribly impatient, but for what, I wasn't sure. I felt like begging someone for something, but the old man was unaware of me. I stepped morosely out into the garden. The grass had eyes and was watching me with long-lashed, doting interest.

I fell on my knees and began to cry, "Oh, don't love me so! I have nothing you need. I am no good at all!"

But the grass only blinked. If I looked into its eyes long enough, I could see how it felt. I stood and dusted off my skirts. Ravens were circling overhead. I sighed, for I remembered that each of the ravens had brought me a death. With every step I took, my heart fell out again, and I tried to carry it, but it slipped between my fingers.

"I can't find my way," I said, and my voice sounded like four poems woven into one. The ravens soared across the sky and a blurry moon appeared. The sky didn't know if it felt sadness or joy, but it gave all it had with a strange, indefinable gesture. I cast my eye upon the distance, where the remnants of a civilization were still standing. The old buildings were gathered together, all facing in different directions, like people who were in one another's way. Each of them was full of secrets, but their sense melted in the mind.

Things were not good enough, no matter how good they were. And they *were* good. Their goodness wrapped around me and made me warm with an electric heat. Influences and details opened up in every pocket of existence like packets of charms. There was a way to reach around the difficulties, and that way lay like a prize at the end of the time of worry.

An old wizard walked beside me. He had been speaking to me for a long time, but I had only just begun to listen.

"Your silence carries no bags, so how can you give to others?" he asked.

I held my tongue, though my hatred was heaving and great.

"You are walking like a beast seeking a sweet carrot," the man muttered. "Always the next carrot. When will you stop?"

I ignored him. The light of the stars poked through the darkness and we walked on, beyond our bodies and down a rippling pathway into a deeper obscurity. The wizard's voice went on reprimanding, but now it resonated in a formless space.

"My dreams are so long and coiled like tape," I said. "I pull at them, but they keep growing and unraveling. I'd rather not!"

"You have forgotten your blessed burden," the wizard said.

"What's that?"

"The responsibility you like to have. It used to be easy. It was simply with you wherever you went, revealing new worlds, courting you like a celebrity."

"And now?"

He laughed, a beautiful blue twinkle in his ancient eyes.

"You're all on your own, falling in love with a bed of rocks. You tell *me* how it's going!"

Anger once more blotted out his presence, and though he continued to walk beside me, I didn't listen to his lectures. "What I know, I know," my heart said. There was an orange wall of certainty, a kind of ochre mud that catches the morning sun. My arms and legs carried on gracefully without any help from a reason.

Each building wore a halo and kept one heel tucked behind the other. When darkness fell the few lights in the windows downtown formed a squinting grimace. Still I walked on the mountain path, but the mountain was growing higher, and it grumbled as I stepped upon its long grey feet. Dirty flags clung to the thin, wet air. I became dizzy and tired.

I ate bags of emptiness for breakfast and drank mountain sunlight for my tea. I was alone except for that pedantic wizard, but then I noticed that there were people in the grass and trees. The mountain streams were dry and inside them were footsteps that walked backwards. I had reached a height where God's big blue face kissed everything passionately, including me. All my friends had fallen into the bottom of the world. My promises were stretched sideways. I squeezed myself into any form I could find. A clay sculpture made by a cookie cutter. A darkness with no location on any map—a roving darkness.

My hands were filled with playing cards, coins, paper flowers, and trinkets. A vague residue of white paint was encrusted in the threadlike wrinkles in my hands. I gathered a generation of spirits into myself and became heavy like a raincloud. An old woman with tiny green eyes like turtles in water listened to my complaints. She would not answer me in the same language I was speaking, but spoke a tongue that has not yet come into this world. I could understand her, but my grief could not be translated into that language, and so it went away.

Still, uneasiness harried my thoughts. A pretty toy was spinning in a golden showcase. The lights were twinkling—each one had a reason for being there, but I used them for my own transcendent purposes. Time stretched around the wondrous evening. Mysteries roamed the streets. What had been ugly in the daytime removed its mask and revealed an exquisite fire. A lover was there, dancing like a mosquito around the corners of my eyes. The haze turned to rivers and trickled out along the highways and flowered past me where I slept in their exhaust.

I slept quietly and out of everyone's way. The rustling of feet, the jostling of trucks, and the sleeptalk of engines sewed themselves together and made a roof over my spirit. Now and then an intrusion destroyed my sleep and I had to move. Moving was not easy because the streets were full of memories. I had to drag myself through abscesses in the flesh of the world. Doors were closed. When I needed them, the eyes of the people were locked against me, but when I was sleeping or minding my own business I often felt their gaze scratching at my sides.

I wasn't permitted to sleep in the good places, but when I slept, the bad places passed through a magenta haze and their nauseating smells became sweet and nourishing. I came to love what was bad and dread what was good. Love became loathsome, like a caress that rubbed the skin raw. I preferred to be detested. Hatred made people look silly and endeared them to me. I saw the heart of all things, the lovable ugliness of that heart.

The streets were filled with moribund effigies and the

masks of people who had stopped trying. They might have been paintings on the pillars of the highway ramp, so still were they where they leaned and watched time thin and blow away. They were green and yellow, with big hopeless eyes and shady cheeks. They watched me struggle through the debris, the great tides of garbage that slowed my stride.

I often forgot where I was. When my mental maps merged and overlapped, strange things appeared. Wolves danced to trumpets while women screamed. There was a man with a limp who kept his hat filled with secret, swindled starlight. Even his broken beauty failed to impress me. Fog wrapped around my ankles whenever I went near the river. Iron railings clambered over the city like ghoulish fingers or like death swallowing something that no longer mattered. The limping man appeared now and then in the dazzling dawns and in the purple nights. I glimpsed a phrase or two shimmering near him, something he had cast upon the air like golden glitter.

"It's better to be under the rocks," he grumbled, "for the shadows of the world don't need any excuse."

He tipped beer into his throat and all were slightly tossed. I adored him, but most people were not like him. When you listened at their faces, you only heard a kind of crunching or the sound of a door clicking shut.

I moved around in circles. The walls of materiality were easily replaced, changing all the time. There was nothing good. Everything was blue and blurry. I trudged through the deep sludge, but I couldn't escape from the labyrinth of highway ramps. Sometimes I saw the river for a moment, and there was a naked strand of sky that blushed and danced. The buildings kept forgetting themselves, and the march of days proceeded in all directions in a disorderly fashion. Choices were placed on hold. The misplaced people hung there like stuffed dolls. Some held placards that were blank. When they tried to speak, they just shook their heads and wiped their thoughts away.

The outskirts of town were eerie and sordid. The grasses clung to me and the little hamlets and cul-de-sacs that were scrawled into the deep dark marshes were scarred and blackened.

"What am I doing out here alone?" I asked. But then I saw a little further into the distance, just beyond the planet, the many souls who travelled with me. It wounded me to know that we were going somewhere, that we were together. For a moment I thought I was leading, but soon I found that I was at the back of the pack. We kept changing direction, like a school of fish, and with each change, the order was rearranged. The shifts happened instantaneously, but the time between them was measured in epochs. I began to wonder if we were going anywhere at all.

My body was made of many bodies, one blooming out of the next. From the ruin of one ending a new life sprang forth. The spaces between dying and living were so small that they were imperceptible. Many lifetimes blurred together, appearing to be one.

I listened carefully. It took many thousands of years for the world to utter one sound, and then it had to take a breath. With patience, I found that existence was speaking words and that the words formed a poem. This poem encompassed all moods, all passions, every possible turn of events. I listened, but after a while I lost touch with the meaning of the sounds I heard. I got caught in one echoing syllable. The poem receded and there was only this sound. On its own, this sound was not quite right. It was slightly North, slightly East, a little too chill and top-heavy.

-●-

It was cold. Inside my clothes there was a damp sweatiness. Outside, there was a hysterical chill. As the sun sank, the people in the street drained away. Everyone good went somewhere else. Those who were left were flawed. There was something sideways and mawkish about them.

The great mother munched on me.

"You still haven't grieved enough," she said. "You taste bitter. You aren't soft." She spat me out of her toothless mouth. Her big head looked like it was made of clay.

"Mother of all things," I said. "Where am I and what is my way?" But her face had closed itself and she was only another wet stone in the edifice of an ugly building.

I got by awkwardly, using the kindness of sideways men as stepping stones. First one, then another took me in. A man with long sorrows found me work. A very young man with one wet eye fixed my status. I listened to their deformed stories, their words that always missed the target. I hated their clothing and even their thoughts. In return, they loved me. They sought my understanding and showed me their secrets. When they saw I was disgusted with them, they tried to change their own nature to please me. They donned strange costumes and assumed new behaviors, as if they were performing on a stage and I was the audience. Their efforts were depressing.

My hatred grew dangerous. Knives lurked between my thoughts, flashing between my glances. I began selling my memories, for the people in the streets had never suffered and would pay a high price for a morsel of the thing they called "authenticity". This paid my way for a few days, but my inventory quickly dwindled. I had only a few strange residues left.

"You haven't lived much," grunted a customer. He was blond of hair and his demeanor undulated between simpering and gloating.

"Does it matter?" I answered, "I'm living now."

I regarded that moment's anguish, trying to discern its shape. I had to step very far back to see its design. It was like a caracol, delicately shaped by many interlocking circumstances. It spiralled out into the distance in all directions. Nothing could be done with it, for no one would ever be able to locate its beginning or its end.

The young man walked off. He was so rich that his purse wept as he walked. I picked up the coins and bills he left behind, fighting with the other vendors. An ugly man spat in my eye.

"Fake!" he said. "Your memories are obscure. No one understands them." The man was bald and several bellies swung from him, one piled on top of one another. Four square amulets hung from long strings around his neck.

"Let me see yours," I said.

Night was drinking the day away in large, painful swallows. A tall woman dressed in black was walking down the street beside me, wailing.

The ugly man said, "Come."

I followed him. His memories were arranged neatly, figurines like thumbprints or labyrinths. I saw in some of them places I had been, people I knew, and the ghoulish faces I had passed on the road.

"Where did you get them?" I asked.

But he shoved me aside, for two customers had appeared and begun fondling his wares. The bigger one wiped some snot from his face with his sleeve. Money was already coming out of his hands. They bought several pieces. I could hear them clattering in their pockets as they walked away.

When I looked back, everything the vendor had sold had already been replaced. He winked at me and kicked a plastic tub beneath the table, wherein hundreds of similar items were stacked.

"But how?" I asked.

"I always keep the originals. Not like you. You sold off your past. Now you're nothing—like the face of an unborn child, or the premonition that it might rain."

"My memories aren't what makes me what I am," I said. "What do I care what happens to them? Let the buyers be entertained for a moment and then forget about them. Let my memories get lost in their houses and kicked by their clumsy children. Even if I gathered all my suffering into a heap and stood atop it, still I couldn't see beyond the city walls."

"If it's beyond the city walls you wish to reach, then it's money that you need. And to get money, you need a product."

The ugly man took me to where he lived, underneath a house belonging to a rich family. Piles of junk were arranged in tight rows along the dirt floor.

"Anything you see here, you can have, as long as you use it to make money," the ugly man said.

There were mounds of spices, red, yellow, brown, and white. I considered selling them as the book of joy, the book of patience, the book of remorse, and the book of grand dreams for the future. Then I saw a pile of skulls. I could tell buyers that from each dead thing a new world would grow, and those who owned many worlds could live in whichever one they chose. Then I saw a box of old postcards, and the utter sadness of buying and selling settled upon my brain.

"Make your choice yet?" yelled the ugly man. He was watching TV, his feet stretched out in a reclining chair. His wife was at the stove, stirring a pot. Through large, watery eyes like china cabinets she looked from him to me.

"Eat something first," she said.

It was very dark underneath the house. Night had fallen and the rich people were eating dinner up above. Their heavy feet crashed over our heads, making the boards groan and tremble and even causing a pot to fall from its hook. The ugly man and his wife settled into their chairs. A dream walked into the dwelling, tall and dressed in white. She rifled through the ugly man's junk as if searching for something. Finally she pulled a small pin from a haystack. The pin was covered in writing. It read:

> I opened doors to windows
> and windows into ovens
> and ovens into cages
> and cages into bones.

> So you open your scissors
> a great yawn
> full of danger
> and causes to die on.

> An object at rest
> must stay at rest
> unless it's asked a question
> and its answer is no or yes.

> Then it must awaken
> and peel its mind

and serve its master
with a darkened smile.

    The words that glinted from the pin could be pulled out
of it like a piece of bark lifted from the surface of a lake. These
words had holes in them and could be worn like masks over the
face where they felt wet and cool. Each mask was unique and
I sold them in the public square for a great profit. Every day I
would pass by the ugly man's house and he would smile. I felt so
much gratitude toward him that a cold hand seemed to squeeze
my heart.

    A river was coiled around the city. The streets were old and
aged poorly by bad sleep. My feelings were sore and alarm bells
were ringing all through my face and limbs.
    "There is no way forward!" cried my body. Tiny devils hur-
ried around inside me, putting up roadblocks on all the routes to
solace. I grew tired and sat like an object beside the water.
    "And yet this world is round," the river breathed. "And so
your misery must always begin again, at the beginning."
    "Not yet," I smiled. "Not yet."
    I heard a few stray notes in the hills. In the way the sky and
water scattered apart I saw that Grandfather Time had grown
young again. I was now his elder. I watched benevolently as his
young dreams were forming. Out of the twilight a few rays of
dawn emerged. They tickled my toes and melted into the subtle
waves at the shoreline. Smells from other seasons were mixed up
in the inconstant breeze.
    I arranged my masks on the sand. People paid for them
and carried them away so that I had nothing left but money. I accidentally sold my own body and face. Realizing this, I put money
where my body should have been and took on its identity. Then I
rolled around for a while in the bed of the world.

    People came to me, one after the other. They tried to keep

me safe. They were glad to see me come. But I always left them, often in the worst moments of their lives.

I passed through brothels and watched the women in their grace and humiliation. I saw how the face of a woman was a story. Like the tide, I was often gathered into that story by a kind of massive gravity. And yet that story was not strong enough to carry me. I kept slipping out through the space underneath the jaw. The bodies of women were like poorly made baskets that unraveled at the touch and spilled everything they carried.

In my body of money, I experienced through a strange poetry. Time had no effect on me. Even when coins and bills were out of circulation, money went on. Even when there were no more buyers or sellers, the accounts waited patiently. The long night of extinction was no more than a beat between business hours. Things promptly began again where they left off, making chimes ring and spinners whir. Some gained while others lost. They were all meat for money's teeth.

One money was all money, so in a sense, I owned everything. All countries were stamped with my name; all borders encircled me in their willing embrace. I traveled effortlessly and gained access to everything. Even thoughts unknown to the thinker were bought and sold, even shades and hues of twilight without a seer. I resided at the pinnacle of existence, so there was nothing to be done with my knowledge and experience, and this made me sentimental.

"Promise me you will sing at my funeral," a boy told a girl. "Your lovely voice will surely triumph over death."

But when the boy died, the girl was nowhere near. Her voice had been lost along the way. Some said they saw it rowing out to sea just before dawn. There was a heavy quiet over everything, instead of a song. I bent the edges of my own logic in order to listen a while longer at the young man's grave. That was how I gave up being money and became part of the landscape.

35

The pepper tree leaned over and smelled my hair.

"I do adore you," she said. Her face was freckled.

"Then make me change," I begged. The willow blew me kisses. All things died and passed away, but I loved them as much as ever. Even when I couldn't remember faces, circumstances, or the way things fit into one another, still I loved them, needed them, called out to them with my words.

Some words I was not sure were real and others thundered like heavy hooves. I appeared in the East and the West. Green monsters appeared in everything. Jewels fell out of my mouth. I laughed at the idea that they were precious. Songs were born and died. It was awful to see their beauty swell up and empty out again.

Sometimes it was safe and sparklingly clean to sit like a crab inside my shell. Sometimes it was agony when I spread everywhere like an oily puddle. Phenomena were painted on the world in strokes of green, pink, pale blue and chalky, meditative yellow. I allowed that, but there were some things I did not allow.

I drank deeply of cruelty, but the space left behind by my victims grew a body of its own. This dark, echoing body danced with me. Our dance ached and resonated. I fell from my red thrones onto a green earth. Nothing was awake within me. A civilization built itself around me. Foundations were laid, new establishments opened. Wooden railings crossed my back like a hatchwork and swinging doors smacked me in the face. I dreamed bitter and honest dreams. I woke up gripping seeds I had not the will to cultivate.

Words grew from the trees, long and winding like tobacco leaves, and they listened like deep ears. Other words settled inside of them and together, they became better words. These new words could only be spoken when someone was ready to hear.

There was sulfur in the air. Time ran through my cheeks, carving gorges and leaving behind dark eddies. My smile was wobbly. A big blue face arose behind the horizon. His edges were rounded. He was a great blob. He smiled and simpered and gave me his attention. Then he ate all the remaining pieces of silvery sunlight and the world darkened.

I encountered nests of worry or malcontent stirring in the trees and dust. A painful transition progressed slowly. I settled into the arms of a stealthy bandit who was carrying me away. He crossed his long arms over me like a harness. I could not have escaped him if I had tried. Still, I knew it was wrong to give up the struggle. A lot of ground was lost while I relaxed in the robber's embrace. I saw the earth skating darkly out from under us as we moved sideways across the earth.

When this fugue ended, I was on another plane, in another life. It was my duty to collect and catalogue human miseries. My wooden desk and chair had been delivered by horse and wagon from the capital. A long line of provincial people had formed before me. They were each waiting to tell their suffering to me. They needed their story to be filed and stamped. This was the only way to get their full ration for the month. My ears were already sore from all the sad truths I had been hearing.

Now a man wearing bangles on his brown arms stood across from me. As he spoke, I accepted his words discreetly, without scrutinizing them. The man's sadness was like a great tower with all of its windows darkened. He finished his story and walked away spilling tears into the dust around him. His shadow jerked across the table for some moments after he had gone. The next peasant had already taken his place, but I watched the man's shadow with a gilded, forsaken feeling.

In my despair I stopped moving, but the world kept its wild pace and wrapped around me. The mountains looked down on me like watchful mothers then slipped under me and carried me on their backs. People swept over me and I knew them only as streaks of colors. I was battered by garlands of flowers and paper streamers and stepped on by the dusty feet of the frail men who swept the shrines. People crossed the material plane urgently, carrying many things that became tangled and had to be left behind. Their activities were futile in a way that should have been funny but was sad instead. So many things began with hope and ended with forgetfulness. There were great quantities of love, but there were always places where there was no love at all.

One world rusted and became a memory. The new people were made from the old people, but they had lost the old ways. The new people did not tell stories about themselves or promise vividly about the future. They had their magic, but they used it right away and often wasted it for no reason.

A cloud passed before the sun and cast deep blue shadows across the liquid sky. Thin cloths hung from the roof beams and billowed gently. My friend was counting coins: for every coin that belonged to a person, another belonged to the government. The soldiers were dressed like beetles. They came to each shop and collected the taxes. They were not the joyful, banal soldiers of other times. These soldiers had no qualities at all.

It was good to be near my friend, but it was not as good as it once had been. Every time he spoke, silence wrapped up his words until they were so small they were not worth listening to. I thought back to the word Grandfather Time had given me. I could not remember how it looked. When I thought of it, I could only think of an egg.

"You are beleaguered," my friend said. "You droop." It was true. I felt like I was in a foreign city, pushing my way through the viscous currents of business hours. But I was supposed to be in my hometown, merely waiting for the rain to pass. Also like an exile I was growing poorer. News drifted in and out of the tea shop like debris pushed by the wind. My friend faded from sight, leaving only a dusty sepulchre and three vague ideas.

One idea said: "Turn your hands to labor day and night. Be more than what you are. Earn your crystal crown."

Another idea said: "You have done enough. The one thing you haven't done is nothing-at-all. This is your real work, but I can see you are much too lazy to do it."

The final idea said: "Excuse my friends. They have no manners! It's a beautiful world and the work has been completed. Don't ruin it with aims or embellishments."

I took this last piece of advice and didn't do anything at all.

When I did something small, like sneeze or stretch my legs, it was not with any particular goal in mind. My actions were like dead leaves falling from a tree.

Tiny fires dotted the horizon. The town was unbuilt again, like a lady taking off her clothes. I was naked too, somewhere in the rubble. The fires grew and walked toward me on tiny feet. Then they walked past me, leaving only green visions behind them. My body was limp and heavy and long like a rag doll's. I couldn't see my feet, they were so far away. I couldn't lift my head, for my neck was thin as the stalk of a flower and my mind was heavy with thoughts.

Wars came marching by me like lines of insects. I tried to bestow upon their phalanxes the words of peace and redemption, but they ignored me as if I were only a mumbling drunk. They passed away and returned while I drifted in and out of sleep. I couldn't care about them because I was so much bigger than they were.

Something happened while I wasn't looking. It was the solution to everything, but I could see now that it was not needed, for everything contained its own solution. There was a healing light inside of all forms, a memory of their own goodness.

Many paths tangled up and involved me. I felt their fiery breaths, their smoky lungs, their bloated blood, their rosy youth, swollen and sunburnt. Hope surged up, wearing a new dress over her chaotic tattoos. I had stopped moving because of the heaviness of my memories. Even the trees moved faster than I did, dancing through me as through the pages of a book. I paid little attention to people and things that changed. They believed I was merely the field that gave rise to them, but for me it was the opposite. Their movement qualified my stillness, making my amazing dance possible.

It had been raining. A deep grey thought, inky blue and green, patient with its sorrow, was alive somewhere near me. The rain had ceased and its memory became an ornament my mind could wear when it wanted to feel distinguished. I felt my aliveness, my warmth, my sensitivity, like a precious thing that could be lost. But then it was already lost and I felt the cold loneliness of its absence. Existence and its opposite walked together like demented twins. Their togetherness was outrageous, so that my mind rejected them both and wandered along by itself, not thinking of them.

Spring played its old memories once more upon the ancient instrument of the world. I was an old woman again. Tiny birds flew back and forth in the cool cement building while high noon burned white fires outside. Time slowed down and each of my feelings reigned for an era. I walked a few paces along the forest path. It was dreadful because I loved myself so much. The trees cupped me in their hands and the sky sipped my thoughts like water. Each footstep was a bead on a necklace, and I recognized that once it was completed, it was not behind me but ahead of me once more.

This knowledge unwound the story from my mind, leaving only silence and the pudgy body of untested hope.

"Fall into the bottom of the poem," a worrier was mumbling. He was a poor grey man in the streets of a dreary city. His advice cast me beyond the help of the long and confusing poem that had been developing around my spirit. None of the letters I had been using to get somewhere could serve as a hand-hold, not even the f's or the r's. Falling, I discovered that the poem was bottomless. The words lay about like ruins. Things occurred around and between them. They got in the way of certain possibilities. They fostered others. Meaning did not depend upon them, but evolved among them. I was disturbed by the way meaning continued to grow, without their help. It was a blue-green feeling that would take some getting used to.

36

A lot of creatures worked on me. They changed out my
parts as if I were an old watch. I had been an old woman, but I
became a little girl. I started walking. I was in a sun-beaten desert
town. It was evening, and the rocks were hot from the afternoon.
I began speaking to my friend.

"You have been through many changes," I said.

"Yet I am still me," he answered.

"How is that?"

"It doesn't matter."

Some people got angry and were wiped away. They had
been little orange people. I knew some of them, but it didn't
matter. I was so tired I was crying. Meanwhile, I kept hearing
footsteps sliding over sidewalks and stairs. Invisible people were
walking through my memories, trying to see their reflections in
glass doors.

I was exhausted. Small people were painting me laborious-
ly. They did not speak. They treated me as if I were not a person
or even an animal, but only a wall. A little bald man pursed his
lips as he worked. At first it was good to be with them, but once I
saw that I was just a job to them, I felt alone.

When the little people were done painting me, they put me
in a cupboard and turned the key. I could sense the little house
around me beyond the cupboard door and the breathing woods
beyond that. In the woods there were giants. I could hear their
minds working like squeaky old doors in the wind. There were
wolves in the forest, too. I was impatient to read the secret hearts
of the wolves, but they remained quiet, distant, elusive. My vows
had been broken and they lay all around me in dull yellow slivers.

It was dark inside the cupboard, but I could tell when the
night came because the whole house began to listen. The floor
grew cold. The darkness was majestic and danced before me like
a red-haired queen. I remembered the details of the house. It was
a small house with an elegant grandeur. The floor was made of

green tiles.

The night seemed to make the room grow taller. The floor seemed so far away that it became difficult to balance overtop of my folded legs. The darkness began to speak:

> A buttered morning
> a fatty noon
> a future hollower
> than a spoon

> too many whats
> such puny whys
> a moon that uses
> spoons for eyes

> and gobbles darkness
> and eats her own hands
> and dries her hair
> in our votive candles

> On the stairway to heaven
> you tried to ascend
> but you found that it wound
> underground again

A family of fairies came home in the morning: a mother, a father, and their young daughter. They were gigantic and their teeth were sharp. They wore feathers and leather and shells and nuts. The daughter shook me roughly until I shed my sympathies. This delighted her, but it exhausted me. Her parents just sniffed me and spoke in a garbled tongue. They sounded as if they were speaking backward.

That night several other fairies came over and played poker. The daughter sat under the table with me while the adults drank and gambled above us. I could not understand what they were saying, but they talked loudly and wept often. The girl pinched and tickled me. Sometimes she put my arm in her mouth and chewed on it gently with her pointed teeth.

Outside, a great sorrow could be heard heaving in the forest. It was as if a sea of metal were being distorted by cruel machines and crying out with human anguish. A red woman came in through the back door and passed through the kitchen without stopping. As she walked through the house, her high heels clicked on the green tiles. She went out the front door and slammed it behind her. No one seemed to notice her, but the merriment of the poker players chilled and began to die.

Suddenly the fairy child wailed. She was looking at me with horror. I saw that my paint had begun to peel away, leaving only the body of the sunken real. For a moment, the idea of shame etched itself upon my mind, but it was mothy and inanimate, like a mummy. Yet the sight of me so troubled the fairy that she made great hiccupping cries. Her parents kicked at her under the table, but their gnarled toes struck me instead. I stared tranquilly into the eyes of the fairy child until she began to return my gaze calmly and attentively. I soothed her by paving her thoughts with the color yellow, so that she could easily walk down any path in her mind without stubbing her toe.

The screaming of metal continued in the forest. The fairy daughter explained to me that a crew of contractors was recycling the dead. A wealthy investor planned to use their ores and ions to build a tower of ripening grief. The fairy parents had been complaining about it all evening. They couldn't help what was happening, for they hadn't kept up with their taxes. Though they lived in the forest and animated it with their magic, they had no claim in the courts.

One of the fairies who had been present that evening was an accomplice of the investor. He was an unawakened, monstrous creature, but he was the only fairy in the forest who had done all of his paperwork. He was making a grand place for himself in the world that was coming. The red woman who had passed through the house was a curse the fairies had raised against him. She would return soon, the fairy child said; her appearance tonight was only the first wave. Although the fairy daughter was hopeful, I had seen it all before. I knew the curse had failed, and now the fairies' intentions were out in the open. The opportunist had fallen asleep laughing darkly to himself.

"I feel like it will always be bad," I said.

The fairy said, "You must find the good in yourself. That is what the dance of darkness is for." She led me out into the spectral forest. There was an intoxicating weight in the air, for a great evil was draped over everything and the air buzzed and vibrated with sorrow like the inside of a cello.

Each of the dead had some piece of me in them. This one had a certain bend of my eye, that one had my sad mouth. They had passed through humiliating experiences and were in the process of being forgotten. A great machine was gnawing at them. I glimpsed its driver, hovering in an illuminated window, grinning wildly. A few other workers hung about in the shadows.

The dead had committed errors and their errors had become their bodies. The evil they had done made it difficult to pity them. They merged together, and from their residues a demon arose.

I saw in the wind and in the clouds eternal symbols that had guided people through long winters. They were broken, yet they still existed. I was tired and ominous. The dead refused to die. They rose up and pelted the wind of the demon, but the wind only brushed them aside. The dead shuddered and wept. They crawled like crabs in the underbrush. The trees saw what was happening and gripped at their own anger with huge claw-like hands. Nevertheless, their feelings were elusive, and soon they were sighing again in the melancholy breeze.

"You have to find the good in yourself," the fairy child repeated. Under her magic, my skin turned grey and I grew cold and heavy. Seeing myself die, I was uncomfortable and bothered. I was sorry for our collective fate and fearful of what lay ahead. And yet there was a red circle of goodness amid the thrashing seas of reckless feelings. I recognized what was good in me because I had known the goodness of others. I knew this to be a lucky gift. I stood upon this small, warm circle of goodness. The disturbance whirled and crashed around me, but from where I stood I could see in it waves of prayer. The demon in her terrible grace writhed from side to side, and inside her ribcage swung a tangled cluster of keys. In her arms there were poems but they were distorted. The demon wore a cloak that pulled at the threads of the world. It was very heavy and tugged at the sky when the demon moved.

I added my prayer to the cloak's heavy folds. The dead fought with their mouths open and I fought among them. Sometimes we were all one wet mouth. At other moments the horror was so complete it seemed that there was kindness in it. A majestic friend took a bow while a great host applauded. At times I lost track of myself and I was nothing but passion and wonder. At one point I was eaten by a bored and panting beast who cared little how I tasted and left most of me to rot. Finding that I was still beautiful and weightless, I felt a kind of guilty coronation taking place. My visages aligned like interlocking rings. A green lady carried me through darkness. A bruised, stupid part of me was still lamenting the dead on the forest floor. Their raw material was gnawed upon by the mechanical jaws of the contractors' equipment. The plans went forward and the dead were swiftly reorganized.

With the green lady I was rising up and could not slow myself or become less buoyant. I called to the bruised, purple body who stayed lamenting and poking at the dead carnage, but she didn't recognize my voice as her own. She looked up and shook her fist at me. I saw the giants pushing their way through the trees. They were beautiful and sick. The sun had browned their skin and their hair swung around them like a bell. Ash fell from their cheeks and landed on the leaves of the canopy.

The wind was moving in one direction, but the river flowed the opposite way. I looked back and saw that the darkness had grown, canceling the distance created by my flight. In the flashes of lightning that threaded through the towering clouds I discerned a huge face—the face of the demon. I knew it also as the face of the world—they were one and the same. The face was a question to which I replied, "Yes." That made me lose everything: pride, security, hope, convictions, the good and the right.

I hung suspended in this disoriented state, amorphous. Everything was equal and washed by me like a soft liquid. My heart was muted. My feeling was neutral. I waited for the stars to come out. When they did, I was sleeping. By the time I woke up, the sun was high in the sky. This kept happening. The face of the villain was always before me. She swished and rippled. The green lady carried me, but I could see now that she dangled from the fingers of the villain. Everything was a part of her, and I was becoming a part of her too. I didn't have the energy to fight. I fell asleep too easily.

Everywhere I went, people were speaking, and in their speech simple and wrong ideas were carried. My own silence was heavy like a blanket. It had many ideas inside of it that were good and many that were nonsense. They were all mixed together, but still my silence sounded better to me than others' speech.

Under the anguished moon, crickets were singing. They spelled my name and placed charms between each letter. The dead had never given up their struggle, but nevertheless, they had become something else. The investors' hands were filled with returns. Their creation was a great tower with hairy crevices and spiders living in its corners. Its eyes didn't blink simultaneously but winked one by one. Its mouth swung around itself salaciously. The dead swam through its cheeks, each soul squirming in its own direction. The tower gobbled up the innocent and mediocre bystanders who stumbled along on the street.

"After all this time, it's a wonder you still find anyone to fill your belly," I remarked. The building laughed, but the dead, swimming in its face, lamented.

"Let me sing you a song I once heard," the tower shouted. His voice lifted stones and caused me to remember long-forgotten sorrows.

> It isn't fear
> that brings me here
> nor seasons swinging
> around the year
> nor teacups filled

with whinging tears
nor thimbles full of
bitter beers
It's you, my dears!

With nibbling footsteps
and swollen packs
with martyred eyes
and curving backs
you trickle out of
funny cracks
so stiff with thrift
so long with lack

You're all I need
and you need me too
I open the door
and you walk through
you offer—
I don't have to guess—
you pay on time
and fill my chest

It's you who trims
the hanging vines
and sweeps the sky
for hidden signs
who pulls the plunder
from the mines
and makes the market
ring with chimes

You carry off
the day's debris
and jingle on
my ring of keys
it's you who paints

my crooked sneer
and stirs the sugar
in my tea
it's you, my dear!

The perverse building stomped off, cackling to himself. The sun swung its mane mournfully and left a residue on the planet. That residue, orphaned, yet madly grew. The demon was a great bowl of a face, smiling and snarling. She grew so big that I could no longer locate her. She was everything and everywhere. A freshness entered the atmosphere. I looked down and saw that Grandfather Time was washing my feet with his long hair. His hands trembled but his face remained earnest. My love for him perfected itself, becoming one dingy tear.

37

I spread out. The clouds piled themselves high and the fronds of the trees and bushes bathed in the indifferent heat. Voices spoke to me, but not of ideas. They spoke for the love of speaking merely. I returned their tidings with little songs of my own. I tarried long in formless places. I fell into a place that was both dream and memory. My wind was foul and dusty. Sweet violet hues swindled unsuspecting fears. I escaped their notice. Things were at one, but falling away. There were good lights and swinging leaves. I was dizzy with the marauding heat. Bells fell over the hills in white chimes. The plunder of laughing kings continued in many rings, spurring unequal crucifixions. I gave myself over to the nauseous, gummy love of the broken-hearted.

There was a quiet in me that was long, like a smooth stair unfolding. People walked upon it wearing hoods and carrying bundles. Ferocious waves of time closed upon it with heavy jaws, but the quiet stair reappeared each time. The sky was scrawled with scars. I tried to read them, but their language was closed to me. I missed my hands. I tried but could not fully renounce intentions or the impulse to unfold them manually.

People no longer existed, but their egos still refused to disappear. Their faces kept emerging everywhere, insisting that they should be real. Consciousness gathered in hard knots that wouldn't break apart. I paved my silence in chalk and resin, but no one would walk upon it. Meanwhile, cities formed. People created themselves again by whatever means it could be achieved. They cared not how nor what it meant. Existence maimed and mutilated them. I did my share of maiming too—an ear here, an arm there. I wasn't the worst of them. That's how I consoled myself.

In this way, a new society arose. Its citizens were fierce and ugly. They speedily clawed through what was soft and good. When only rugged beings with claws were left, they complained about getting scratched. I was not ferocious enough to last long in this world, but for a while yet I survived, for the skillful and ruthless monsters had set up a system by which I could subsist on the scraps of their predation. This was how I acquired certain substances that held me together. They came from the bodies of others whom I had never met. Sometimes I heard these strangers rollicking through my own thoughts or tickling me around my waist. Consuming their ill-begotten substances kept me alive, but it confined me to a low and unimportant caste. I paid for my share of the spoils through drudgery and humiliation.

I didn't have time to clean the white stairs in the wilderness any more. I didn't know what had become of the wilderness, for the city had grown fatter, its waist expanding and its head lolling like a big baby's. Among the servants it was rumored that the wilderness was empty now of echoes, that it no longer remembered the other times, the many worlds it had eaten. It was said that the wilderness had become another stupid servant of the city, a lackey with its tongue hanging out.

The high-castes were big and fat. They pushed out their chests as they passed. They bumped into one another with their big rubbery bellies as they climbed in and out of their cars. They grew so large that they needed more space. We cordoned off their areas with velvet ropes. Outside of these areas, it became very crowded for the meagre low-castes. We had to push each other out of the way in order to get to our tasks.

One day, in the crush of the crowd, I became frustrated and stopped moving altogether. I stood and thought, my mind drifting among complicated orange clouds. I noticed how several dimensions overlapped and imbued one another with meaning. I was reading this meaning as if it were a book in which an answer to an indefinable longing might be found. But in a moment I was shoved carelessly by another worker. I was in the way.

"Make your choice now," the worker said. "You can always get out; just cease to be yourself and you will have escaped."

I saw the beauty of his argument. Yet I was already hopping to, for there wasn't a moment to spare. Survival overpowered philosophy without any discussion.

I showed up and demanded my pay at the end of the week,

and yet I still hoped for more. When I said my own name and the words that were mine, I expected something in me to respond. I knew that the cruel machinery that fed me would some day cannibalize me, and I fantasized about that day. When it arrived, I imagined I would have lots of attention and sympathy. I would be on the news and my vicious end would become big-time entertainment.

As it happened, there was no fanfare. I was smashed mercilessly by hard realities. My grand ideas were turned into small metal coins and deposited into all kinds of slots to make things whir and moan. It was a morbid laughter, this jiggling of coins and vibrating of machines.

A round face arose in the theatrical darkness. He wore a toothy smile and there were jolly creases in his jaws. I was like a broken umbrella—the rain fell through me, though some relic of my structure yet existed. The giant face, burnt like toast, worked its mechanical jaws and said in a mellifluous voice, "The way from here to there can be danced as easily as walked." Garbled music arose. The face lit a cheroot and the whites of its eyes turned green. He smoked the cheroot until he burned his lips, then ate the butt and demanded another from the concierge. I tried to wrap my belly in a towel because it was so wet, but it was no use, for there was nothing but water and more water.

"My dear, you are bottomless," the big face said. "There's nothing that can plug you up, no satisfaction for you."

I wanted to answer, but I was in too much pain. With my substance had gone my memories. When I dreamed, I spoke in someone else's voice into someone else's microphone. When I reached back toward my origins, I found no nourishing matrix to inform me of who I was. Even the sand underfoot cursed me as it met my body's weight. It seemed that it would always be this way. As long as I had believed that happiness was possible, still longer I would know that it was not. I sang a little song in order to encourage and comfort myself:

That's enough of that:

just sit and be empty a while
it doesn't matter who you are
or if you have your mother's smile
it doesn't matter how you feel
no one cares whether you're real
the bottom is very like the top
when it comes to the turning of a wheel

Cataclysms struck like cymbals, but the machine marched on. Bits and pieces of me were distributed among the pockets and bodies of the rich. My ghost wandered in the shadows in inescapable mourning while tiny feminine spirits fed me on rice wine. I reeled and cavorted, drunk and starving.

The world for which so many small beings had been sacrificed was big and fat. Trumpets were blaring. Juicy, incandescent lights crawled through the fog. The streets were wet with a milky glow. Poker games were played and big fat chips rolled between bulbous fingers. I lived sometimes in the crevices that formed in a fat man's face and sometimes in the unsettling cool grey of his bedclothes in the morning light.

When the high-castes had gotten as fat as they could, they decided to go on a diet. Their violence perfected, they became as docile as grandmothers. They took great care not to cause one another harm, but the truth was that they didn't like each other. They were cruel gossips and merciless critics. When they passed one another in the street, they cursed and grumbled. They loathed one another because they reminded one another of their own ugliness.

I know this because I was lurking in their thoughts, peering into their darkened yards, opening their rusted and wheezing gates of regret. I and the other ghosts of their victims were condemned to haunt them. We slapped our fingers against the metal bars around the high-castes' hearts. We echoed and rattled around in their consciousness. When they undressed in their shadowy rooms and hung up their clothes, we also hung shapeless and brooding in the gloom. When their daughters turned sixteen, we smiled from inside their faces and animated their parties with a lurid panic.

There was one particular monster in whose house I habitually lurked. He had yellow eyes like a cat. His bald forehead was shaded with the purple of twilight. He had survived because of his heinous crimes, but when the new world came about he foreswore brutality and became a gentleman. He wore a long blue tie that covered his bulging belly. Gradually, he slimmed down and seemed quite harmless. He would stand in front of his oblong mirror and while he looked at himself, I would drink up his reflection like a jackal sipping from a lake. Soon there was nothing left of him but a pale blue scar, shaped a bit like his ridiculous cravat.

The man didn't seem to notice the change. He drifted around his apartment, brushing up against ghosts and bad memories, humming to himself, and lit a cigarette. He was unaware that he had become no more than an odd blue scratch, or that his cigarettes were only pieces of chalk.

When he went out to tea, I lingered in his footsteps. At banquets I heard the man explaining to his colleagues how it was that he remained so charmed while madness and horror pervaded the world. He called his terrible resiliency "optimism".

"I'm always optimistic," he said. "It's a choice, to be sure. Perhaps it is the most important choice we have today..." He made speeches about optimism in crowded theaters. His words had a hypnotic quality. Like a spell, they harmed and distorted me each time I heard them. I stumbled about with the man's optimism weighing down my head. I kept falling forward onto my face, my little body flinging to and fro helplessly as I rolled along.

The same plight had befallen all the ghosts and wraiths who had heard the man's ideas. His theory destroyed us. We became ineffective. Too late, we realized that we had been too lenient in our work of tormenting the high-castes. We hadn't sincerely meant them any harm. We had secretly enjoyed their victory, as if we were somehow part of it, as if we shared in its glory just by being near them. The optimist in particular had become our god and our beau. We had even overlooked his hideous moustache.

Desperate for another chance, I tried to take apart this maddening word, "optimism," that had swollen our brains. The "o" was so big and round, I couldn't grip it. It seemed to swallow everything and it smirked while doing so. The gospel of optimism spread and inoculated the once fearsome monsters. That "o" hung like a wreath from all their doorways, bringing cheer and fellowship. Although they still secretly despised one another, they tipped their hats and smiled. We foundered helplessly in their enormous new gutters, trying to claw our way back into their windows, their breaths, and their creaking staircases of shame.

We were repelled. It was hopeless. Finally, we gave up hope completely. At that moment, we saw that the "o" that had caused us so much pain and consternation was really a great wound, the inside of which was filled with yellowish-green pus. This wound ate our enemies from the inside. One day they were singing their carols of optimism, and the next they were boring their own eyes out. The "o" had destroyed everything in the world except for them, and then, inevitably, it destroyed them too. The "o" had boasted of eternal fullness, but now we realized that it was a terrible, wonderful zero. It encompassed all things, like the grave. The gentleman with yellow eyes blew away like the husk of a seed. I thought I saw him winking as he went, wearing a somber and elegant smile, a smile of sagacity and ease.

As for us ghosts, in the place in our skulls where all that optimism had throbbed, there was now only a whistling emptiness. The whole world whistled through these holes, making music like a flute. It was beautiful. The killers who had passed through that mystical O-shaped doorway joined us, their victims, in the realm of the unreal. Stripped of their big, healthy bodies, their spirits were weak and helpless. We who had merely lurked in their shadows now saw that we were more capable and fit than they had ever been. We looked upon their pathetic, vulnerable spirits and were compelled to help them, so confused and trembling were they. We fed them on vapors and the colors that exist behind and between things. We gave them of ourselves and they were grateful. Into their emptiness we poured something, and in the fulfilling of a need, joy itself was found.

Somehow, in this way, all beings got by. At first, every-thing was dead and dry and brown. There was nothing to look at but the papery wind. Slowly, with no sense of urgency at all, we created a way forward. Cycles of birth and death were initiated. Family and community arose. Bonds of love and affinity formed. Time moved gently like the murmuring sea. I allowed myself to be rocked by this soothing, meandering rhythm. Sometimes I was mother and sometimes I was daughter. The cruelty of the killer caste appeared now in my right eye, now in my left. Every new generation carried a sickness inherited from the one before it. Yet love encased evil in its balm and carried it onward, cushioning its fall, absorbing its pain, and transmuting it into the precious experiences and substances of the many worlds.

38

I was a daughter once more. I had eyes of earth and a wild gaze upon the hills. As my mother rocked me, she recounted the myths of love and hate and how the killers of everything had become everything's children. I couldn't make sense of her words. When I spoke, ancient sorrows streamed from my mouth. The priest came to collect them and made of them a tincture. In return he gave me a strange tattoo on each of my hands. He tattooed me while my mother was sleeping, and when she awoke, he told her the marks were a sign from God. The sign meant I was to be his servant for seven years. My mother was too tired to argue. She waved her hand and the priest carried me off.

When I could walk, I walked into the mountains. Great knifelike boulders stabbed the earth. I read on every stone the story of past suffering. Playing over the painful grooves were the ecstatic songs of crazy joy. I added and subtracted, and using myself as an unknown entity I performed a mysterious algebra. Still, I could not balance the equation. I went to sleep inside the little bed formed by the equality symbol. My dreams were so good they made up for my lack of understanding.

I walked through a field of white lilies. Snakes crossed my path as silently as the distant comets flying through space. Words met with me in the primeval purple twilight. The word "martyr" bowed gracefully and carried me on his back over silver ribbons of mountain. The word "clown" took me on a drinking spree in the gutters of a desert town. The word "mercenary" made three cuts in the earth: one for profit, one for loss, and one for the man in the middle.

A prophet met me on the path and tried to give me teachings. While he spoke I cast a red stone into the canyon below, but it did not give me the satisfaction of an echo. The prophet puffed up until he filled up the sky. He was robed and hooded in clouds and his eyes were like distant storms.

"Can't you see my greatness?" he said.

"Yes," I said, "You're making quite a scene."

"I can see you don't need my blessing," he said hotly, and the sky emptied itself of his face. Still, I saw that he left his blessing for me on the mountainside. It was a box with a red path inside. The red path was wherever people were and everyone was walking on it. Sooner or later everyone would have to step off of this path, but they didn't know where it was leading, when they would leave it, or why they were traveling on it. The path was both a gift and a curse and so I wept both with joy and with sorrow.

I brought the box to the the market. At the market, the fashionable people passed me by. Because I only had one article to sell, they assumed I had stolen it and they turned up their noses. I noticed that there were many pitiful vendors with only one item in their store. A man in a hat was selling a cooking pot. A woman with a gold tooth sat before a single chicken. A little boy tugged at the sleeves of passersby and waved a single silver watch in front of them. To make my business look more legitimate, I added some of my own kitchen items to the box. After that, a few of the vagrant women stopped to inquire about pots and spoons, but they weren't interested in the box or the red path inside it.

When the evening came, the street emptied. I swung from the branch of a tamarind tree, fantasizing about selling the box for a fortune so that I could pay my debt to the priest. A foreigner came along, stirring clouds of orange dust behind him. He stopped and looked at the box.

"My wife will like this," he said.

"How do you know?" I asked.

"Because she is dead and the red path is life."

"What will you give me for it?"

The man paused. His face was oddly familiar. I peered at him but his eyes flashed like lightning and sent a ringing pain through my head.

"I can tell you where a treasure is hidden," he said, "but you must find it for yourself."

"What treasure is there in this world worth having?" I asked.

"Are you so depraved? Then let me tell you: it is only by having it that this question can be answered. The answer depends on you rather than the treasure."

I sold the man the box and in return he gave me the name of a holy ground where the country's heroes were buried. I went there at night as he instructed.

The dreams of the dead men were murmuring underground, unfulfilled. I could hear their dead fingers clutching at their unrealized intentions. The orange earth squirmed around their guilty omens while the larvae of winged insects transformed quietly in the roots of the grass. I heard the politicians of recent times conversing with the kings of the distant past. They were all speaking at cross-purposes. Their antiquated ideas were absurd. Their voices overlapped, becoming an unsettling noise.

The talk of these dead kings and politicians revealed the secrets of history. They said:

> Our brides were wrapped
> in tasselled cloths
> like city lights
> in veils of moths
>
> from dust they shaped
> a water jar
> and raised us sons
> of silk and yarn
>
> we swiftly filled
> their minds' blank walls
> with playbills
> for entertainment halls
>
> with cannon balls

their bellies swelled
their hearts crossed
with ammunition belts

the mules were strong
the railway was fast
but none lived long
for they were not made to last

I gleaned from the conversations of the dead that the
mythology I had cherished in my youth was only propaganda.
The men of power laughed bitterly, recounting the tricks they had
played on the people. They desecrated the heroes I had learned
to admire and the great acts of love I had been taught to emulate.
In the absence of these reference points I felt my mind groping
shapelessly for its own meaning and nature. Between and among
the vociferous men, the women of history clicked their tongues
and rattled their knitting needles.

The foreigner had instructed me to wait in the holy
ground, but waiting proved difficult. Now and then a shiver traveled through me, as if a cold wet thing was splashing through my
flesh. I felt stiff and creaky. I was hungry and lonesome. Errands
called to me back in town. It seemed that just now it would be a
good time to pass by the main square. At home, I had many little
tasks to accomplish. I thought of them lovingly, as if I would
never experience them again.

All the while I waited, I felt an evil intention organizing
itself. Gnomes and minions were gathering around me and peering into me. In the darkness, the borders of my flesh disappeared
and my spirit was revealed. My consciousness was a labyrinth
with a red path to the North, a yellow path to the West, a blue
path to the South, and a purple path to the North-East. The paths
squirmed and contracted. They pulsated painfully.

Still I waited for the promised prize to appear. The voices
underground crowded together so that they became vibrations
and even gathered into solid entities. They crawled and slithered

into my mind by every opening. Whatever loose odds and ends they found within me, they used according to their own designs. They populated my thoughts with dark songs and awkward burdens. Betrayals lay like cold silver knives between the bonds of warm flesh. The sea was there, curling around everything and covering me in its riotous beauty. My feet brushed against the fuzzy heads of murdered men beneath the waves. On the beach, several generations of outcast royalty sat back, chuckling. Time oozed onward, dragging with it an immense cargo of death toward an unknown and unknowable destination.

Behind the row of gap-toothed, gangly princes an old hotel was decaying. The royal heirs yawned and leaned back on their asymmetrical limbs in the shade of a shaggy tree. They guffawed and brayed, condemned to eternal boredom and incessant entertainment. The galaxies far beyond their sight watched them with a hungry indifference. Still I waited, but in the face of their horrendous cynicism, the love I had always carried within me seemed futile. I saw its meaning float away in ribbons. What I had understood to be myself was inverted, like a glove turned inside-out.

What was left of me was not a treasure but a hideous hollowness into which the cackling fiends rushed, chattering remorselessly. I saw them yanking at my sister's bones and dancing with dirty feet upon my mother's yellow dress. They parodied my ideas, strutting like pompous clowns. They satirized my sincere feelings and used my prayers as slogans to manipulate poor and gullible people.

When the dawn came, it bore no light, only a kind of mechanical energy. The fiends had successfully mined my secrets and worked my weaknesses into their larger schemes. I searched for my old habits and motivations, but I found myself cut off from my trajectory, adrift and purposeless. With my ideals slashed and my merit plundered, all earthly accounts had been settled and all past conditionalities abolished. The priest had been paid, not only in this lifetime but in all lifetimes. The fates were satisfied and nothing further was required of me. I was free.

I wandered about the graveyard and then the edges of the town with a sullen aimlessness. That night I slept on the stone steps of a chapel on the eastern side of town, surrounded by stray cats. The next day, I inhaled fumes with the street children until I forgot my own name and the names of the colors that danced before my eyes. The following day was much the same. Sometimes I couldn't walk at all, but could only laugh. One tooth fell out and then another. Blindness came and went.

At the same time the earth, water, and air grew prickly and hostile to human flesh. It was something about the stories we had been telling ourselves. I couldn't keep the facts straight, but I knew we had been tricked. The sources of our life had been contaminated by people who believed they were doing good.

It amazed me that in such times there were still intrepid working citizens who went on striving toward the ideals they had been taught. They were dressed up like buffoons as their bosses demanded, and they groveled and cowered as they hopped about. They often went out of their way to step on my fingers or kicked me as they passed, but they could not destroy the spirit of renunciation that gave me and the other street children our grace. Thousands of these model citizens fell ill and disappeared, but the rest still planned on futures that would unfold fulfillingly unto the horizons of time.

I went in the opposite direction. I became a stupid baby. I didn't demand a mother who was pristine and primordial, capable of nourishing me infinitely. I knew that that mother was exhausted and dying, but another mother was there to take her place. The new mother revealed herself through all that was pernicious, all that was horrifying. She killed me, rather than making me live. She ate me from within, causing gruesome pain. My new mother could be counted on to carry me every day into new depths. I gave myself to her completely, and she reciprocated unsparingly.

There is a cruel bottom of things where existence and its opposite meet but still cannot agree on even the smallest questions, and so they descend into nonsensical debates like two madmen scratching in the mud. Things fizzled about in that realm uncomfortably and inconsequentially. Inside that seething buzz I heard voices like whispers in the rain. My heart was completely broken, useless as a cracked clay pot. There was nothing to do but think, and by thinking long enough, all things change, as they change when the sun moves from East to West.

39

The sickness that fell upon the planet broke the people down to their elements until we were nothing but a many-colored dust. Yet the dust still remembered. The planet went through a sour period in which it seemed to be considering giving up. After all, it was very old and sometimes it felt it had seen enough. There were great tremors in which the planet threatened to let go of itself and break apart. But there was always something poignant about the way the rocks and debris settled back together, embracing one another naturally, by their mutual gravity. The earth's patience gave rise to pink and purple beasts who were unlike people in every way. These simple animals were kind and melted together like water. They took their time and yielded easily. In other epochs, we would have killed them for their meat, but now we saw their beauty from below. Even the touch of their shadows was ennobling.

These creatures walked through us and we stirred, strange songs emanating from us. Our dust sang:

Gifted, wise, and erudite
in harmonies we used to sing
in iron ships we used to sail
in robes of white with diamond rings

such wondrous things we used to do
but left undone what mattered most
and now we stick to others' shoes
and swish and scatter to and fro

If the earth had a sister, she was so far away that she could not be seen. The mother of all things spread her mute mouth over what was alive and what was unfeeling. Wherever she kissed, green arose, but grey followed in its wake. Things were small and wanted to be eternal but could not and so they turned bitter. These bitter, impermanent beings said:

> A woman I once knew
> let's call her the dainty wind,
> spilled in my direction
> and gave me a spare name.

> But that one is worn out
> so how will you summon me
> when the woodsmen come
> looking to cut me down?

I told these voices to have patience. They laughed at me in their bitter way. The ground was dry and the dust was restless. Everywhere there were cracks and fissures. All that was forgotten fell down into the cracks and its mad laughter echoed up from below.

Some sad eternal woman was always there, putting bread in everyone's mouth. When I asked her why, she smiled and mumbled nonsensically. Her smile was lovely and it brought me peace. It was that peace that made me special. The terrors I had seen repeated geometrically throughout every dimension rested easily in this peace. This dark, loving indifference lay between each particle of existence, separating each page of the book and balancing the river lights that fell into my left eye and my right eye.

"Yes," I said to the erotic sprites dancing in the halos of street lamps and barge lights. "Yes," I said to them, "I know."

These lewd lights fertilized one another and placed furry seeds in my mind. The seeds said:

> Swing slowly
> for whenever you're near
> I get where I'm going
> but I take wrong turns

and my hands can't steer
my destiny spurns
a path that is clear
and every way out of this song
for it would just be wrong
to be anywhere but here

you don't have to be in a body
to be burning bright
you can be dead or alive
or even unborn
or recently torn from your warm home
you just have to want love
to be on my side
and everything else will turn out right

When these seeds fermented I wept. I emerged from my
bath of tears in many different forms. Uniting these diverse bodies was a blessed forgetfulness, a kind, grandmotherly veil cast
over the long shadows of grim and ruthless causality.

"I have no patience for you," a little boy said, stroking my
cheek.

He was raising me backwards so that I would become a
baby again after being very old.

"Thank you, my son. Just be patient. I will do my best. I
promise."

"No!" He shouted. But he went on stroking my cheek. Tiny
people climbed ladders from my shoulders to my hair, and tinier
ones climbed ropes between my wrinkles. Small plants were
growing from my shed memories, and my regrets made them
strong and picturesque.

I fell into the mouth of the world and for a moment, I was
what the world was saying. I sounded funny, like an old song
people used to sing in a smudged town. How could I have forgotten that softness, that greyish-yellow tone? The crows kissed
my cheeks even though they had no lips. They clicked whenever
I walked by. The rain walked all over the world but wouldn't let

me walk alongside it. I fed my prayers to an old chimney and they became another ragged stain in the sky.

Then I fell out of the world's mouth and stood beside language. I was a tall watcher on the pilgrims' path. I stood still while the seekers passed by, propelled by hopes of finding. I allowed their energy to push past me but stayed in the place where there was nothing to be found. There, I experienced peace. Peace was a being who was born and grew strong, but later peace grew old and weak and finally expired. Still I remained.

My sister had passed by several times on the path. She carried boons or traveled in penury, begging. I was unmoved when she was attacked by bandits or torn apart by wolves. I lit a candle for the bandits. The wolves were my pets.

Grandfather Time was taken prisoner by a terrible fiend in a mountain stronghold. I knew this as dust knows things, humbly and prostrate. Impotence gave my existence a quality. I experienced my helplessness in tragicomic tones. Eventually, these vibrations were borrowed by minstrels and a music arose that mellowed and confused its audience. This music spread through the population and finally reached Grandfather Time's captor in his cave of stone.

The gigantic personality who had arrested Time became feckless and vaguely angry. He was trapped in his mood, so his intentions were not actionable.

"Where did I leave my pipe?" he grumbled, stroking his long red beard. He shuffled papers about on his desk. Grandfather Time failed to notice that his captor was hopelessly distracted. He was idly kicking at toy bells on the floor of his cage and reciting to his captor a dry text: the rules of the universe. I saw this from where I languished in the dust, generating the mocking energy of a meaningless victory.

The shadows deepened. It was the deepest of darknesses. I was more lost and forlorn than ever. In this ultimate darkness, I was aware that I was alone. Everything I had seen and known was annihilated and extinguished. The finality of its annihilation proved that it had never existed. The world I had experienced was vacant, a darkened puppet theater, and I realized with chagrin that I had always been the puppeteer. Ruefully I reviewed the memories and experiences I had believed to be real. The earth itself, the past and future, extinctions and regenerations, ideals and corruption—they were mere delusions, colorful bubbles in the froth of my infantile consciousness.

I considered the possibility of another existence, an existence free from the dictates of my flawed subjectivity. Where could such a world be found? What qualities might it have? For a long time, there was no answer. My friends danced before me like dead icons. My enemies giggled at me using my own voice. The enormity of my solitude blanketed and crushed me until I emerged in another form, only to be crushed again.

Then, inexplicably, it was there: kindness, like an enormous thumb or a gigantic worm, pushing into the darkness with its innocent, silly face. Was this another of my play-things, a part of me pretending to be real? The truth was that I was part of it, but it was also something else. How this was so was a beguiling mystery. From this mystery, manifestations emanated. There were mountains and shorelines, organized beings and mixed motivations. I relaxed and allowed it to happen. Awkwardly, I played at helping it, interacting with manifold beings, no longer alone. These multitudes allowed me to become also, and through their gifts and their bad and good advice, I formed a body from what was left of the darkness.

There were many things to be done: Grandfather Time had to be rescued from the mountain-top. My sister was out there somewhere, carrying a piece of my unfinished poem. I made sure to snatch enough shadow from the night to shape myself a hat and a suit of clothes and I began walking toward the morning as I had done many times before.

"Do you really think things will turn out differently this time?" crooned an organ grinder. I tossed him a coin. Tired servants sat on the stoops of the houses where they worked and wiped their faces with white cloths. Their sadness cast colored lights into the stubborn black sky. In the market, merchants were piling shrunken heads into neat stacks and hanging pineapples at the corners of their stalls. A sleep-walker was standing blankly on the sidewalk. I crossed the street to avoid him. A group of angry men rushed by wielding clubs and irons, as if headed for a brawl.

The river was full of gold by the time I crossed the levee. Maniacal men and women accosted me, raving about imminent terrors. I placated some and evaded others. I marched on. The river was sobbing pathetically. I was moved, but I remembered how it had sneered in other times and I closed my ears to its pain. Several soldiers stumbled along, their faces hollow as skulls. A few angels fell out of the sky and plunged, flaming into the river. Angry jeers called after them from heaven until it closed up again like a surgical wound. The many voices of the sea called to me but I turned my back and walked into the heart of the land, where the mountain was giving birth to a stream.

I walked one way, but my thoughts walked the other way. Beauty split us apart and was inexpressible and silent.